HIDDEN

Books by Fern Michaels

Books by Fern Michaels (Continued)

Fast Track
Hokus Pokus
Hide and Seek
Free Fall
Lethal Justice
Sweet Revenge
The Jury
Vendetta
Payback
Weekend Warriors

The Men of the Sisterhood Novels:

Hot Shot
Truth or Dare
High Stakes
Fast and Loose
Double Down

The Godmothers Series:

Far and Away
Classified
Breaking News
Deadline
Late Edition
Exclusive
The Scoop

E-Book Exclusives:

Desperate Measures
Seasons of Her Life
To Have and To Hold
Serendipity
Captive Innocence
Captive Embraces

Captive Passions
Captive Secrets
Captive Splendors
Cinders to Satin
For All Their Lives
Texas Heat
Texas Rich
Texas Fury
Texas Sunrise

Anthologies:

Home Sweet Home
A Snowy Little Christmas
Coming Home for Christmas
A Season to Celebrate
Mistletoe Magic
Winter Wishes
The Most Wonderful Time
When the Snow Falls
Secret Santa
A Winter Wonderland
I'll Be Home for Christmas
Making Spirits Bright
Holiday Magic
Snow Angels
Silver Bells
Comfort and Joy
Sugar and Spice
Let it Snow
A Gift of Joy
Five Golden Rings
Deck the Halls
Jingle All the Way

HIDDEN

FERN MICHAELS

KENSINGTON
PUBLISHING CORP.

www.kensingtonbooks.com

KENSINGTON BOOKS are published by

Kensington Publishing Corp.
119 West 40th Street
New York, NY 10018

All Kensington titles, imprints, and distributed lines are available at special quantity discounts for bulk purchases for sales promotion, premiums, fund-raising, educational, or institutional use.

Special book excerpts or customized printings can also be created to fit specific needs. For details, write or phone the office of the Kensington Sales Manager: Kensington Publishing Corp., 119 West 40th Street, New York, NY 10018. Attn. Sales Department. Phone: 1-800-221-2647.

Library of Congress Control Number: 2020952481

ISBN-13: 978-1-4967-3145-6
ISBN-10: 1-4967-3145-X

First Kensington Hardcover Edition: June 2021

10 9 8 7 6 5 4 3 2 1

Printed in the United States of America

HIDDEN

Prologue

Boston, Massachusetts
Millstone Manor

"What do you mean you still don't know where it is? I'm paying you good money to find it." The decibel level of his rage almost shook the walls. "Just find it! And fast!" Arthur Millstone hurled the burner phone across his desk, causing his wife, Rowena, to flinch. After years of marriage to Arthur, she very rarely flinched anymore. "I told you to oversee the estate sale!" The vein in his neck was pulsing as he unleashed his fury at his wife. She could have sworn there was spit coming out of his mouth.

Rowena calmly flicked the ash of her cigarette into the Burj al Arab ashtray from the world-class hotel in Dubai. She leaned back into the sumptuous leather club chair facing Arthur's desk and crossed her long legs, which were shod in a pair of Christian Louboutin shoes. "You do realize there was a lot of furniture involved in that sale. *A great many pieces.* And they were sold to a multitude of buyers. Whatever piece of furniture that document was stashed in is long gone. Somewhere. Anywhere." She let out an annoyed huff.

"Well, that's just not good enough, *darling*," he said, his voice dripping with sarcasm.

"May I remind you that you were the one who insisted I use Amber. The aspiring art curator from your club." Another drag of her cigarette, then a long glare, as Rowena waited for Arthur's response.

"I'm not in the mood for your snide remarks," he hissed. He pointed to her shoes, one at a time. "Those? *Those?* And that Chanel bag? Remember where the money came from. And if we don't find and destroy that document, all of it will be out the window." He slumped into his chair. "Must you smoke those filthy things in here?" he barked.

"It's *your* ashtray, *darling*. And these are no worse than your horrid Cuban cigars." Another flick of ash.

"I don't have time to quibble as to whose nasty habits are worse."

"Oh, Arthur, take a chill pill, will you. It's lost, gone. *Fini. Finito.* It is never going to turn up," Rowena said, calmly stubbing out her cigarette to emphasize her remark.

"Don't be so sure. If we don't get our hands on that thing, this multibillion-dollar empire will no longer be at our disposal. And I doubt they have designer jumpsuits in prison."

Buncombe County, North Carolina
Stillwell Art Center

Cullen Bodman wiped his hands on the work apron that protected his pants. He stepped back to look at his latest handiwork. The sign read: THE B.A.R.R.N. It announced the Bodman-Antiques-Retro-Restoration & Namaste Café. His sister, Luna, looped her arm through his. "Nice work, Cul. Just in time for this weekend's grand opening of the art center. I have to admit, the adjacent café was a brilliant idea."

"I had to get you out of my hair somehow." He lightly elbowed her in the waist.

"Aren't you the funny man?" Luna returned the affectionate nudge.

Luna and Cullen had grown up in a modest middle-class community. Their parents were antique dealers who were planning to retire. Cullen had graduated from college two years before Luna and had worked for a large development company for ten years. When their parents announced their retirement, Cullen saw it as an opportunity to use his hobby of restoring furniture and embark on a new career, beginning with what was left of the inventory from his parents' shop. They had been able to negotiate a space for Cullen's workshop and showroom, and an adjacent shop for a small café.

Luna was a free, creative soul. Given her paranormal endeavors, she used Bodhi as her last name in honor of her alter ego. The word meant "enlightened" in Sanskrit. But when it came to working with Cullen, she was a Bodman through and through.

But it was her interest in human behavior that had led her to earn a degree in psychology with a strong focus on parapsychology. Luna was also astute at kinesics, the interpretation of body language. Both of her skills, learned and intuitive, allowed her to do freelance work with local police departments, handling missing persons cases, including a big case for the U.S. Marshals Office of Missing Children.

Now the plan was for her to set up shop at the adjacent café, doing readings for those who inquired, and consulting with Cullen's clientele when it came to helping pick out pieces that would conform to their particular tastes. It was the best of both worlds for her.

Cullen was all business when he wasn't in the shop stripping old furniture and bringing it back to life. Though in a lot of ways opposites, he and his sister made a good pair. Always had.

The beeping of a truck backing up signaled the final delivery. Cullen had purchased several items that were in dire need of restoration from a dealer in Reston, Virginia. The original estate sale, in Boston, Massachusetts, consisted of dozens of pieces ranging from a rococo ormolu commode that had fetched $10,000, a Louis XVI marquetry armoire that had gone for $6,000, and a Louis XVI sideboard that had sold for $5,000. But Cullen was much more interested in the old, dilapidated objects that came from the garage of the estate. With some TLC, it would give him a great deal of pleasure to bring the four items back to life and sell them to good homes. In all honesty, Cullen was hoping to move further away from the antiques business and make restoration his only focus. He just didn't have the heart to tell his parents that yet.

Cullen had the business head and the restoration expertise. He would leave Luna to her many talents. Together, they could make this "crazy idea" work, which was what their father had called it when they decided to open their business at the art center.

Luna and Cullen worked their way through the pristine shop, in which dozens of restored pieces waited for a new home. Four more pieces would fit perfectly in the thousand square feet of space at the front.

A ramshackle ash-blue farm table with drawers was the last thing off the truck. Luna moved toward it as if it were a magnet. When she touched the top of the table, she got a shiver. She wasn't sure why, but the shudder led her to believe something wasn't quite right.

Chapter One

North Carolina

Cullen Bodman was a typical, clean-cut, all-American guy. He was nearly six feet tall, with sandy-brown hair and green eyes. True to his name, he was a "good-looking lad." He had a lean and trim build. Physically fit. Woodworking had made his biceps the envy of most of the guys at the gym. They were toned and sinewy, something that came from physical labor rather than barbells. He loved to work with his hands. Build things. But his parents had encouraged him to get his degree in business administration. "You can take that anywhere" was his father's advice.

He was right to a certain extent, but working in the business world was not anything for which Cullen had any real desire. He wanted to be enthusiastic about his work, something he shared with his sister. They were both creative and sensitive; and they felt smothered if they couldn't express themselves. However, unlike his sister, Cullen often disguised his compassionate and sympathetic side. He needed to be level-headed. Responsible. But underneath the cool, contemplative exterior was a kind, considerate, and tender man. It had been a long inner quest to be able to merge the two.

Now, at thirty-five, he could look forward to something exciting. *Not* looking at spreadsheets and tracking costs per project. Other people's projects. Bor. Ing. But *this*? *This* was exhilarating. Even with the financial risks involved in starting a new business, he was happy to wake up to a new day every morning.

Cullen was equally thrilled to have his sister working in close proximity. Growing up, he had always been his sister's protector. He knew she could take care of herself, but he also knew that she had a kind, vulnerable soul. Her empathy could lead her down paths where people did not appreciate her generosity.

Funny. Despite being psychic, she very often found herself bailing people out of tight messes while getting herself into one. He thought of the adage about the shoemaker's kids who have no shoes. He recalled the time when one of her college roommates needed to borrow some cash. Luna couldn't get to the bank and foolishly gave her roommate her ATM card. Luna had no reason not to trust her. They had been roommates for almost four years. But the next morning, she discovered that her roommate had cleaned out her account and skipped town. Cullen gave her the $3,000 she had stupidly let slip through her hands without a lecture or reprimand.

Or the time when someone spray painted big, black letters on Luna's apartment door with the words *Weirdo. Luna-tic!*

It took several days of interrogating the neighborhood and looking at whatever surveillance video was available, but Cullen finally identified the graffiti artist and tracked him down. It took little convincing from Cullen for the Keith Haring wannabe to decide he would be retiring his can of spray paint.

Cullen smiled to himself recalling the confrontation. The

kid was around twelve years old. Cullen followed him home from school. When Cullen rang the doorbell, a very tough-looking woman with a large mole on her chin answered. A large black hair, the size of a cat whisker, protruded from the mole. It completely caught Cullen off guard, and he almost burst out laughing. Instead, he regrouped and began his lecture. "Mrs. Rector, your son defaced my sister's front door."

She immediately became defensive, but Cullen put an abrupt halt to her tirade. "While my sister may have beliefs different from yours, I can assure you she is not weird. In fact, she is a highly spiritually evolved human being. Much more than I can say for you, given your lack of tolerance. I don't know what you are teaching your children, but if I so much as see your son, or any member of your family, near my sister again, you will wish you lived in another country. Harassment and hate are not welcome here." He stared her down. "Do I make myself clear?" Her lower lip twitched as the mole danced up and down on her face.

Mrs. Rector answered with a meek, "Crystal." Cullen turned on his heel, eager to leave the scene before he burst out laughing. With that mole on her face and her hair wrapped up in a babushka, she reminded him of *Strega Nona*, the famous award-winning children's book by Tomie dePaola. It had once been banned for showing witchcraft and differences in spirituality in a positive light. *How ironic*, he thought. *Luna will certainly get a big kick out of this.*

Throughout high school and college, Cullen and Luna had remained close. Neither had married nor entered into a committed relationship. At least not for any length of time. Luna would give Cullen her take on the latest girlfriend. One time, it resulted in a heated argument when Luna warned Cullen that Nora was a cheater. "You have no proof of that," he bellowed.

"No. Not yet. But mark my words, Cullen Bodman." She slammed the door on her way out.

They hadn't spoken for almost a month. Luna was not only his sister, but she was also his best friend. He felt terrible about it. Then one day his phone beeped, indicating an Instagram message was waiting. It was from Luna's friend Barb. He furrowed his brow. Barb rarely, probably never, sent Instagram photos to him. Her text read:

Where are you in the photos?

He peered closely. It was a photo from a recent party. Was that Nora? With her arm around some dude? She was hanging on him like a Christmas ornament. It was the party at the Biltmore Estate Winery, the weekend he was in New York on a business trip. He stared at the photo again and again. He didn't recognize the guy, but Nora seemed to know the guy rather well.

He phoned Luna right away. "Hey, sis. I want to apologize. You were right about Nora."

"Oh? How so?" Luna could barely contain her excitement. Her plan had worked. When Luna had received the pic from Emily, she didn't want to confront Cullen herself, so she asked her friend Barb to forward it, asking where he was in the photos. Luna never told Cullen that she had asked Barb to intervene, but after that incident, Cullen never questioned his sister's sixth sense. Even if it made no sense to him.

Luna Bodhi Bodman had long, wavy, ash-blond hair. Occasionally, she would put colored streaks in it. Red for Valentine's Day. Green for St. Patrick's Day. Pink for Breast Cancer Awareness Month. Whatever the holiday or cause, you could see it in her hair. She would often wear it in a braid when not wearing a headband around her forehead, harking back to the 1960s and the 1980s. The granny-style wire-rimmed glasses and hippie-type bohemian wardrobe emphasized her spirit. *No pun intended.* She had a keen eye for design and a talent for charcoal drawing.

As a child, Luna was incredibly creative. Her imaginary playmate, Debbie, was a big part of it. Luna was convinced that Debbie wasn't imaginary at all. She was simply invisible to anyone who didn't believe that she existed. Luna was quite adamant about Debbie being real, so her parents decided to let her have her fun. They hoped she would eventually grow out of it. What they had not expected was how soon that would occur.

The night before her first day of school, Luna's father sat her down and explained that Debbie couldn't go to school with her. Luna confidently replied, "I know, Daddy. She's moving to California to play with another little girl who is lonely." Luna's dad was taken aback. He had no idea his five-year-old daughter knew there was even a state called California. Luna also seemed totally fine with her playmate's moving away. "I'll have other friends to play with, and Debbie needs company. So does the little girl in California." She was very matter-of-fact about the whole thing.

Her big brother, Cullen, was also relieved. He didn't want to get into any fights on the playground defending his kooky sister. He loved her to pieces, but sometimes she could get on his nerves, as undoubtedly happened with all older brothers and younger sisters. But as they got older, he began to appreciate her knack for "knowing things." When they were in junior high, Luna had a "feeling" about one of Cullen's pals, Harry Johnson. She couldn't explain it, but she had "bad vibes" about him. He was the Eddie Haskell of his class. Always putting on an obviously feigned, polite front. At least it was obvious to Luna that it was just a front. So she argued with Cullen, telling him he should keep away from him, but Cullen was a very loyal friend, always assuming the best in people. A week after her warning, Harry was arrested for breaking into an electronics store and stealing a few thousand dollars' worth of inventory. An electronics store. Didn't Harry realize they would have extreme security? Not only was he a thief, but a stupid one at that. Cullen shrugged it off as a wild guess on Luna's part, but in his heart of hearts he knew she had sensed something.

As they matured, Cullen knew not to argue with his little sis's woo-woo messages. Growing up, there had been too many incidents where those messages were right on the mark. The most common type was when she would make a phone call, and the person on the other end would exclaim, "I was just thinking about you!" It became so commonplace with her best friend, Barb, that Barb would answer the phone with a witty, "What took you so long?"

Luna could pick a winning racehorse by going to the paddock and looking into the animal's eyes. Cullen referred to her as "Dr. Doolittle," among other things. Her percentage of being right was better than Michael Jordan's basketball shots, something she would remind her straitlaced, basketball-crazed big brother about from time to time. The words "woman's intuition" had been said in the house way too many times to ignore. Eventually, he learned to trust her intuitions. He didn't always act on them, but then again, many people don't listen to their doctor's advice, either. "Eat less meat." "Stop smoking." "Get more exercise." And that advice came from people with degrees!

In college, Luna's undergraduate psychology curriculum offered several electives in the paranormal, a phenomenon beyond the scope of scientific understanding. It included extrasensory perception, telepathy, clairvoyance, telekinesis, and psychometry. She was particularly fascinated with psychometry, leaning on the theory that since everything is made of energy, one could get "vibrations" from inanimate objects. When asked for an explanation of the phenomenon, she would quote Sir Isaac Newton's law of universal gravitation, or cite Neil deGrasse Tyson, the director of the Hayden Planetarium and successor host of the TV series *Cosmos*, first developed by Carl Sagan. If neither of those worked, she would talk about electroencephalograms and brain activity, the development of neuroscience, and electromagnetic impulses. After the first minute and a half, the eyes of whoever had asked about it had glazed over and they had moved on to a different subject.

When she was in her teens, she had worked at her parents' shop during the summer and weekends. Her eye for art and décor did not go unnoticed by customers.

But for the most part, she kept her interest in "the unknown" on the down-low.

When Luna graduated from college, she had no plan. When people asked, "What are your plans?" she would answer, "My plan is not to have a plan. I'm just going to be goin' with the flow." The idea sent shivers up and down her parents' spines, but they knew she would be OK. How? They weren't sure, but Luna was resourceful and perceptive.

They breathed a sigh of relief when she got a job with the county doing evaluations for children's services. She also interviewed potential foster parents. With her insight and understanding of body language, she could spot an abuser more easily than most. When she could match families with kids, she was overjoyed. But when it came to the ugly situations, of which there were many, she was thrown into a black hole. One of her coworkers, who also understood a bit of psychic stuff, would remind Luna of psychiatrist Judith Orloff's definition: *An empath is an emotional sponge.* Orloff felt so strongly about the vulnerability of overly empathetic people that she had written a book about it, *The Empath's Survival Guide.* "I'm surprised you haven't read it inside and out," the coworker noted.

Luna had read the book. Many times. But it was a good reminder.

Chapter Two

North Carolina

In Luna's third year of working at children's services, an AMBER Alert had gone out to the surrounding area. A three-year-old girl was missing from her yard. The local sheriff's office conducted an extensive hunt of the area and came up empty. After twenty-four hours of searching, the authorities were beginning to suspect it might have been an abduction. Even though there hadn't been a ransom note, they called in the U.S. Marshals Office of Missing Children.

Luna volunteered to help with the search, taking her dog, Wiley, a border collie she had adopted from a shelter, with her. The original owner had thought the dog would make a good "tracking dog," but Wiley had other ideas and been surrendered to the shelter. Wiley must have sensed Luna's innate ability to communicate with animals. On more than one occasion, he found her purse when she had left it in the car. It was another example of those unexplainable things. Luna would be rummaging through the house when Wiley would run to the front door and start to bark softly. "What is it, pal?"

Wiley would scratch at the door. Luna would let him out, and he would run to the rear passenger door of her car. Naturally, Luna would follow him. And, sure enough, there her purse would be on the floor in the back.

"How did you know I was looking for my purse?" He gave a soft woof in reply. "And how did you know where it was?" Another woof. "OK. But we have to keep this between us. Enough people think I'm a little loony. We don't need them to know that I carry on a two-way conversation with my dog." Wiley nudged Luna under her arm. Luna gently grabbed his ears and kissed him all over the top of his head. She wasn't sure if he could help finding Avery, but even if he couldn't, he was good company.

When Luna and Wiley arrived at the search party base, she was introduced to U.S. Marshal Christopher Gaines. The minute she shook his hand, she got all goofy. His deep, dark blue eyes were framed with thick black eyelashes, the kind women pay a lot of money for. He reminded her of the actor Jay Hernandez, who played the new Magnum P.I. on television. And that smile. Even though it was a somber occasion, his smile was warm. He exuded authority in a very nonchalant way. Confident but not cocky. Luna estimated he was maybe a couple of years older than Cullen. Gaines had a hint of gray at his temples. He was slightly taller than Cullen and a little more buff. Fit but not a muscle head.

Gaines gave her the two-handed handshake. One on top of the other. She got what she would often refer to as the jolt. It could be a good thing or a bad one. In this case, she wasn't sure. It was a bit unnerving for her normally grounded but eccentric persona.

"Thanks for coming out. We need all the help we can get." A genuine smile crossed his face. "And who do we have here?" He bent a little closer to Wiley, who sat still like a good dog, with his tail going a mile a minute. Wiley held up his paw.

"This is Wiley." Luna could barely get the words out. The jolt she had felt was physical chemistry. The kind that makes you giddy and excited.

Gaines bent over and took the dog's paw. "Nice to meet you, Wiley." Wiley woofed a sound of approval. "Border collie, eh?"

"Ye-yes," Luna stuttered. "He was trained to be a tracking dog, but his original owner couldn't seem to get him on track, so to speak." Now she was nervous, trying not to sound trite or daft. "At least the owner had the good sense to bring him to a shelter, where he could be adopted."

"And that's where you came in?" His smile broadened.

"Yeah. Let's just say I'm a sucker for animals. I seem to . . ." She let her voice trail off. No sense in scaring this hunk away with her woo-woo stuff. At least not yet.

"You seem to what?" Gaines encouraged her to continue.

"Oh, nothing."

He tilted his head. "I'm an investigator. Don't make me interrogate you." He chuckled.

"My brother. Cullen. He calls me Dr. Doolittle. Talk to the animals. Like that." She was keeping it together as best she could. There was a very disarming attraction she was feeling coming from him. *Maybe that's what made him good at his job. His chemistry. A secret weapon.* She gave a slight smile.

"I get it. Animals are very smart. They have to use their instincts to survive. Their sense of hearing and smell can mean the difference between life and death." He cleared his throat. "Sorry. Didn't mean to get so dramatic."

Luna giggled. "No. No. It's perfectly fine. A lot of people don't understand how intuitive animals are." She looked down at Wiley. "Right, pal?" He woofed in response.

Gaines chortled, then touched the back of her shoulder. "Come, follow me. I'll get you signed in."

Luna's legs turned to rubber and the hair on her arms stood at attention. She thought she was going to faint.

Gaines took a tight hold of her forearm. "Are you OK?"

"Yes. Yes. I'm fine." *And stupid, and clumsy, and a total idiot.* "I'm just a bit tired. Had a long night of paperwork," she lied.

"I know what that's like." He still kept his hand on her arm. "I'll get you a bottle of water while you sign in." Gaines guided her to the table. "Minnie? This is . . ." It was then that he realized they hadn't introduced themselves to each other. Quick-witted, he continued and pointed to the dog, "Wiley." He hesitated for a second. "And this is his mommy."

Minnie looked up from the clipboard. "Hello, Wiley. And you are?" She turned her head toward Luna and continued in her Yorkshire English accent.

"Luna Bodman, or Bodhi. It depends on what day it is." She laughed nervously. *Shut up. You sound like an idiot.* "Kidding." She flashed her best smile at Minnie. Wiley sat obediently.

"Oh, hon, I have those kinds of days myself." Minnie winked conspiratorially at Luna and spun the clipboard around. Marshal Gaines set a bottle of spring water on the table and headed toward the tent being used as their base.

"Just print and sign your name. You can read it, of course. Just says you won't hold anyone responsible, including property owners, if you should fall on your face or other such problems with coordination. Also includes falling tree branches, bee stings, or getting sprayed by a skunk."

Luna laughed. "Oh, that would be so gross."

"Wouldn't it, eh?" Minnie replied. She handed Luna a bright yellow vest and a lanyard with a laminated card that read VOLUNTEER and a whistle attached. Pulling a second vest out of the box, she slid it across the table. "Now, let's see if we can fit one of these on your pooch." Wylie wagged his tail with enthusiasm. He, too, would be part of the official search party.

"Marshal Gaines is about to give everyone an update and instructions." Minnie nodded in the direction of a tent. "By the EMS truck."

Wiley stood proudly as Luna managed to wrap the extra vest around him. "Thanks very much," she said to Minnie.

"Thank you, hon. And thank you, too, Wiley." He gave a little bark and followed Luna on his leash.

Luna approached the group that had gathered inside the tent. There was a screen on the far wall with a satellite photo of the surrounding area. Gaines began speaking. "Avery Tucker was last seen at her home playing in the yard. He pointed the laser pointer at the map. "As of now, there haven't been any ransom demands; but that doesn't mean there wasn't an abduction. Local police officials conducted a search in the nearby area. Yesterday, we had helicopter surveillance, which turned up no sign of the little girl. The density of the trees and the rolling hills made it difficult for them to get a good look. Today, we are extending the perimeter as far as we think she might have wandered on her own. We need to cover all of the ground area in grids. Minnie tells me that there are twenty-three of you. I want you to split up into six groups of four. I'll be the fourth in one of the groups. Each group will be issued a tablet with a map and grid. If you spot anything that could be a clue, tap that spot on the tablet, and an agent will meet you.

"The girl's name is Avery Tucker. Age three. She is approximately thirty-nine inches tall, with short brown curly hair and is wearing a pink romper, white T-shirt, and pink sneakers. She could be frightened and hiding somewhere, so keep calling her name. Any questions?" There were none. The seriousness of why they were there surrounded them like a black cloud.

"Brennan's Deli has provided box lunches. We also have water, but let me remind you, there are no bathrooms in the woods. And, gentlemen, I suggest you keep it zipped." A small chuckle moved through the crowd. "OK, folks, please break up into groups of four. Thanks again for your help." He was articulate and well-spoken, and the authority in his voice garnered respect without making him sound like Joe Pistone, aka Donnie Brasco. Luna was reading his body language. *Nothing to hide. Self-assured.*

Luna took a deep breath, pulling in as much positive energy as she could suck in. She was determined to find the little girl. Her gut told her she could find her. *But how?* Well, that was always the fifty-million-dollar question. *Or had it inflated to a hundred million?* Luna felt that Avery was hiding somewhere. Scared, hungry, and most likely dehydrated. Luna spotted a small sweater on one of the tables. "Is that Avery's?" she asked.

"Yes. We were counting on a tracking dog for today's search, but owing to budget cuts, we have to wait another day for them to bring him over from Charlotte."

Wiley made a bit of a whining sound and jumped up and sniffed the sweater. Luna tried to pull him back. "Wiley, behave yourself." He looked at her and wagged his tail.

"You said he was trained to be a tracking dog?" Gaines eyed the sweater.

"Apparently he didn't like to hunt," Luna said apologetically.

"Let's see what he's got." Gaines smiled at her and let the dog get a better sniff of the sweater.

As the rescuers divided into groups, Luna realized she was one of only three. That meant Marshal Gaines would be in her group. Her knees got wobbly again. As each group moved in assigned directions, both Luna and Wiley got a "pull" toward a grove of trees that was not on their grid.

"Excuse me, Marshal Gaines?" Luna thought about how she was going to approach the subject.

"Yes, Luna?" Gaines stopped to listen.

"I don't know how to say this, but—"

He interrupted her. "Go ahead." He didn't smile, but his face was soft. "Over a decade in the Bureau, I've probably heard it all."

"Then I'm sure you've heard of a woman's intuition." Luna looked up and gave him her sweetest smile.

Gaines smirked and nodded.

"Can you indulge me for a few minutes?" Luna tried not to sound like she was pleading.

"OK. Let's hear it." His tone was even.

"Would it be all right if Wiley and I headed into those woods on the other side of the meadow?" Wiley was tugging on the leash, pulling her in the same direction Luna was pointing.

"That was going to be next after we scoured this area."

Wiley was pulling Luna along.

"I can't afford to have another missing person, so I can't let you go there alone."

Luna scrunched up her nose. "What if our group goes together?"

"I don't want to break protocol. I'll go with you and get someone from another group to track our grid." He pulled out his phone and pinged a lead tracker in the closest group.

"Ray? Send one of your people over to me."

Within a few short minutes, a local librarian joined Luna

and Gaines's group. Gaines handed the tablet to one of the remaining people. "We're going to check out another area. Should take us about an hour. I have my cell phone. Just hit the button that says GAINES on the upper-right corner of the tablet, and I'll answer. Everyone OK with this?" Nods and mumbles went around.

"Thank you for indulging me," Luna said in a hushed voice, as they moved quickly across the small open field that had once been a sheep farm. She stopped suddenly and pointed. "Over there." It was a thick grove of oak trees. She started calling Avery's name. Wiley let out short whoops. Luna stopped again. "This way." They moved through the thicket of trees when Gaines spotted a large felled oak. Must have been over a hundred years old. Gaines spotted something pink among the dead branches and the hollowed-out trunk that was resting horizontally on the ground. The three ran swiftly to the spot, praying it would be Avery, alive and unharmed. Gaines and Luna were calling her name as Wiley barked and yelped. The pink object moved slightly as the trio got closer. Gaines moved a large branch out of the way. The little girl's eyes fluttered, then shut again.

"Easy does it." With Luna's help, Gaines kept moving the branches.

"Avery? Honey? Can you hear me?" Luna said tenderly. A moan came from the child. They moved the debris as fast as possible, Wiley barking them on. Gaines knelt next to the tree trunk and began removing the leaves covering most of the little girl's face.

"Avery? I'm a policeman." Gaines wanted her to understand he was one of the good guys. He doubted a three-year-old would know what a U.S. marshal was, but he showed her his badge anyway.

"Mama," the girl whispered.

"Yes, honey. We're going to get your mama, but first we have to get you out of this tree. OK?" Gaines said reassuringly. He checked her for fractures, cuts, and bruises before trying to move her. There were a few superficial lacerations, probably sustained while stumbling through the woods.

How Avery got wedged inside the oak was a good question, but at that moment, they needed to get her to safety. Gaines pulled out his mobile phone and hit a speed-dial button. "We've got her. She's conscious but slightly dazed. A few cuts and bruises. She seems to be breathing normally and is asking for her mother." He listened for a moment. "Roger that."

Luna immediately whipped off her bandana, poured some of the bottled water on it, and began to clean Avery's face. "You OK, sweetie?"

"I want my mama." Tears rolled down her face. And then Luna's face. Luna could have sworn she saw Gaines's eyes well up, too.

About eight minutes later, a medevac helicopter landed in the small field. Two EMS attendants ran toward the thicket with a stretcher.

"Hey, how would you like to go for a helicopter ride?" Gaines smiled at the little girl.

"Mommy?" she squeaked. "Where's Bunny?" she gabbled.

"We're going to get her. OK?" Gaines reassured her. He furrowed his brow and mouthed, "Bunny?"

Luna shrugged, kept wiping Avery's brow, and murmured, "Who is Bunny, sweetie?"

The little girl could barely whisper. "The bunny. I lost bunny." Then she closed her eyes and began to doze off.

Once they secured Avery in the helicopter, it rose slowly and took off for the nearest hospital. Gaines was on his phone giving updates to the base. He was grinning from ear to ear. "Minnie, you know what to do. We should be back at the base in about thirty minutes." He could hear Minnie on her walkie-talkie spreading the good news to the others. Gaines could hear cheers and hoots in the background.

On the walk back, Gaines put his hand on Luna's shoulder. "How did you know?" He looked at her in amazement.

"I wish I could tell you how." Luna shrugged and smiled. "It's a gift."

"Indeed it is."

"So you're not going to say it was a wild and lucky guess?" Luna gave him an affectionate elbow jab, which she regretted immediately. *What was I thinking?*

"Nope. I'll take whatever help I can get. And Wiley did a great job, too. Didn't you, boy?" Wiley kept trotting ahead, proudly wagging his tail.

By the time they arrived at the base, there was already a news van waiting to interview the search team. Shoving a microphone into Gaines's face, the reporter fired off questions.

"Was she hurt? Was she assaulted? How did she get here?"

"I'll take your questions in the tent. Excuse me." Gaines pushed past the gathering crowd. He looked at Luna. "Follow me."

"Oh, wait." She stopped abruptly. "I'd rather we keep my 'lucky guess' between us. I do a lot of work with children's services. Don't need the publicity. Just say we found her. Please. Is that all right with you?"

"Are you sure? How about Wiley? Can he get some of the credit?"

"Wiley? Absolutely! Just leave me out of it." Luna gave his arm a squeeze. *Again with the physical contact.* She was mortified.

He patted her hand. "Your secret is safe with me. Although I don't know if I can leave it out of the official report."

"You seem like a pretty smart guy. I'm sure you'll think of something." She was hoping for a dinner invitation, never mind the official report.

Gaines chuckled. "I'm sure I will." He paused. "I'll be heading back to Charlotte in the morning." He pulled out his wallet and handed her his card. "If you are ever in the neighborhood . . ."

Luna took the card. "Thanks. You never know."

"I have your contact information, so if I'm ever in the neighborhood, I'll give you a shout. Thanks for being so assertive. And accurate." Gaines bent down to give Wiley a good head rub. "And thank you, too, Wiley." He gave her a short salute and began answering questions. "We don't know how she got into the woods. We found no wounds except for a few scrapes. From what we could tell, she simply wandered away and got lost."

Luna heaved a big sigh. *Maybe I will be in Charlotte one day.*

After many phone calls and much television coverage, they learned that Avery had spotted a rabbit in the yard and managed to crawl under a ridiculously small hole in the ground under the fence. She had followed the rabbit into the woods and lost her way. The doctors said she was suffering from some exposure but was going to be fine and could be released in a day or two.

The next morning, Luna went to the hospital to check on Avery's condition. On her way there, she stopped at a local children's store and bought a plush bunny for Avery. As she pulled into the parking lot, she spotted Gaines carrying what looked like a stuffed animal. She got goose bumps. *Good-*

looking, smart, and sensitive. Definitely crushworthy material. She looked at herself in the visor mirror. *Wish I had primped a little more. Oh well. What you see is what you get . . . even stuff you don't see.* She smirked. She decided to give Gaines a head start to the pediatric floor. Not simply out of courtesy, but her legs were betraying her again, turning to rubber. She hoped a few minutes would help restore her nerves.

When she arrived at Avery's room, the little girl was surrounded by balloons and her doting parents. They were overwrought that something like this could happen but also very thankful she was safe.

Luna stood tall, pushed her shoulders back, and entered the room. "Hi, Avery. Remember me?" She handed the pink-and-white rabbit to the little girl.

Avery looked up with a sweet smile. "Uh-huh."

Her mother was clinging to a wadded-up tissue. "Thank you so much for helping with the search. I don't know what I would have done if anything . . ." Her voice trailed off, and she broke down in tears. Avery's father put his arm around his wife.

"We're all OK, hon. We're all OK." He introduced himself and thanked Luna for her participation.

"It was my dog Wiley. He has a thing for kids," Luna said modestly. "And, of course, the leadership of Marshal Gaines." *Oh my God. Am I flirting?* She tried to look away but noticed a slight blush on Gaines's face. Concerned she was about to make a total fool of herself, she quickly added, "I'm so glad everything turned out well. I have to get to work. You take care now. And no more chasing bunnies. OK? Now you have two!" She nodded at the one Gaines had set down on the bed.

A meek little voice thanked her, and Avery's parents gave

Luna a big hug. She nodded at Gaines. "Have a safe trip home."

On the way out, she bit the inside of her lip, wondering if she had imagined the chemistry between them. *I guess I'll find out eventually. If I'm ever "in the neighborhood."*

Several months later, while she was still working for children's services, she got a call at work. It was U.S. Marshal Gaines. He wanted to pick her brain over another missing-person case. She was delighted to help. He asked if she could come to Charlotte to sit in for an interview with the siblings of a young man who had gone missing. "We'll pay you, of course, and for your stay at a hotel."

Luna was taken aback. "Pay me?"

"Yes, as in paying for your time. Do you have a daily fee?"

Luna quickly tried to calculate her pay for two days, plus the two readings she had scheduled. *The total came to $150 per day plus $100 for each reading she would have to reschedule. Should she charge them for that? She would eventually get paid when she did the readings.*

"Luna? You still with me?"

"Oh yes. Sorry, someone popped their head into my office."

"Would five hundred dollars for the two days plus hotel and meals be amenable?" Gaines asked, wanting to get this settled ASAP.

"Let me check my schedule. I'm assuming you want me there tomorrow or the day after?"

"The sooner the better. The brother has been missing for a week. And the longer the disappearance lasts, the less likely we are to find him. The siblings think he may have been abducted, but there have been no ransom requests as yet."

"Got it. Hang on a minute?" she asked. Luna put him on hold and dashed into her supervisor's office. "Chaz? It's the U.S. Marshals Service."

Her rumpled boss looked up from the pile of papers on his desk. "What have you done now?" He was half joking.

"They want me to go to Charlotte tomorrow to sit in on an interview. A missing high school kid."

"What do they need you for?" he snarled.

"Maybe because I helped with the Avery case? I'm not totally sure. I only have two appointments tomorrow, and I can reschedule them." She wanted to get on her knees and plead.

He plunked the glasses off the edge of his nose. "Yeah. OK. But don't make a habit of it."

"Thanks, boss." She wanted to kiss him. Not really.

"Get Gladys to take your appointments. If anything seems off with either of them, you can discuss it with Gladys when you get back."

"Thanks again." Luna spun around, her long skirt swirling like a whirlpool.

Over the next two years, Luna worked with Gaines on several cases. They developed a casual friendship, but the chemistry was always there in the background. One night after dinner, they ended up walking extremely close to each other. She could smell the hint of aftershave and feel the heat from his breath. It was all she could do to remain vertical and not swoon. For a very brief moment, she thought, hoped, he would kiss her. But he didn't. Maybe that's what they meant by "professional courtesy."

During the few times they were together, they shared a little bit of personal information. He was thirty-nine, two years older than Cullen. Divorced with a ten-year-old son. No serious relationship. He didn't have time. It was one of the reasons he was divorced. But Luna knew one day she would have to put on her big-girl pants and make a pass at him before he got involved with someone. The thought of both of those things made her cringe, making a fool of herself for trying or being a fool for not.

Chapter Three

Buncombe County, North Carolina

Ellie Stillwell would be considered a dowager by some, but much of her wealth came from her own family. The origin of her wealth was something she kept under her red hat. In the late 1950s, North Carolina had begun to focus on economic development, which had the effect of increasing the value of land as it became more scarce and developers were willing to pay more for it. Her family had purchased large parcels, mainly to assure themselves that they would have a say as to how the land was developed. Part of her family's estate was a large tract situated several miles from the downtown area of Asheville, North Carolina. No one had thought much of that parcel until Ellie secured a permit to build an art center on it. Some local politicians were adamantly opposed, complaining that it would mar the countryside. The center was to sit on fifty acres within a larger section of one square mile. Though most people in the area thought of it as farm country, there hadn't been a farm on the property since the end of the Second World War. But Ellie was on a mission.

She thought the land was going to waste. She also thought

all the government cuts in funding for the arts was a crying shame. Too much talent and not enough support. Her goal was to build a dedicated area for the arts.

She was inspired by the Torpedo Factory Art Center in Old Town Alexandria, Virginia. In November of 1918, the U.S. Navy began construction of the factory on the banks of the Potomac River for the production of torpedoes. Over the years, the building had had many incarnations, ranging from a manufacturing plant to a storehouse for government documents.

In 1973, the building was purchased by the Art League; it was renovated in 1982. At present it housed the largest collection of working artists and studios to be found under one roof. Ellie liked that idea very much. She was also partial to certain antiques and wanted a designated space for them. But she didn't want it to be a mishmash of things that looked like someone's garage sale. No, this was going to be a new, clean, bright space for artists to unleash their creativity and sell their work.

In the beginning, a handful of local community members took her to court to try to stop what they deemed would turn open land into commercial, industrial space. *What's wrong with these people?* she wondered. Ellie enlisted the talent of a local architect to design the space with an ambience similar to that of the Torpedo Factory Art Center. The lower level would have an interior courtyard with an atrium feel, surrounded by workshops.

Ellie was also a staunch supporter of the environment. The entire building was planned to be eco-friendly, using solar energy to power the entire building. She took every measure to assure the county that this would be something they could be proud of and which would encourage other communities across the country to support the arts. *And* the environment. She knew intuitively that she was doing the right thing. When she submitted the plans to the county board, they could not find a single reason to stop her from going forward with the project.

The two-story building included skywalks connecting the various sections, anchored in the center by a staircase. The ceiling would have skylights, giving the interior a sense of openness and space. The natural light was ideal for the interior landscaping created by a local landscape artist.

When complete, the building itself boasted fifty thousand square feet and an outdoor Belgian-block patio. It was surrounded by several acres of landscaped greenery and open space. Three sides of the first floor were devoted to workshops and art studios facing inward toward the courtyard. Each had glass sliding doors to offer the most exposure and allow for secure closing overnight. The fourth side consisted of specialty shops selling food items and straddled each side of the large folding doors leading to the patio.

There was a spot for artisanal cheeses and a café that served and sold specialty teas and coffees. Another sold baked goods. There was a shop selling handmade ice cream, a gourmet sandwich shop, and a wine cellar. Not wanting to deal with kitchen issues, and to minimize her interactions with the Board of Health, all food was brought in freshly prepared, daily. It was a grab-and-go style. Patrons had the option of grabbing something on their way out or sitting at one of the small café tables dotting the interior courtyard. The outside courtyard also held several tables with umbrellas for al fresco dining, weather permitting.

Ellie wanted the center to be a destination, a place where you could bring the family for an inspiring day, a good sandwich, and a great cup of coffee. In the evening, art events could make use of the wine cellar, and she would rent out the space for private parties and musical events. She viewed the center as a new location for community functions as well as a place to support the arts. All of them.

The second floor concentrated on vintage stores, each with a theme, including Christmas items, collectible dolls, perfume bottles, nautical merchandise, neon signs, and vintage handbags.

Ellie was also cognizant of artists' fluctuating incomes. She knew the money wasn't much and not consistent. In the spirit of fairness, rent would be a small percentage of their monthly sales. It was somewhat of an honor system since many of the tenants dealt in cash, but Ellie had faith in the better part of human nature.

The Stillwell Art Center was going to be Ellie's legacy. She hoped at some point it could become a co-op, where the artists each had a stake in the upkeep, but when or if that happened, she would bequeath it as part of her estate.

The center had been two years in the making, and during that time she had scrutinized every applicant who wanted a space in the building. She had a glassblower in the front corner and a pottery thrower in another. In the far corner was the quirky man who made pieces of sculpture out of cut-up beer cans. Across from him, a brother-and-sister team had a restoration business adjacent to the café. By the time of the grand opening, the Stillwell Art Center was home to over thirty artists and vintage shops and a half dozen food vendors.

Ellie Stillwell came from a long line of landowners. They were conscious of maintaining the integrity of the county and its resources. They were also benefactors of the local libraries and animal-welfare organizations, but for the most part they didn't flaunt their wealth or their generosity. They preferred to be low-key. Her father had once told her that if people think you have a lot of money to give away, they also think that you should give some of it to them. Not for any particular reason. Just because you have it.

"It's none of anyone's business how we spend our money," he would say. When there were events that listed the names of the patrons, her family's generous contribution was always listed as coming from Anonymous.

She had met her husband, Richard, when they were both attending Duke University. He was in the law school, and she was working on her PhD in art history. They had been married for forty-five years when he had died of a massive coronary. *At least he didn't suffer. At least not for very long.* That was how she consoled herself. They had had no children, so now, a widow at age seventy, Ellie was going to put her own resources to work.

Richard had been one of the highest-paid real-estate lawyers in the county. They had lived a simple life, spending very modestly, and Richard had been a keen investor. When he died, Ellie was stunned, but not totally surprised, that her net worth, including what she had inherited from her family, was over fifty million dollars. Even after using half of it to fund the arts and support animal causes, she was still left with enough money to last the rest of her days, which had become boring without Richard. However, with the arts center project, she and her two German shepherd dogs, Ziggy and Marley, had something to do every morning. She and Richard had taken one of their vacations in the Caribbean, where Richard had developed a love for reggae music. Hence, she had named the dogs after the music icon, Bob Marley, one of the pioneers in the genre, and his son Ziggy, who has continued spreading the sound and following in his father's philanthropic footsteps. Ellie liked both the music and the sentiment.

One of the must-haves for the art center was for part of the open area to be used for a dog park, where well-behaved pooches could mingle and play. A cleanup station was also available. During the construction, Marley and Ziggy had marked their territory, giving it their seal of approval.

Ellie thought it was amusing that the politicians who had originally fought her efforts were now clamoring for an invitation and photo ops. The social climbers were also green with envy. For decades, they had ignored Ellie. Plain Ellie, the art professor. Now, they were also kissing her you-know-what for that coveted, colorful, translucent, glassine piece of paper saying:

We request the pleasure of your company for the grand opening of the Stillwell Center for the Arts.

Of course, the governor would be there, as well as the state's two senators, and the mayor of Asheville. It was shaping up to be a momentous occasion in the history of North Carolina. Ellie had to admit, she was enjoying every minute of every aspect of what she hoped would turn out to be a life-changing event for the area. But there was no way she could know exactly how life-changing it would be, both for her and so many others.

Cullen was pacing the floor, trying to decide what to wear to the opening. Should he look like someone from HGTV? The *Property Brothers*? Flannel shirt? Jeans? Blazer? Clearly, the enormity of their new venture was in his face, and face it he would. For the first time in his life, he understood why women get anxious about what to wear for events. He laughed at himself. *Take it easy, buddy. It's going to be great.* He finally opted for a pair of nice jeans, an oxford shirt, and a blue cashmere blazer. Neat, casual, approachable.

*   *   *

Luna was about to incorporate several skills in her and her brother's new endeavor. She promised her colleagues at the Children's Center she would always make herself available if they needed her, and she made sure Marshal Gaines knew of her plans. At least some of them.

Luna had been reluctant to tell Ellie Stillwell of her extra-curricular activities and decided to keep it to herself until it was absolutely necessary to bring it up for discussion. She did not advertise or promote her psychic gift. She would only take referrals from former or existing clients. As much as Cullen was her protector, she, too, wanted to protect Cullen from any ridicule or embarrassment due to her penchant for the paranormal. Not that it was a huge secret, but Luna felt it was in Cullen's best interest if she didn't shove it in every passerby's face.

Inside the Namaste Café, there were four small café tables and a wall of design and art books. A counter held baked goods supplied by the Flakey Tart, which also had a shop at the arts center. Among the pastries, scones, and muffins, there was a selection of three blends of coffee and an assortment of teas. Aside from being Luna's part of the overall family operation, it would provide a small income stream, not just a place to hang out and eat great flaky delights with a robust cup of freshly roasted coffee. A large easel with a sketch pad sat in one corner. It was a divination device she would surreptitiously use when she was doing a reading. It was almost as if she were doing automatic writing, but in her case it was automatic drawing.

Her level of excitement was reaching enormous heights. It was a new day and a new beginning. The grand opening for the art center was that evening. Several weeks ago, she had sent Gaines an invitation, saying, "In case you're in the neighborhood," which had become a playful joke between them. Even though she hadn't heard back, she was hoping for the best.

Luna dug through her chest of favorite kitschy outfits and decided to tame it down for the evening. Well, not too much. Sliding her long dresses across the closet pole, she discovered a long, pale yellow lace dress that flared at the hem. She could still twirl if she wanted, something she was known to do when leaving the room, or when she was spot-on with something she had predicted. It had long, lace-belled sleeves that matched the flow of the skirt perfectly.

She peered into the mirror, scrutinizing every inch of her face. First thing was to ditch the granny glasses and opt for the contact lenses she rarely wore. On a normal day, she wore a lightweight foundation to cover some of her freckles, a bit of blush, and a smear of lip gloss. That night, she wanted to be a bit more radiant, just in case. Just in case Marshal Gaines made an appearance, she was going full-on makeup makeover. Not too freakish, but a lot more glam. Luna drew on her creativity and applied each stroke as if she were creating a work of art. The amber eye shadow made her hazel eyes stand out, and the shimmery copper eyeliner framed them beautifully. A coral-bronze blush enhanced her cheekbones, and the neutral lipstick was a nice contrast to her dazzling eyes.

Now for the hair. Earlier, she had noticed that it didn't look healthy. She hadn't been paying much attention to it over the past few weeks as they were getting ready for the grand opening. It was time for drastic measures. Well, maybe not too drastic.

Luna darted into the other bedroom, which served as her yoga retreat, sewing room, and art studio. She dug out a pair of shears and chopped three inches off the bottom. "Much better." Now it was only three inches below her shoulders but had movement and looked lush. She ran a brush through her waves and decided on a bohemian-style updo with a side braid. One side of her hair was swooped over the top into a side braid at the base of her neck with a small ribbon, then allowed to flow freely at the bottom. A few wisps on each side. Perfect. She still looked respectable yet a bit eccentric. She popped on metallic ballet-slipper-style shoes. She took a spin in front of the mirror. "Wow. Who knew I could look this good?" She chuckled out loud. Now she really, *really* hoped Marshal Christopher Gaines would be able to get a good look at her.

Chapter Four

Boston, Massachusetts
Millstone executive offices
Earlier that day

Arthur Millstone was pacing the floor. Rowena was smoking her third cigarette while nonchalantly spinning her stack of David Yurman Cable Spira bracelets. She hated it when Arthur was in a mood. Normally, she would pour herself a single-malt scotch, but it was still too early in the day, even for her.

Rowena was Arthur Millstone's trophy wife and she knew it. She was tall and slender, with platinum hair cut in a short, stylish, chin-length style, one side longer than the other. Rowena had had one mission in life. To marry a rich man. Mission accomplished. It had taken a few years for her to wangle her way into the top echelon of old-money families. She had done it the hard way. On her back. The problem was that men with the kind of fortune she was after were usually married, and divorce was too costly. She had been around that block more than once until she met Arthur Millstone.

Arthur was sixty when he began his affair with Rowena.

She had been thirty-five. Like the other men with whom she had dallied, he was married at the time, but Rowena fixed that. His divorce was swift, and new nuptials were shared immediately thereafter. It was now three years since Rowena had become Mrs. Arthur Millstone.

Rowena jumped when the phone on Arthur's desk rang. She just knew there was trouble ahead. If they could get past the reading of the will, everything would be fine.

"What?" Arthur barked at his assistant.

"Mr. Millstone, Mr. Dunbar is on the phone for you."

He pressed the flashing button. "Clive? I hope you have good news for me." He feigned lightheartedness.

"Hello, Arthur. I'm afraid we are going to have to postpone the reading of the will for at least another thirty days."

Arthur kept his temper under control. "But why?"

"Your father was supposed to meet with me the day of his heart attack. He indicated he wanted to make some changes in his will. Unfortunately, we never had the opportunity. He said he had everything on paper and the document was signed and witnessed by the house manager, Colette Petrov."

Arthur was seething. He knew that the Petrov woman was going to be a problem. His father, Randolph Millstone, had been too fond of her. Not in a salacious way. It bothered Arthur that Randolph had treated Colette warmly. Randolph had reminded Arthur time and again that the staff was there to accommodate the needs of the *manor,* and that Arthur or his gold-digging wife could handle whatever Arthur needed.

Arthur resented everything about Colette. She was efficient and kept the staff humming. Arthur knew that he could be demanding, but Rowena's behavior made Arthur look like a saint in comparison. On many occasions, his father reminded the two of them that as long as the house was running smoothly, Arthur and Rowena had nothing to complain about.

But they did. Repeatedly. Constantly. Again and again. Arthur wished that he could have fired Colette months ago, but she was off-limits, at least until his father passed away. In point of fact, after Colette had arrived, the power to hire and fire was hers or his father's. Arthur no longer had any say in the staffing of the manor.

"I don't understand, Clive. You have his original will, correct?"

"Yes, but I'm bothered by the missing document. It was unfortunate that he never regained consciousness."

"Yes, very." Arthur's mood was taking a turn for the better. "I don't see why this needs to be delayed any further."

"I'd like to have the opportunity to speak with Ms. Petrov, but I understand she is no longer in your family's employ."

"That is correct. Rowena caught her looking through her dresser. Probably trying to find something she could sell."

He glanced at Rowena. She rolled her eyes, knowing it was all a lie.

"I can't speak to that. Did she leave any forwarding information? Where she could be reached?" Clive pushed.

"Not that I know of, but perhaps Rowena might. I'll check with her when I get home."

Rowena lit her fourth Treasurer Aluminum Gold cigarette. At sixty bucks a pack, twelve dollars had gone up in smoke in less than a half hour. Arthur waved the smoke away from him, giving Rowena a disgruntled look. She took another long drag.

Clive continued on the other end of the line. "Arthur, as trustee and executor of his estate, I feel obligated to be certain his final wishes are met."

Arthur sat up straight in his chair. "I know you are trustee and executor, Clive. Isn't there a time limit for how long you can postpone the reading of the will?"

"It could take up to several months, Arthur. That's why it's important for me to locate Ms. Petrov to ask her if she did, in fact, witness his signature, and if she has any idea where the document is. If she did not witness any such document, then we can proceed."

"Clive, you know it wasn't in the safe, and we searched the entire house but came up empty-handed." That much was true, but for a very different reason. He huffed. "Very well, Clive. I'll see what I can find out." He hung up without saying good-bye.

"We have to find that woman before Clive Dunbar does. Or before those documents show up somewhere. One or the other. Preferably both."

"Darling, if you recall, we gave her a very generous severance package, including a one-way ticket to Buffalo for her and her son, with the understanding that she would go live with her sister." Rowena lit her fifth cigarette. She was chain-smoking now.

"Yes, Rowena. It was I who gave her the money and the send-off. You were nothing but a bystander during the transaction. So, yes, my dear, I do recall." He was losing his patience at record speed.

Randolph Millstone had been the CEO and majority stockholder in Millstone Enterprises, a global business started three generations before. Arthur's mother had died when he was twelve, and his father had indulged him ever since. Arthur had dropped out of college a few times, wrecked expensive sports cars, and spent two years as a world traveler. He had played the role of playboy rather well. But pressure had been put on him to settle down. When Arthur met his first wife, Sylvia, Randolph thought he would settle down, so he gave him a job at the family business, hoping it would inspire and motivate him.

At present, Arthur was sixty-three, almost sixty-four, overweight, and out of shape. His once full head of wavy hair had receded to parts unknown. He wasn't aging well. Arthur was standing on the precipice of total failure or serious bodily harm.

He furrowed his brow at the sound of his cell phone, which had landed on the sofa. He lumbered over to pick it up. "What now?" he growled.

Chapter Five

Boston, Massachusetts
Millstone Manor

Rowena didn't think it possible, but Arthur was in a worse mood than he had been earlier in the day. He had received a phone call from Jerry Thompson, a private detective on the Millstone payroll, that was disturbing. Arthur gave him the assignment to find out where the estate furniture had landed. Arthur was convinced his father had left a copy of his latest will somewhere in the house. But his father had suffered the heart attack in the garage. He should have had the will on his person. But no document was found, and the Petrov woman claimed she had never seen the document again after she had witnessed his father's signature. She insisted she hadn't read it. Simply witnessed his signature and signed on the dotted line.

Arthur was pacing the floor with a glass of single-malt scotch in one hand and a cigar in the other. Ordinarily, he would be sitting in his Eichholtz Highbury Estate tobacco-colored leather chair, puffing away on the hand-rolled Cuban. Rowena thought Arthur was so cliché. God, how she hated his old-fogey tastes. He should have kept all of his father's furniture. But his father, Randolph Millstone, had not been an old fogey. He was one of the last members of the Greatest Generation. His style was fashioned after Winston Churchill and Ernest Hemmingway. It was a man thing. Back then, it was fine. Now? Why couldn't he get over it? What was the point in selling his father's furniture if he was only going to replace it with some of the same or similar things? If anyone was to blame for the will's going missing, it was Arthur. Had he not been in such a hurry to scrape up some cash, maybe they would have found the missing document already.

It hadn't taken long—a little over two years of married whatever—before Arthur was constantly getting on Rowena's nerves with his pompous attitude and constant reprimands about her spending habits. She put up with his gambling and cavorting, which she figured was a fair trade-off for being a rich man's wife. Yes, she knew about his extracurricular activities. Hadn't she been one of them when he was married to Sylvia? In truth, Rowena was grateful for his dalliances. Though she had no plans to have sex with him again, she still hoped he had the good sense to use a condom, if only to protect his partners and avoid lawsuits.

Thanks to his many affairs, Rowena no longer had to sleep with the boor. Arthur was a lot of things, but a passionate lover was not one of them. Another cliché, she thought. Fat, rich, and bad in bed. At least that was her experience with the many wealthy men she had had affairs with before she married Arthur. And now she settled for being a trophy wife. She was in her midthirties when she had met Arthur and was seeing a new generation of gold diggers snapping at her heels. Younger, more nubile, a lot dumber, but smart enough to know what an older man wants. Damn that little blue pill.

She had been acutely aware that if she didn't land some

old bag of wind with money soon, she could be looking for a real job in the not-too-distant future. She had to admit, she was just as much a cliché. Rowena calculated how long she would have to live the stereotypical life of a trophy wife before she could depart with a nice sum of money, assuming that Arthur did not blow it all first. The estate sale was supposed to help pay off some of his debts, but then he had gone and spent the money on *things*. Lots of *things*. And he had the audacity to chastise *her* for her extravagance? Some nerve.

Rowena thought about Arthur's ex. She wondered who had gotten the better end of the deal. Sylvia Millstone had received a very hefty settlement upon becoming the ditched wife—the equivalent of a golden parachute. She appeared to be extremely content to leave with a settlement of ten million dollars. It was half of Arthur's net worth at the time, most of which consisted of his stake in the family business, which itself depended upon the provisions of his father's last will and testament.

Sylvia might have seemed to be the silent, dutiful, and now-scorned wife, but she was shrewd. Sylvia had moved to Portugal with her substantial settlement. For one thing, Rowena knew that Sylvia wouldn't want to be hanging around town while she and Arthur were the new "it" couple. Little did anyone know that Sylvia would be doing cartwheels if she hadn't torn her rotator cuff. Sylvia was fifty-five years old and had a whole lot of living ahead of her. She had bought a villa, drank wine, ate good food, and had the company of a man ten years her junior.

Rowena suspected that Sylvia had known about Arthur's serious gambling problem. Sylvia must have sensed the oncoming train wreck Arthur Millstone represented and had probably been greatly relieved to get off those tracks. Thinking about her current situation, Rowena was almost envious of Sylvia.

Rowena was beginning to wonder how long Arthur could sustain his lifestyle, and *her* lifestyle, before his debts caught up with him. At the moment, Rowena couldn't dump Arthur. There was a little matter of the prenup. Sure, she'd get a tidy figure, but at present she had access to the wealth of the family business, Millstone Enterprises International. Rowena suspected that Arthur was dabbling in the culinary art of cooking the books. There was no other way he could cover the tens of thousands he lost every month. Of course, she wasn't supposed to know about Arthur's association with the Irish mob, but she had overheard more than one conversation. At the moment, as she watched her husband pace the floor, she knew that her future was hanging in the balance. Pulling another cigarette from her inlaid mother-of-pearl-and-silver case, she thought, *Arthur is right.* If they didn't find and destroy that second will, or Colette Petrov, Randolph's girl Friday, they both could be checking in to the Graybar Hotel.

Rowena sat on the arm of the leather chair and took a long drag. "I think we should call Amber. I know we scoured the receipts, but maybe she'll remember something. Something someone said. It's worth speaking with her."

Arthur stopped abruptly. "You were supposed to handle this."

"I know. I know. But, like I said earlier, using her was *your* idea. Maybe *you* can jog her memory." She let out a plume of smoke.

Arthur looked as if he were going to snarl, but immediately thought better of it. He needed to think. Get a grip. He knew there was an imminent deadline in the murky future. Even though the deadline hadn't been revealed, it was out there. Looming, like a large, dark shadow.

"Call her," he barked.

Rowena flinched. Again. The second time in one day. That was a record. If she flinched once in a decade, that was one time too often. The fact that she was thirty-eight meant she didn't do it often. She stared blankly into space.

"Rowena!" Arthur screamed at her. "Get on the damn phone and get Amber in here!"

"But I thought—" Rowena tried to interrupt him.

"Damn it! Do I have to do everything?" Arthur yanked the telephone handset off the cradle. He punched a few buttons on the phone.

Like a coin flip, Arthur's tone changed. "Hello, Amber dear. How are you?" Rowena felt the bile sour in her throat.

"I'm very well, thank you." He paused a moment. "I realize it's a tad late, but would you be available to stop by this evening? Rowena and I were going over the receipts for the estate sale and we have a few questions." He listened, frowned, and responded, "Tomorrow morning? How early can you get here?" Another pause. "Yes, eight o'clock will be fine. I'll have Rowena fix us something to eat." He glanced up at his wife. Her mouth dropped. She gave him an incredulous look. Arthur waved her off. "Yes. We're on a limited staff now. We are reevaluating our needs." He listened again. "It's no trouble at all. Fine. See you in the morning."

Rowena was livid. *Rowena will fix us something to eat?* "When did I become the chief cook and bottle washer around here?" She stomped over to the credenza and poured herself some good old Kentucky bourbon. Three fingers' worth.

"Listen, Rowena, we need to figure this out before Clive tracks down that Petrov woman, or worse, that document turns up somewhere. So you're just going to have to play the happy little housewife for a while." He clasped his hands and tightened his fingers. "We can't let anyone wander around this house until we resolve this mess. I don't want anyone having access to anything."

"What about the cleaning people?" Rowena's voice had

gone up an octave. "Certainly, you can't expect me to mop the floors and dust?" She was close to shrieking. "Look around. Marble floors. Twenty thousand square feet. More pieces of furniture than you got rid of. No, sir. You need to come up with a better plan than making me Cinderella before her fairy godmother showed up." She stomped back to the chair and flopped into the big leather seat.

"Oh, stop pouting." Arthur's voice was more even now. "You can keep the cleaning staff, but I want you supervising every move they make. And I mean every move. I don't want another debacle. We don't have a lot of time. I know that Clive is anxious to get to the bottom of the mysterious will. How long will it take him to think of learning where Colette is by going to her parents?"

He unclenched his fingers and buried his head in his hands. The vibration from his burner phone made him sit up. He groaned. "Now what?" he barked, then sat up taller. "Really? Where?"

Chapter Six

Charlotte, North Carolina

Marshal Christopher Gaines had been born in Tuckahoe, New York. His father was a police officer whose ancestors had come from Scotland. His mother, Bettina, was from Brazil. She was a stunning woman, with black hair and blue eyes. The family often joked how lucky Christopher was to inherit his mother's good looks. And most likely her intuition, or at the very least, to respect it.

Growing up, he had been a good student and a fine athlete. His speed and coordination won him a baseball scholarship to Vanderbilt University in Nashville, where he majored in criminal justice. Much to his father's chagrin, he had no interest in pursuing a career in professional baseball. It was grueling, controlled your life, and was tenuous. Gaines wanted something stable and interesting. Professional baseball might be exciting, but it wasn't stable. But doing the same thing every day for forty years was not his goal either. He wanted a career where he could make a contribution and still be invigorated. He wanted to be involved in something larger than himself, something for the greater good.

When he graduated from college, he enrolled at John Jay College of Criminal Justice in New York. The masters of arts program offered a variety of areas of study. Criminal investigations was the direction he wanted to go, and he hoped to eventually get a gig in the U.S. Marshals Service. Not an easy task.

While he was studying for his master's, he worked for the Manhattan District Attorney's Office three days a week. It was a lot of drudgery, but he believed it would pay off eventually. If you wanted experience in a cornucopia of crime, he was truly in the right place. Once he completed his course of studies, he became a paralegal in the DA's office and began to apply for positions with the U.S. Marshals Service. It had taken almost two years, but he had finally been offered a position in the Mobile, Alabama, field office. He was twenty-six years old. It wasn't an ideal location, but it would do. He would continue to prove himself to his superiors until he could apply for a transfer to a location that was a little less humid. He took on every assignment he could to move ahead. Consequently, it took its toll on his marriage.

He had met Lucinda Dawson when he first arrived in Alabama. She was a bouncy blonde. Cute. Of course, he was attracted to her. And she was smitten with his worldly ways. The fact that he was a federal marshal scored him a lot of points with her. Little did she know how demanding his work would be and that she would begin to tire of his never being around enough. She thought that if they got married and had a child, he might be inclined to be more family-oriented, but she was wrong.

For Gaines, getting married seemed like a good idea at the time. He adored Lucinda but always questioned if he genuinely loved her. He liked her. A lot. And not unlike women, men also felt their biological clock ticking. Or maybe it's their social standing. At twenty-seven, he thought it was time to settle down despite not having the slightest inkling as to what that really meant. Lucinda got pregnant right away. Both of them thought it would make things perfect.

They could not have been more wrong. It only put more stress on their relationship. Gaines thought a change of scenery would improve their crumbling marriage. A new town. A fresh start, so he applied for a transfer, which he ultimately received.

After they moved to Charlotte, North Carolina, both of them realized they were better at being friends than spouses. She needed more than he could give. When Carter started school, Lucinda got a job working as a dental hygienist, which gave her something to do. But eventually, they separated. Not that they had spent much time together anyway. It was as amicable as a divorce could be. Their main concern was for Carter's well-being.

Gaines rented an apartment while they shared joint custody of Carter. In the beginning, Lucinda tried her best to gain full custody, citing his workload, but Gaines's supervisor promised they would make every effort to schedule him to make sure he had time for his son. It was tricky at times, but they were managing. Lucinda had already moved on to another man, the dentist she had been working for, but there were strict rules about sleepovers. For her and for Carter.

The time had come for Gaines to get a bigger place, one that was closer to where Carter lived. It was a short fifteen-minute drive, but Gaines didn't feel it was close enough. Carter was getting old enough to play outside without supervision, and he desperately wanted a dog. Gaines wanted to provide a comfortable home for his son. After attending a number of open houses and scrutinizing websites and the local newspapers, a house three blocks away from where Lucinda lived became available, and Gaines jumped at the opportunity. The place was a wreck, but it was habitable, and because it was in a state of much-needed repair, he got it at a good price.

Gaines had gained the respect of his superiors and his peers. He was well regarded and established in the Charlotte field office and was able to manage his schedule better.

Carter was jazzed at the idea of a new house with a big yard, and trees, and a big dog. He hoped. Carter liked the outdoors. Even though the house had a basement, he wasn't a gamer-basement-dweller. He preferred sports. It was clear he had inherited his father's athletic ability.

Gaines had been in good spirits recently. He felt a current moving. Things appeared to be shifting in a positive direction. He couldn't quite put his finger on it. Then he thought about that wistful woman who had volunteered during the search. Bright. Funny. Interesting. Certainly quirky. For the most part, he hardly noticed women, although a lot of them noticed *him*. With his work and his son, particularly his relationship history, he didn't pursue anything that resembled one. But that woman, Luna. She was different. Special. A little kooky, but that was a major part of her charm.

The day they were looking for Avery and Luna asked to go to the grove, he knew she was onto something. At least he knew she *believed* she was onto something. If Gaines had learned one thing in his years of law enforcement, it was to always trust his gut.

During his second year on the job, he had been on a stakeout at the harbor in Mobile. He was supposed to go down the side of a particular pier, but a voice in his head shouted, *STOP!* He ducked around a corner and pulled out his weapon. It was the only time in his career he had shot someone. Gaines was glad he hadn't killed the guy, but had he not listened to that voice in his head, he would have been the one lying in a pool of blood that night.

Gaines was delighted that Luna had agreed to work on the

missing-high-school-kid case. Luna spotted the lie after the first question, and she made a few notes. After about an hour of questioning, they took a break. Gaines left the interrogation room and went into the room on the other side of the two-way mirror, where Luna had been observing. He nodded in Luna's direction. "Do you want to tell me what you think or what you feel?"

Luna rolled her eyes. "First, she keeps trailing off. She doesn't complete her sentences, then regroups. Second, she is responding to direct questions with phrases that appear to be answers but aren't."

Gaines's smiled widened. "Continue, please." He wanted the other two law enforcement people in the room to learn a little from this avant-garde psychologist.

"Here's an example of what I mean. When you asked her 'Do you know if your brother has a special hangout? A place he frequents?' she answered with, 'Sometimes he goes out with some kids from school.' That did not answer your question. Of course he goes out with some kids. But where do they go? You don't have the answer to that because she neither acknowledged nor denied there was a special place."

"What do you suggest?"

"I suggest you send in Sergeant Hunt." She nodded to one of the other officers in the observation room. "She's a woman and perhaps can relate to the sister with how much a pain it is to have a brother. Try to gain her confidence." Luna looked down at her notes. "Then ask her the same question but pose it differently. Say something like, 'Does your brother ever talk about his friends and tell you what they usually do when they hang out?' She may or may not realize she actually knows the answer to the question, but revisiting the same subject in a different manner might get the results you're looking for. Either by tripping her up, or, as I mentioned, triggering a memory."

"Thank you. Anything else you want to add?" Gaines asked.

"She knows something. She's holding back. I'll bet on it," Luna said with confidence. Her knowledge of body language coupled with her intuition made the odds that she was correct particularly good.

Gaines looked at the other officers. "Hunt? Got it?"

"Got it." Hunt stood and went to the other room, where the missing teen's sister sat nervously. She was fidgeting much too much for someone who wasn't trying to hide something.

Hunt entered the room and began questioning the sister, again pretending that she had no previous information. "I'm Sergeant Hunt. Marshal Gaines got called away. I hope you don't mind going over the questions again. I need to get up to speed." Hunt began with similar questions: "When did you see your brother last?" "Who was he with?" "Does he normally disappear for a more than a day?" Hunt got the same answers as Gaines had. Then Hunt came to "Does your brother ever talk about his friends and what they usually do when they hang out?"

The sister squirmed in her seat. "He likes to play video games."

"Who does he play with?"

"A lot of people, like, online."

"Anyone local?"

"Yeah. He hangs out with Don Guesser. They rigged up some WiFi in an old garage, like near Guesser's father's autobody shop."

In the other room, Luna popped out a quiet, "Bingo."

A few minutes later, the sister was spilling her guts to Hunt about her brother's transgressions and possible whereabouts. The sister knew exactly where her brother was and why. He was hiding out in the garage everyone presumed abandoned. Only he and Guesser knew about the secret gaming shack, and Guesser hadn't yet been officially questioned. He was conveniently out of town visiting relatives. Then the *why* came out in a flood. Her brother owed another kid money for drugs.

Gaines was standing behind where Luna was sitting. He put his hands on both her shoulders and gave them a gentle shake. "Bravo. Excellent work."

Luna spun around in the chair. For a nanosecond it felt like they were going to kiss each other with delight. "Case closed!" But it was an awkward moment. And there were other people in the room. Gaines was relieved he wasn't alone with her. It was obvious that both of them felt a little clumsy, but the electricity between them was undeniable. It was the jolt. He finally recognized the feeling.

Once the police retrieved the kid from the abandoned garage, they informed the parents that he was safe and they should pick him up at the police station. They were relieved he was OK but furious when they knew why he had disappeared. Gaines and Luna agreed that there would be fireworks at that house later that night, and not the enjoyable kind.

"How does a fifteen-year-old kid from a nice family get into debt with a local bully?" Luna asked.

"Haven't you noticed? We are becoming a culture in which there are few if any consequences for our actions."

"People forget about karma." Luna sighed, then smiled.

Gaines had finally realized that he was quite taken with Luna, but he would never admit it. He knew it wasn't good policy to fraternize with coworkers even though she was technically a subcontractor. A consultant. Still.

After the interview was over, Gaines invited Luna and two others from the office to grab a bite for dinner. Luna was happy to be spending more time with Gaines but disappointed she would have to share his company. But it was better than nothing.

Over the next two years, they shared a few meals when they were working on a case, but it never led to anything. Gaines usually invited others to join them. He felt safer that way. Not that he thought Luna would do something to make him uncomfortable, but he wanted to avoid those tricky moments of sexual tension he felt when they were alone together.

There was one night when he almost kissed her. Then he put on the brakes. They had a nice friendship and a good working relationship. He didn't want to mess that up by coming on to her. *Wouldn't she have dropped a hint by now if she was interested?* Then, much to his pleasant surprise, the mail arrived with a very artsy invitation to the grand opening of the Stillwell Art Center. He had heard about it from a number of sources, including Luna when he had seen her earlier in the year. It was an unexpected pleasure when he opened the invitation. He would definitely work it into his schedule. He was certain that he could figure out a number of excuses to be *in the neighborhood.*

Gaines wanted to bring something to wish her luck and remembered that she adored sunflowers. He drove to three different florists until he could find some. He knew that if he didn't hustle, he might miss the opening entirely.

Chapter Seven

The Stillwell Art Center
Opening night gala

Ellie stepped into the large walk-in closet of her bedroom. She didn't have the kind of wardrobe one would expect from a multimillionaire, but Ellie had never lived extravagantly. She was often seen wearing the same dress at more than one event. Not necessarily in the same year, but she couldn't see the point in spending a lot of money on a dress if you were only going to wear it once. Ellie wasn't cheap, but she was practical. *So what if I look the same in different photos at different events?* The only two things that would change would be her hairstyle and her jewelry. She was comfortable in her own skin and her own choice of clothes.

But tonight was special. In the theme of artistry, she had had a local seamstress make something for her. It was similar to the first little black dress designed by Coco Chanel in 1926. The length was midcalf, with long sleeves and a low-belted waist. The deep V-neck was trimmed in silver brocade instead of the original one in gold. She wore a pair of black kitten-heel pumps by Stuart Weitzman, and her bag was a vintage Chanel she had purchased from Forever Fashion, the vintage handbag vendor who was opening her shop at the art center. Her pure white hair was cut in a chin-length bob with bangs, and she had added a silver metallic streak about two inches wide on one side. The hairdresser matched it to the silver on her dress. Tonight, she pulled one side of her hair behind one ear, and the silver streak was on the other. Diamond studs and a diamond tennis bracelet completed her simple yet elegant outfit. She puckered her lips for a coat of gloss over the cherry-red lipstick.

Ellie stood in front of her mirror and sighed. How she wished Richard could be with her. He would be so proud of her. She could almost feel his presence, looking over her shoulder as the two would check themselves in the mirror before a night out. She stiffened for a moment. She could have sworn she smelled his cologne. Kiehl's Musk. She had loved burying her nose in his neck. It was masculine without being overpowering. And she loved how it blended with his own natural scent. If there were such a thing. Ellie thought it *was* a thing. After all, people had body odor, right? The trick was to catch it before it went afoul. She was confident cologne was invented for that very reason. Odoriferous camouflage. It was common knowledge that was why women had carried posies or nosegays since the fifteenth century. Personal hygiene was a luxury for most people. She chuckled to herself. *Now there's a spray for every part of the human body.*

Ellie turned quickly as she thought she saw something move from the corner of her eye. "Take it easy," she said aloud. She had to admit she was more than a bit nervous. The project had been an enormous undertaking. Aside from the actual construction, she had done almost all the heavy lifting herself. The planning, the meetings, the negotiations, the interviews. She also wanted it to stay under wraps. No one was to get a preview or sneak peek. That night would be the Great Reveal. It would only be fair, to the artists, the media, and the community. Everyone gets to see it for the first time at the same time.

The press had been hounding her for weeks. She was glad she had hired one of the local college students to help her with the arrangements for the event. Working on the project didn't seem half as stressful as balancing caterers, getting tenants settled, fielding questions, and managing those much-sought-after invitations.

She indulged herself by renting a limo for the evening. Just a town car. Not a stretch. That would have been ostentatious. The groomer had dropped Ziggy and Marley off an hour before, both dogs wearing bow ties and berets. Ellie had the clever idea to cut holes in the berets to fit over their ears. Neither seemed to mind. Ellie wondered how long their getups would last.

As Ellie left the house, she was taken aback by the clear, late-summer sky. The stars shone brightly. The air was dry and crisp. Just enough to make it a perfect evening.

"Come on, guys." The driver opened the rear passenger door, letting the dogs in, then went to the other side to open the door for Ellie.

The dogs were extremely well behaved but took up much of the rear. Ellie wiggled herself in next to Marley. Thank goodness it was only a few minutes away. During the day, she and the dogs walked to the center, but tonight was different. She was wearing her good shoes.

When her car pulled up to the front, the valet opened her door and helped her get out while the driver let Ziggy and Marley out. They quickly moved to Ellie's side. For the most part, if you didn't like dogs, you weren't about to have a conversation with Ellie. At least not in person.

There was a small space next to the massive front doors

where guests were having their pictures taken before they entered. It was truly a *grand* opening.

The courtyard had been transformed into a tropical paradise, with high tables decorated with orchids. A small jazz combo played under the staircase as waiters carried and passed hot and cold hors d'oeuvres. The Wine Cellar provided several tasting tables. Champagne-filled glasses were scattered about.

All the gallery doors were wide-open, with many pieces placed around the courtyard and the patio. And, of course, everything was for sale. That particular evening, a portion of the proceeds would go to the Art Fund, Animal Care, and Children's Services. The George Wall Lincoln car dealership would match every dollar collected. They had even donated a new Lincoln Corsair to be raffled off at the end of the evening.

The place was packed with people. It was possible they had reached maximum capacity. Ellie had sent invitations to the top brass of the community but also offered the public an opportunity to attend for a fee of $25.00. She felt it was a fair price to pay for free food and drinks and to be a part of an exciting event. Ellie wondered if any of the invited guests would pony up a donation. She was curious to see the receipts and pledges at the end of the night.

When the jazz combo finished its set, a string quartet began to play. After their hour of music, a guitar virtuoso played classical guitar in the style of Segovia. Ellie was pleased with the variety of music, food, drink, and, of course, the works of art on display.

She floated through the crowd, making sure she said hello to each and every one of the guests as well as all the artists and vendors. Ziggy and Marley were getting bored with the chitter-chatter and made noises to go out to the dog park. Ellie had had the foresight to hire two assistants from the animal hospital to be "doggie-sitters" during the event. She knew Ziggy and Marley would be antsy and would want some fresh air.

Ellie was happy to see Wiley, Luna's dog, scampering about. She liked Luna. There was something about her that was special. Different. Ellie couldn't quite put her finger on it, but she sensed that Luna was an acutely sensitive person. On more than one occasion, she thought Luna was about to say something, but then Luna would quickly change the subject. Ellie hoped once the center was up and running, she and Luna could have a cup of tea in the charming space Luna had created.

Ellie also liked Cullen. A handsome gentleman. Ellie knew Cullen was single, and she strained to think of someone who would be a good catch for him. As far as Luna, well, she was different. Ellie knew it would take a special man to understand the current that ran through Luna Bodhi Bodman. True, Ellie did not know her well. Not yet. But there was something about that young woman that made Ellie want to get to know her much better.

Cullen and Luna had arrived an hour before the announced beginning of the event just to be sure everything was in place. Cullen's showroom space was well lit without looking like Madison Square Garden. A dozen antique chandeliers were connected to dimmer switches, showing off their illumination. Most were turn-of-the-century lights that had originally been designed for candles. One of Cullen's first projects was to wire them and turn them into functioning twenty-first-century ceiling fixtures. He had done a meticulous job with each and every one. Most had begun as broken pieces of tarnished brass tossed into a bin.

Cullen thought this was an interesting phenomenon. People didn't want to take the time or spend the money restoring things, yet they didn't have the heart to part with them either. At least not to throw them into the trash. It was always in Cullen's favor when he went to garage sales. People were willing to sell the box of junk in return for a few bucks. *One man's trash is another man's treasure.* But it wasn't the money Cullen would make after restoring the piece. It was the time he spent re-creating something that gave him a sense of fulfillment, especially when he was finished and could step back and observe the results of his own personal artistry.

Cullen was explaining the origins of one of the pieces to a guest when Ellie made her way into the room. Cullen had been in awe of Ellie since the first time he had met her. She was spunky, bright, and had a great sense of humor, with a robust laugh to match. It was almost as if she were impervious to aggravation, yet he was sure she had experienced a great deal of it during the construction of the center. Heck, even before they broke ground, she had had to overcome many obstacles. But she was an unstoppable force of nature. Cullen recognized a similar trait in his sister.

Ellie seemed to glide across the floor. "Cullen! The place looks superb!" She took his hand, then pecked him on each cheek.

"Thanks, Ellie. I'm happy you like it." Cullen was almost blushing.

She couldn't help but notice several SOLD tickets on some of the items. "Well, certainly looks like you've had a few customers already!" Ellie was truly delighted. She wasn't quite sure how his antique/restoration business would do with so many original artists, but Cullen had made arrangements with some of the other tenants. He would display pieces of their art in his showroom and they could borrow pieces from his. It was already turning into a cooperative enterprise. Ellie was quite pleased.

Even Jimmy, the odd beer-can sculptor, had made something for all of the other tenants. They were metal tulips made from the red-and-white Budweiser cans. The leaves were from green Heineken and Dos Equis cans. Ellie wasn't sure where Jimmy got all his materials, and she really didn't want to know. As long as the place didn't smell like stale beer she was fine with what he did.

All that anyone knew about Jimmy-Can-Do was his name. That was it. Except for Ellie, no one knew his real last name. No one knew where he lived or where he had come from. He was rarely seen on the premises. In the morning, he would open his gallery, hang price tags and item numbers on his work, and disappear. A yellow pad and pen sat on the top of a box that read:

> *We work on the honor system. If you want to pay by credit, please leave your name and contact information and the item number you're taking. Someone will contact you. Otherwise, please deposit cash or check. Thank you.*

The fact Ellie had installed the newest, most high-tech security systems in the state was a big plus. If anything went missing, they would eventually find the culprit.

When Jimmy first approached Ellie, she wasn't sure what to expect; but she was immediately fascinated with the six-foot-tall palm tree he had made from beer-can cuttings. Once he had finished a piece, he coated everything with a type of polyurethane to smooth the edges. Ellie thought it was just a matter of time before beer-can jewelry became all the rage on Instagram. Ellie knew Jimmy wouldn't show up for the opening, but his work was on display. The dozens of creations from floral arrangements to lamps, to coffee tables, gave the corner of the center a whimsical feel. She was pleased at the interest the guests had taken in a new way of recycling.

Ellie made her way through the crowd and into the café. Luna was standing next to the credenza, speaking to several people about different types of teas and their benefits. Her easel was set up in the corner, with a rough sketch of a coffee cup with swirls of steam on it. The place had a warm and welcoming feeling to it. She guessed Luna was a part of that warmth. And the yellow dress? Well, that made for a ray of sunshine. Ellie was quite impressed at how lovely Luna looked that evening. Luna excused herself from her guests and walked over to Ellie.

"Ellie. Congratulations. This is more than I even imagined. It's fantastic. What a vision you had!" Luna was almost gushing. But she was totally sincere.

"Luna, you look lovely." Ellie kissed her on both cheeks.

"I clean up real good." Luna laughed.

Ellie took both of Luna's hands, stepped back, and gazed at her. "Indeed you do. I don't think I would have recognized you."

"Oh, thank you." Luna was doing a half twirl, swinging from side to side. "And you look beautiful, Ellie. I love the dress. Very Chanel."

"Yes it is. I had Lily make it for me."

"It's spectacular." It was Luna's turn to admire Ellie.

"I'll have to get Lily's information from you. I have a bunch of skirts, circa 1960s, but they are in dire need of help."

"If anyone can breathe new life into clothing, it's Lily."

A few more minutes of small talk, and Ellie was on her way to the other shops before she had to make her welcome speech.

About an hour into the extravaganza, Ellie picked up the microphone and began to speak. She was surprised how emotional she was feeling. With the two years of working on the project, and the last few months of final preparation, she hadn't had the time to absorb the Herculean feat she had accomplished. Not until just then. She had a small speech she had prepared, but she couldn't quite get the words out.

After a few deep breaths, she started. "Good evening, everyone. Words cannot express my gratitude for the support we have received in making this vision, this idea, a reality. I wish all the artists the absolute best and hope this is the beginning of a long relationship with you and the arts. Thank you." Applause, hoots, whistles, and hollers bounced off the glass. It was thunderous. Ziggy and Marley came running in, with Wiley following behind, all three barking up a storm.

The evening flew by, and Luna was acutely aware that Marshal Gaines was nowhere in sight. There was only a half hour left before the event was over. She started to wash out the coffee and teacups in the small sink when the hair on the back of her neck started to rise. She whipped around and saw the tall, dark, and handsome marshal pushing his way through the crowd, Wylie leading the way. Luna was trying not to shake and fumbled with the china. He caught her eye and gave a wave. She smiled back and motioned for him to come in.

As he approached the doorway, she noticed that he was carrying a bouquet of flowers. Sunflowers. *He remembered.* One evening, when they were talking about some of their favorite places, Luna mentioned Tuscany because the hillsides were alive with sunflowers. *Wow. I'm impressed. Shocked. Stunned. Verklempt.* Naturally, she didn't want to sound like an imbecile and utter those words. As he got closer, her knees were hammering out a rhythm of their own. *Easy. Steady. Smile.*

"Congratulations! The place looks great. The whole place is great. Wow. I'm really impressed."

Luna trembled at his words. *Didn't she just think those*

same words only a moment ago? "Marshal Gaines. So nice of you to come."

"Sorry I'm late. Work stuff and then there was construction on I-26 near Hendersonville." He paused. "These are for you." He handed the flowers to her. "You look quite lovely this evening."

"Why, thank you, Marshal Gaines." She smiled coyly.

"Oh. I hope you don't mind me paying you a compliment. It's hard to know. Being PC and all." He sounded very official for a minute.

"Don't be silly. Kindness doesn't cost a thing." She held the flowers up to her nose. "Sunflowers. Reminds me of Tuscany." Another wobble in her knees. "They're beautiful. Thank you. Let me see what I can find to put them in. Can I get you a cup of tea? Coffee?" She gestured for him to sit at one of the café tables.

"A glass of wine would be better." He smiled. Luna thought it was the biggest smile she had ever seen on his face.

"I assume you are off duty, Marshal Gaines?" she teased.

"For the night, yes." He nodded assuredly. "And you can just call me Chris, if you don't mind."

"Sit tight. I think I know someone who knows someone who can help us out." She laughed. The phrase *I know someone who knows someone* was a favorite joke among criminals and law enforcement.

Luna went into Cullen's studio to fetch something that would work as a vase. She didn't want to use any of the artists' pottery. She didn't want to be responsible. Display, yes. Usage, no. She knew Cullen had a few glass vases in his storeroom. When she entered, she stopped short again when she saw the old table, the one that had given her the weird vibe earlier. She approached it gingerly, as if it might bite her. The closer she got, the stronger the feeling, but much to her surprise, it wasn't as ominous as before. It was almost as if it were calling to her. She moved closer and touched the top. "I'll be back, but not tonight." Luna had a habit of talking to things. Scientists call it anthropomorphizing, giving human qualities to inanimate objects. It is not an unusual occurrence with highly sensitive people who also experience great empathy. She wasn't embarrassed by it, either, which simply added to her charm.

She grabbed a tall clear vase and headed back to the café, winking at Cullen as he was showing someone a rocking chair he had restored. He gave her an odd look. She winked again.

With the vase in one hand, she tagged a waiter with the other. "Could you possibly bring two glasses of red wine to my shop?" Gaines wasn't the only one with a good memory. Luna recalled his interest in wine, particularly red.

"Sure, Luna. Be right back." The waiter, who was also a student, knew Luna from his teenage years in foster care. She was aces as far as he was concerned.

Gaines was casually leaning into the back of the chair, scratching Wylie's ears. Both of them were people-watching. Gaines was also good at reading body language. He had to be to do his job, which also added to Luna's nervousness. She was extremely conscious of her gestures when she was around him. At least in the beginning. And tonight. But tonight was different. It was not related to work. It was personal. And she was elated.

Luna filled the vase with water, cut an inch off the stems, and arranged the bouquet. "These are beautiful. Thank you again." She set the vase in the middle of the counter between the coffeemaker and the boxes of tea. Perfect.

"I'm so glad you could make it." She pulled up the chair next to him as the waiter brought two glasses of cabernet sauvignon.

"It's the good stuff. Ellie went all out for this shindig." Luna raised her glass, as did Gaines. "So what brings you to Asheville?" She was hoping he was going to say "You" as she gazed at the sunflowers.

"I know someone who knows someone who was opening a shop in an art center."

Luna almost spit out her wine while trying to keep it from spewing out of her nose. She regrouped quickly. "No, seriously. Are you on a case?"

"No, seriously. I. Am. Not." Gaines's eyes went soft. "I really wanted to see you, as well as this massive project the whole state is talking about." Gaines swirled the wine in the glass.

"Is there time for you to give me a tour?" Gaines looked up.

"The plan is to shut down at ten."

Gaines looked at his watch. "Doesn't give us much time, does it?"

Luna hoped this was not going to be the end of his visit. "Not really, but I'll gladly show you my brother's space next door."

"What about tomorrow?" Gaines asked pointedly.

"What about it?" Luna was puzzled. Would he make the two-hour drive back if he wasn't in town for work?

"I'm scouting out the Village Hotel at Biltmore for a retreat for some of the marshals."

"Ooohh, fancy. Is this where our tax dollars go?" Luna gave him a sideways look.

Gaines chuckled. "No. It's a grant, and it's only eight of us. Kind of like a think tank. And we'll be bunking two per room. Fun times."

"Well, I'm glad you were able to fit in a visit here to the art center."

"So what about tomorrow?" Gaines repeated his question.

"Uh. Sure!" Luna remained cool despite her excitement. "Come on. Let's go see what Cullen is up to." Luna needed another person in the room with her and Gaines. *How many times had they been together? Four? Five?* She knew she should be over the willies by now. She tried to convince herself it was all in her head. The attraction. The pull. The energy. There was no denying something was reverberating between them. She could feel his body heat. Wiley followed happily behind.

Cullen strode over to them as they walked into his showroom. "Marshal Gaines! Good to see you, man. What brings you here?"

"Doing a little scouting. Decided to mix business with pleasure."

Pleasure? That was almost fainting words. Luna got goose bumps. What kind of pleasure did he mean? She certainly wasn't going to ask him. She tried the Jedi mind trick from the *Star Wars* series, beaming thoughts to Cullen. *Ask him. Ask him.*

Cullen gave her a strange look. Luna opened her eyes as wide as her lids would stretch, hoping Cullen could read what was inside her head.

Cullen crossed his arms and leaned against a newly restored farmhouse table. "Which is which?"

"Which is what?" Gaines looked a little puzzled.

"Which is business? We're not under surveillance, are we?" Cullen joked. *Good save, bro*, Luna thought.

Gaines laughed. "I'm scouting for a site for a weekend retreat"—he turned to look at Luna—"and your sister sent an invitation to the opening."

Cullen smiled and nodded. "Glad you could make it."

"That's a nice-looking table." Gaines tilted his head toward the piece on which Cullen was resting his butt.

Cullen immediately jumped away and grabbed one of the decorative towels Luna had placed on a baker's rack and began rubbing the area where he had squatted. Luna couldn't help but giggle. Then she thought about butt prints instead of fingerprints and started laughing harder. Both men stared at her as she got more hysterical, pointing to the table. She finally caught her breath. "I guess you could substitute them for fingerprints!" By that time, she was howling. Of course, most of her reaction was nerves. Her mind swiftly went into *I'm such an idiot* mode.

Gaines let out a guffaw. "I'll keep that in mind. Imagine if we still had to use ink pads?" Luna and Cullen were almost doubled over. For well over a decade, prints were taken electronically with a scanner. "Although I don't think the scanners they're using now could capture a whole lot of data."

"Here's an idea." Luna snickered. "You put people on a conveyor belt like they do at the grocery stores!"

Everyone was having a good, hearty laugh. Wylie lay on the floor and put his paws over his face. That brought on more hilarity.

It took several minutes for the group to regain some degree of poise. The air was electric with delight. Luna could feel it. As did Cullen and Gaines. Cullen squeezed his jaw tenderly. "My face hurts." Gaines blinked back tears. That moment created a bond among the three of them. Luna recalled a famous line from Victor Borge: *Laughter is the shortest distance between two people.* Even three.

"As I was saying," Gaines snorted, "that's a fine-looking table. I like the whitewashed finish. Maple?"

"Yes. I wanted to give it a bit of an updated look. Anyone can find a maple farm table anywhere. I put my own spin on things."

"I can see that." Gaines noticed the barn door that led to the back room. "Workshop?"

"It is. Wanna take a look?" Cullen was happy to share and discuss his work. Especially with a dude.

They moved through the showroom, Gaines stopping to admire a few other pieces. "I like to tinker. Well, I used to, but work takes up a whole lot of time."

As the two men started to talk man-tool-speak, she felt like the little sister tagging along. Maybe that wasn't so bad. It took some of the pressure off her. She tried to read Gaines's body language. All she could decipher was a man of confidence without arrogance. Open. Honest. At least that's what his body language was telling her. She wondered what her body language was telling him. She quivered at the thought.

When they entered the workshop area, Luna was once again pulled toward the mysterious table.

Cullen followed her. "Here is something that came in earlier today. Pretty sad-looking. Needs a lot of work."

"How old do you reckon it is?" Gaines peered at the drooping trim.

"Great Depression. Mass-produced. Veneer over plywood."

Gaines stood up straight. "What are your plans for it?"

Luna suddenly felt protective of her new inanimate friend. "I think I might adopt it," she broke in.

Cullen gave her a curious look. "But didn't you say you—"

Luna interrupted him. "I said I had a 'feeling' about it. That's all." She folded her arms across her chest and immediately unfolded them. She didn't want to appear defensive. *Relax*, she told herself. Even if Gaines wanted that piece, it would be months before Cullen would get to it.

Cullen continued. "It has that greenish tone that I want to recover. I'll strip it down, fix the wood, prime, stain, wax. Not sure until I get started."

"Well, if Luna decides to pass on it, let me know. I bought a house and it needs furniture. After my divorce, I moved into a furnished apartment until we got past the legal stuff."

Luna was about to blurt out, "More!" but she didn't. She appreciated Gaines's not wanting to air his laundry, dirty or otherwise, in public.

"It's not a big place. Two bedrooms, den, kitchen, two baths. The usual post–World War II ranch. It needs some work, too. Actually, it needs a lot of work. I figured it can be something my son and I work on together. Granted, he's only ten, but he could be a good helper, and it's an opportunity for him to learn how to use tools safely." Gaines smiled, thinking about his son, Carter.

Luna appreciated the affection Gaines had for his son. There was something soft under that masculine skin.

"So, Luna, are we going to have a bidding war over this?" Gaines joked.

"TBD. To Be Determined," she said, with a sassy tilt of her head.

"What are your plans for the rest of the evening?" Cullen asked Gaines. Luna thought that perhaps her Jedi mind tricks were working.

"I was about to ask you the same thing," Gaines said.

OK, this is getting a little freaky, Luna thought.

"Even though there was plenty of food, I didn't have a chance to eat," Cullen said. "Or have a drink."

"Your lovely sister was able to wangle a glass of wine for me, but food would be good. I haven't eaten since lunch. I think. The day has been a bit of a blur." He checked his watch. A little after ten. "Is there someplace that's still serving food?"

"Three Brothers Pizza is open until eleven. I'll let them know we're coming. Let me go lock up. I'll be right back."

Luna snapped her fingers, and Wiley stood waiting for Luna's next move.

Luna was feeling a sense of relief. She was tickled pink

that Gaines had showed up, and even more tickled that he seemed genuinely interested in her. Normally, as whimsical as Luna might behave, she had it together in a kooky sort of way. She was rarely intimidated and decided to take her own advice. *Go with the flow. What will be will be. And be yourself.*

Luna checked the lights and plugs, making sure nothing was left on except the alarm system.

Cullen and Gaines were back in the showroom area. Cullen turned to Luna. "Since we each have a car, how about we follow you to your place so you can drop Wylie off? I'll bring you back home later."

"Sounds good to me." Luna was already trying to figure out how to get Gaines to bring her home instead. Maybe another Jedi mind trick? She laughed to herself.

They exited through the back door of Cullen's shop and drove to Luna's house. Gaines suggested she ride with him so there wouldn't be three cars heading to the same place. Dropping her back wouldn't be an issue since it was on his way to the hotel. Well, not exactly, but close enough to make it an acceptable alternative.

Gaines opened the passenger door for her, and she slid into the seat of the Jeep Cherokee. Gaines did a little jog to the other side of the vehicle and hopped into the driver's seat. He started the engine and turned down the music that he had been listening to earlier.

"The Dales?" Luna asked, but she knew the answer. Gaines looked surprised. *He wasn't the only one with a good memory.*

"Yes, it is."

The title track "Easy Times" was wafting from the speakers. The new band had just been starting out and was reminiscent of early Crosby, Stills & Nash. Luna commented on their sound. "It's something about the harmonics—the overtones created when their three particular voices mix." She listened again. "It's interesting."

"What?" Gaines asked.

"Vibrations." Luna wasn't sure how much further she wanted to take that conversation. *Vibes. Energy. Woo-woo.*

"The Law of Perpetual Transmutation of Energy?" Gaines glanced at her, waiting for a reaction.

Luna thought she was going to pee her pants. "Let's throw in the law of electromagnetism, shall we?" She was cackling. "How about the laws of karma?"

"Which one?" Gaines kept his eyes on the road.

"How about the law of force?" Luna suggested.

"Seriously? Do you really want to have such a heady conversation? Now?" He looked in her direction.

She snorted. "No, not really. But thanks for asking. Maybe some other time."

"Good, because I was grasping at straws!" He howled.

"Oh! You!" She gave him a little smack on the side of his arm. Just like she did with her brother. Except her feelings for Gaines were not at all fraternal.

"Ouch!" Gaines faked being hurt.

"Such a baby," Luna fired back. She was genuinely enjoying their repartee. *Go with the flow, girl.*

Gaines seemed quite relaxed and talked about his new house and all the work he had to do on it. Luna was happy to listen to his smooth, even voice, with the sweet-sounding music playing in the background. It was a nice blend.

"Well, if you need any restoration tips, Cullen is your man."

"I most definitely got that impression. He's quite talented."

"He is indeed. It runs in the family." Luna smirked.

"*That* I have no doubt about." He turned to smile at her. *That smile. Yikes.* Luna had to catch her breath.

Luna continued to give him directions as they headed to Three Brothers. When they arrived, Luna was greeted by Louie, one of the brothers. "Luna! Nice to see you!" He nodded to Gaines. "Good evening."

Luna introduced them. "This is Christopher Gaines." She hesitated with any other information. Luna wasn't sure if Gaines wanted his profession known.

Gaines nodded in return. "Smells fantastic."

"Follow me." Louie escorted them to the table where Cullen was sitting.

Gaines moved swiftly to be sure he pulled out Luna's chair before Louie had the chance. Chivalry was not dead. Maybe a little pale but not dead. Louie handed them the plastic-coated menus.

"Don't let the ambience fool you." Luna was referring to the pizzeria décor of red-and-white-checkered tablecloths, straw-covered Chianti bottles with melted candles, which served as centerpieces although they were never lit. From where they were sitting, they could see into the kitchen, which was still bustling at that time of night.

Gaines looked around. "They're pretty busy for this hour."

"It's a favorite stop after the early movie," Luna advised him.

"So what do you recommend?" Gaines was perusing the menu.

"Their eggplant rollatini is fab," Luna suggested. "But if you are in the mood for pizza, I have to say this is probably the best pizza you're going to get outside of the New York metropolitan area." She chuckled.

"I could go for a slice. Maybe three."

"I'm with you on that," Cullen added. "We should order a large pie. Do you like anything on it?"

"Anything but bell peppers."

Luna clicked her tongue. "I want a slice or two myself. But I like spinach on mine." She looked at both men.

"OK with me," Gaines said.

"And an antipasto," Luna added. "I'm hungry!"

Louie came back to the table, and they placed their order. As Louie was about to turn away, Cullen said, "Don't forget the garlic rolls with the antipasto!"

Luna thought to herself, *Garlic rolls. Great. I love them, but my breath! Ugh*. Then she reminded herself *to go with the flow*.

There was a lot of conversation about Cullen's work and Gaines's dilapidated house. Luna was enjoying the banter between what were becoming her two favorite men.

As the meal was winding down, Gaines admitted that it was a great-tasting pizza. He then ordered spumoni and coffee for dessert. "I don't remember the last time I had spumoni." He leaned back against the chair, looking very satisfied.

"So what's your plan for tomorrow?" Cullen asked innocently.

"Your sister is going to give me a tour of the art center."

Cullen seemed a little surprised. "Is she now?" He felt Luna kick him under the table and tried not to wince.

"Yes, since I arrived so late, there wasn't much time. I've heard a lot about the place and want to see it for myself."

"I wouldn't have figured you for an artsy kind of guy," Cullen joked.

"There are a lot of interesting things I want to see. The glassblowing, and the dude who makes art out of beer cans, and a few others. Ellie Stillwell set the state on their asses with this project. Just goes to show you what can be done when someone puts their mind to it."

"Yeah, too bad it always has to come from the private sector," Luna retorted. "No offense, you being a government employee."

"No offense taken. Believe me, I have my frustrations with the bureaucracy. But for the most part, I do my job, and people generally leave me alone," he explained. "But that doesn't mean I don't get aggravated when things don't move fast enough."

Luna was enjoying getting to know Gaines on a more personal level. He had ethics and was extremely conscientious.

"I can only imagine. I have a lot of tolerance, but patience is a virtue I have a very hard time cultivating," Luna replied.

"When have you ever tried to cultivate it?" Cullen teased. "This woman is one of the most impatient people I know."

Luna couldn't help but give him a playful slap on the arm. "Don't believe a word he says."

"Yeah, right. When Luna wants something done, she wants it done *now*."

"Not true." She smirked. "OK, once in a while, but it's usually important," Luna defended herself.

"I've seen you in action. You do have a way of taking control of a situation if it's not moving fast enough for you," Gaines commented. "I remember our first encounter. You wanted to go to that grove right away."

"And I was right, wasn't I?" she taunted.

Gaines nodded in agreement. "You certainly were. And who knows how long it would have taken us to get to that grove?" He smiled at her.

Luna cocked her head toward her brother. "See? Sometimes it's important. And I'm usually right." She folded her arms across her chest, then quickly unfolded them. She had to keep reminding herself of her own body language.

After dessert and coffee, Louie returned to the table. "Can I get you anything else?"

"No, thank you. I'll take the check, please," Gaines offered.

"Oh no, let us pay. You drove all this way. It's the least we can do," Cullen protested.

Gaines pushed his blazer aside, displaying the badge on his belt. "That's an order." He gestured to Louie. Louie was slightly taken aback, but then understood it wasn't meant to intimidate. It was the marshal joking with Luna and Cullen.

"Official business."

Louie bowed in accord. "Coming right up, Officer."

Luna, Cullen, and Gaines got a kick out of the exchange. "Thanks, Christopher. It has been a pleasure." Cullen added, "Next time, it's on Luna."

Luna rolled her eyes and shook her head. "My brother, the big spender."

Guffaws came from both men. "Seriously, next time you are in town, we'll take you to a nice place."

"This was great," Gaines replied. "But I just might take you up on that offer next time I'm around."

Luna got wobbly again. *Next time.*

After Gaines paid the check, they stood and headed toward the door. Cullen turned to both of them. "Want me to drop you off, sis?"

She thought she was going to punch him. But before she could respond, Gaines chimed in. "I'll take her back. It's on my way."

"Cool. Thanks," Cullen responded, as if he didn't know it wasn't exactly on the way, but he was happy his sister was in such a playful mood.

Cullen and Gaines shook hands. "Good luck with your place," Gaines said sincerely. "Maybe I'll see you tomorrow."

Cullen replied with, "Enjoy the tour!" and walked toward his car as Gaines and Luna strolled to the Jeep.

Again, he opened the passenger door for her. *I could get*

used to this. It was an act of kindness and courtesy. Being weak or feeble had nothing to do with it. There should be no shame in exhibiting good manners.

In spite of the hectic and exciting event, Luna was still bouncing with adrenaline. It was as if she and Gaines had known each other before. *Maybe*, she thought. *In another life?* She smirked.

Gaines looked over at her. "Care to share?"

"Huh?" Luna was off in her own little world; her thoughts were spinning, recounting the frenetic day and the wonderful surprise of Marshal Gaines showing up. "Just thinking about today. It was exhilarating."

"You must be beat," Gaines offered.

"No, not really. That was why I smirked. It's as if I've drunk a gallon of coffee."

"Adrenaline," Gaines commented.

"That's *exactly* what I was thinking." Luna was astounded at the way they were in sync. But that wasn't anything new. She had felt that way from the day they had met.

He smiled but kept his eyes on the road. "Turn here, correct?"

"Yep." Luna was sorry the evening was coming to a close as he pulled into the driveway and put the Jeep in park. She acquiesced to her new approach of being cool and calm. But also being herself. "Hey, thanks for coming. And the sunflowers." She leaned over and gave him a peck on the cheek. He froze for a moment, then jumped out of the driver's side and walked over to hers. He opened the door and held out his hand. She took it gladly. Once she was on solid ground, Gaines kissed the back of her hand. She swooned.

Gaines broke the mood. "See you tomorrow?"

Luna was floating on air. "Absolutely."

"Good." He let go of her hand. "What time should I show up?"

"Ten? I'll have coffee and scones waiting." She gave him a warm smile.

"Sounds good. Sounds delicious." He waited in his Jeep until Luna was safely inside her house.

Wiley was expressing his joy at seeing his mommy. Luna flashed the porch light once, indicating all was well.

And it was.

Chapter Eight

The Stillwell Art Center
The next day

Most of the artists and vendors arrived at eight thirty to set up before the center opened at ten. There had been people gathering outside since nine o'clock. Perhaps it was the Lincoln Corsair they were raffling off that brought the visitors. Ellie had decided to wait another day to pull the name of the winner, allowing for more contenders and proceeds to go toward the foundation. Entrants wrote their contact info on their tickets so they did not have to be present to win, which satisfied the prior evening's participants.

The gala drew a lot of ink in local print, as well as social media bombardment. Still, Ellie was thrilled beyond belief at the turnout. She thought about the initial interaction she had had with the Bodmans. He was gentrified, cordial, and warm without being smarmy. The sister was quirky, funny, and astute. Interesting combination. Ellie remembered at the end of the interview that Luna took Ellie's hand, and said, "You are doing a wondrous thing. Have no fear. It will all work out." And she gave Ellie a kiss on the cheek.

Though it was the innocent gesture of a kind and loving young woman, Ellie felt it was some kind of omen. A message. It *was* going to be all she imagined. *Gosh, how she missed Richard.* This was spectacular, but it would have been much better had he been there to watch the development of Ellie's vision. On the other hand, if he were still alive, would she have had the passion, vision, and fortitude to pursue such an undertaking? She pondered that thought. They say that everything happens for a reason. Well, if the reason for her inspiration was Richard's death, she wasn't keen on that reason. Whatever the case, she had to accept it and be grateful. And grateful she was.

Ziggy and Marley made their way to the open doors on the west side of the courtyard and out to the dog-park area. There was always someone on duty for doo-doo patrol. It was usually a student, looking to pocket some extra cash for making sure that people picked up after their dogs. And people were happy to tip the pooper scooper. The area was kept immaculate.

Ellie decided to make her first stop at the café. A good cup of coffee was always appreciated. Plus, she wanted to chat with Luna a little more. Luna was conversing with Lebichi (Chi-Chi) Stone, the Nigerian silver-jewelry artist who had a gallery on the south side of the building, across the courtyard from the café. Her name meant *Look Unto God.* Chi-Chi had come to America with her father and mother when she was nine years old. Before moving to the States, her father had worked in Kano, Nigeria, one of the few places in Africa where silver was to be found. He had been employed by a company that made ceremonial bowls, and Chi-Chi had shown an interest in the craft at an early age. As she grew, so did her fascination with jewelry, using her father's knowledge to make handcrafted items. After high school, she studied metalsmithing and fine-tuned her craft. During summer breaks,

Chi-Chi would visit Nigeria and bring gemstones back to incorporate into her work.

She started displaying her pieces at jewelry trade shows, where she received high praise and a lot of sales. Her jewelry prices ranged from $500 and up for a bracelet, $200 for earrings, and upwards of $1,000 for necklaces. For the holidays, she would make smaller, less expensive pieces that sold out within days. Chi-Chi didn't want her business to become a jewelry manufacturer. She wanted to remain an artist, so she jumped at the opportunity to secure a space at the Stillwell Art Center. She had an apprentice working with her, but Chi-Chi would design all the pieces put up for sale.

Chi-Chi was a work of art herself. She was tall, with a honeyed complexion, a high forehead, and high cheekbones. Her hair was in long braids, often wrapped over her head and ending in a collection flowing down her back. She regularly wore colorful caftans with matching head wraps. Each day, she would wear one of her stunning bracelets, a pair of earrings, and a lavish necklace. Invariably, she would end up selling what she was wearing that day to a customer. In some ways, Chi-Chi reminded Ellie of Luna. Both were free spirits. Creative. Sensitive.

"Good morning, you beautiful women." Ellie gave each of them a peck on the cheek. "We have quite a turnout today!" Ellie gave a sweeping look across the courtyard.

"We sure do, and last night was fabulous," Luna gushed. She had reason to. The night before revealed something she had hoped for, a positive indication that Marshal Gaines felt something for her. As a person, *and* a female.

Chi-Chi spoke with the slightest accent as she offered her enthusiasm. "I sold over three thousand dollars' worth of jewelry last night and took orders for another five thousand dollars' worth."

"Wonderful!" Ellie clapped her hands. "Last night was a

roaring success. I had no idea people would be digging into their pockets to support the center."

"Yes, but a lot of these people thrive on telling their friends how much money they donate." Luna sighed.

"Well and good, because we raised over seventy thousand dollars! Let them talk as much as they want as long as they keep writing checks!" Ellie guffawed.

Luna and Chi chuckled in response.

"I'd better get back to the studio," Chi-Chi announced. "Lots of work to do. Ta." She blew a kiss and floated across the courtyard.

"Chi-Chi is so beautiful," Luna observed. "Inside and out." She turned to Ellie. "Kinda cool that *chi* means 'life energy.' Even if it is her nickname. It fits."

"Speaking your language, eh?" Ellie smiled.

Luna cocked her head. "I am sensing you want to ask me something." She used air quotes for the word "sensing." "Come. Have a coffee."

Ellie looked around and noticed the large bouquet of sunflowers. "They are beautiful. Not easy to find this time of year."

Luna blushed. "A colleague of mine brought them."

There was a couple sitting at one of the tables in the corner of the café. They were far enough away for a private conversation. "Cappuccino?" Luna asked Ellie.

"That would be great. Thanks." Ellie took a seat in the corner opposite the other couple, next to Luna's easel.

A few minutes later, Luna brought the steaming coffee to the table.

Luna blew on her coffee and took a sip. "So, what's up, Miss Ellie?" She smiled, peering over the mug.

"You said something to me yesterday that stuck."

"And what was that?" Luna truly couldn't remember. So much had happened in the past couple of weeks.

"You said 'Have no fear.' I thought it was a little odd. Don't misunderstand me. I got the intention, but it was those words. My late husband used that expression often." Ellie waited for a reaction from Luna.

"Huh. Interesting." Luna kept sipping her coffee, waiting for Ellie to reveal more.

"Luna, dear, I know you have a penchant for spiritual things. Psychic phenomena, telepathy. It's not a big secret. A bit on the down-low, but not classified information." It was Ellie's turn to pause.

Luna pursed her lips. "You are correct." Another pause.

"And?" Ellie pressed on.

"And?" Luna echoed.

Ellie huffed. "Dear girl, I know about your extracurricular activities, if that's what you're concerned about. I can be quite open-minded about those things."

"Oh, Ellie. I wasn't sure how to handle this. I do have a small clientele, but I hadn't decided what to do about them. My plan was to continue to do readings at my home or at the client's house. But I was apprehensive about meeting them here." Luna was almost apologetic. "You see, when I do a reading, I usually sketch at the same time. It's almost like automatic writing, except I draw."

Ellie leaned in closer to Luna. "Fascinating. Tell me more. Or better, show me. Please."

Luna was stunned at Ellie's interest and likely acceptance. "Are you sure?" Luna looked around the café. The couple who had been sitting earlier had left, and the place was empty at the moment. "I wasn't quite set up to do it here. At least not yet. I wanted to find someone who could be my backup as a barista so as not to leave customers in the lurch."

"That's an easy fix. I'll get one of the pages to stand guard, so to speak."

Ellie had hired art students to work as pages at the center. They would be a source of information and assistance to visitors. There were usually two on the main floor and one on the second. She pulled her small walkie-talkie out of her tote bag. "Sabrina? Can you make coffee?" Ellie listened. "Splendid. Can you come over to the Namaste Café and hold the fort for . . ." She looked at Luna for a sign. Luna mouthed *half-hour*. ". . . a half hour?" Ellie nodded at Luna. "Thanks, Sabrina." Within a couple of minutes, Sabrina appeared in the large glass doorway.

"Hey. What can I help you with?" Sabrina was a second-year art student at the university and eager to please her boss. A good recommendation from Ellie Stillwell could go a long way when she applied to renew her scholarship.

Luna got up and walked over to the counter. "You know how to run one of these?" she asked, jerking her thumb toward the cappuccino machine.

Undaunted, Sabrina gladly took charge. "I sure do. I did a short stint at Starbucks until I got the job here."

"Fab. We'll be over in the corner just in case." Luna moved the easel to the other side of the café. "Follow me." She motioned to Ellie.

Luna stood in the corner with the easel between her and the table where Ellie was sitting. "May I have a piece of your jewelry?" Luna asked from behind the sketch pad. "It's how I do this. It's called psychometry."

Ellie removed a ring from her right hand. She had never taken off her wedding band and wasn't about to do it now. But it didn't matter which ring she chose. Luna was going to get some sort of energy from the ring. That's how it worked for her.

Ellie handed the ring to Luna, who held it in her hand for what seemed to be an eternity but was in actuality less than five minutes. Luna held the ring in her left hand and began to draw with her right. She began to speak. "I see a retro, 1950s Formica table. On the table are piles of coffee cake. The table is in the kitchen next to the basement stairs." She kept drawing. "I also see something that looks like a big black box in the basement. But it's not a box. It's more like a small room. And what's up with the TV set? Keeps going on and off."

Luna tore off the sheet of paper and rested it on the table in front of Ellie.

Ellie sat silently. The drawing was of a table that looked like the one that was in the kitchen of the house in which she had grown up. Complete with the pink chairs and a stack of cake. There was a large square with a smaller black square inside it. She stroked the page and looked up at Luna. "My mother used to bake coffee cake for every occasion. And my father had a darkroom in the basement." Tears started to well. "And the TV?" She pointed to a sketch of a television with rabbit-ear antennae.

"My late husband had one of these in the garage. He refused to part with it. Kept insisting he would refurbish it. But it never happened. Every time I go into the garage and see that set, I think, 'Richard, how could you leave me with this thing?' And then I chuckle." Ellie pulled an embroidered handkerchief out of her bag and dabbed her eyes. It had the initials *RS*. It had been one of Richard's. Ellie looked at it in disbelief. She always carried a handkerchief, but never Richard's. She couldn't recall how it had gotten into her handbag. She shrugged it off as something that could be easily explained. But for the moment, she was much more intrigued with what could not. How could Luna know about the coffee cake? The darkroom? And the television? She was nonplussed. Stunned. Speechless. She looked at Luna. "How?"

Luna shook her head. "I can tell you what, but it's impossible to say 'how.' How is it possible? I don't know for certain. But I do know that everything is made up of molecules, and molecules vibrate at different frequencies. Somehow, I am like a radio receiver and I pick up the frequencies that are being emitted from your ring."

"This is fascinating." Ellie stared at the rough sketch in front of her. "But how did you get all that information from a ring?"

Ellie puckered her lips. "On the one hand, it's complicated physics, but on the other hand, it's about tuning in." Luna took the seat next to Ellie. "I like to compare it to cable television. Some people have premium, others have basic. But we all have a connection. It simply depends on what channel you tune into." Luna looked at Ellie. "Does this make any sense?"

"Yes it does. I like that analogy. Cable TV."

"Unfortunately, there are people who forget to turn on the set or forget to plug it in," Luna joked.

Ellie patted Luna's hand. "Can you tell me more? How do you interpret this?"

Luna thought for a moment. "In a nutshell, I think it's your late husband letting you know that he's with you in spirit."

Ellie laughed softly. "Do you know that he begged me to bake my mother's coffee cake recipe hundreds of times? I never wanted to because they were so fattening!" She sighed.

"And the kitchen and darkroom tell me that your parents are with you, too."

A small stream of tears ran down Ellie's face. "Oh dear. Just look at me." She sniffled and dabbed her face with Richard's handkerchief. "And this." She held it up. "I have never touched Richard's handkerchiefs. They are still in the top drawer of his chest of drawers. At least they were." Ellie looked confused.

"Oh, and then there's kinetic energy." Luna took a sip of her lukewarm coffee. "That's a whole other complicated subject. But did you ever think you saw something move? Not a shadow, but let's say a teapot?"

"A what? Teapot?" Ellie was curious.

"Yeah. Once I was standing in the kitchen with my friend Charlie, and suddenly the teapot was whistling and the water was boiling. But . . . neither of us had filled it, put it on the stove, and turned it on." Luna leaned back in the chair. "We both looked at each other wide-eyed and said, 'Did *you* do that?' Nope. Neither of us had touched the kettle, and we had been standing there for a good fifteen minutes talking. It was really bizarre." Luna shook her head in disbelief. "What can I say? It happens."

"That's very interesting. Once in a while, I'll find something in the house that I could swear I hadn't put where I found it. Especially my keys. But I always chalk that up to my age."

"Did you and Richard joke or argue about keys?" Luna asked.

Ellie let out a guffaw. "Yes! He could never find his, and I would tease him about it. I even put a silver dish on the table next to the front door. I'd leave notes. *Keys go here.* I cannot tell you how many times we were late to an engagement because he couldn't find his keys. We would invariably end up using mine."

"That's another way of him connecting with you." Luna tilted her head. "Do you ever feel his presence?"

Ellie looked up from the handkerchief, which was now in a big knot. "Sometimes. In fact, I felt it last night. I could have sworn I smelled his cologne. Kiehl's Musk."

Luna got up and wrapped her arms around Ellie and whispered, "Have no fear."

Ellie hugged her back and thanked her for the insight and inspiration and assured Luna that unless Luna wanted to make her extra talent known, Ellie would keep it to herself.

Luna was relieved that her secret side wasn't off-putting to Ellie. In truth, Luna was thrilled. That was an issue Luna was tormented about. *What would Ellie say? What would she think? Would she kick her out?* Luna's instincts told her that Ellie would be supportive, but sometimes Luna's talents were not self-serving. Otherwise, she would have won the lottery by now. She was eager to tell Cullen that the cat was out of the bag with Ellie. But she didn't want to get interrogated about the night before. Besides, Marshal Gaines should be stopping by any minute.

Luna was dressed a little more casually than the night before. She was wearing a cream-colored gauze maxi dress trimmed in green embroidery, with green tassels hanging at the cuffs and two hanging down from the hand-stitched collar. Bronze metallic gladiator sandals adorned her feet, and a bronze fabric was woven into the long braid that fell over her right shoulder. Her fancy do was a bit disheveled from the night before, but it still looked pretty and feminine. Bronze-and-brass bangle bracelets with matching earrings completed her upscale bohemian look. She checked her reflection in one of the mirrors on the wall. She felt comfortable. Sorta. Anxious? Maybe. Terrified? Probably. Over her shoulder, she spotted Gaines's handsome face as he moved through the crowd. She liked the way he walked. Long strides. Not rushed. A man who appeared to know where he was going.

"Good morning!" Gaines strode into the café, wearing jeans, a chambray button-down shirt, and a navy-blue corduroy blazer that set off his blue eyes.

"You look very pretty today." Gaines smiled at her.

"Thank you, Marshal Gaines." She was being coy, but neither of them seemed to mind. It was cute. Flirty.

"Sit." Luna gestured to a table that had a basket of scones and muffins. "How do you take your morning coffee?"

"American, with a shot of espresso?"

"Coming right up. Cream or froth?"

"Talk about fancy. Just a dash of cream, please."

Luna quickly made the coffee and brought it to the table. Gaines was about to get up, when she said, "Sit." Then she giggled. "I didn't mean it as in 'sit' like I tell Wylie."

"You're funny. You know that?" Gaines was amused by her for sure.

They sat for about a half hour as Luna described some of the artists and their work. He definitely wanted to see the beer-can art. *Must be a guy thing, but Jimmy's work was genuinely interesting.*

Luna leaned in closer, lowering her voice to almost a whisper. "That Jimmy Can-Do artist? He's an enigma. No one ever sees him. He gets here before the center opens, puts his stuff out, then disappears. I don't think anyone has ever spotted the guy. I know I haven't. Weird."

"Want me to do a background check?" Gaines was only half kidding.

Luna laughed. "Not yet. But if things start getting a little hinky, I'll let you know."

"Good deal. Shall we get going? I have a meeting in two hours."

"Sure thing." Luna picked up the basket and the coffee cups. She rinsed the cups and tossed the remaining crumbs into a separate basket she kept for the birds. At the end of each day, whatever crumbs were left she would bring out to the back and toss near the bird feeders. Yes, Ellie had thought of them, too.

They made their first stop at Cullen's. He was working in the back, getting some of the recent items organized.

"Hey." Cullen looked up and wiped his hands on a towel hanging from the pocket of his work apron. "Good to see you, man. Thanks again for last night."

Gaines extended his hand. "Don't mention it. My pleasure."

"So what are you two up to?" Cullen grinned.

"I'm giving him a tour." Luna stuck out her chin as if to say *What about it?*

"Oh. Right. Well, I'm sure if she tries to give you any trouble, you'll be able to handle it, Marshal." Cullen smirked.

"See. Always the comedian." Luna stuck out her tongue. She grabbed Gaines's arm. "Let's blow this Popsicle stand."

"You heard her. I guess I am at her mercy for now. Catch you later." Gaines almost stumbled as Luna tugged him harder.

Luna spent a delightful morning with Marshal Gaines. He was fascinated with the glassblowing place called Hot Sand. They made everything from bedazzled pumpkins to tableware. He purchased a set of blue drinking glasses for his new house. His other fascination was with Jimmy Can-Do's art. He couldn't resist the baseball bat that was made of hundreds of pieces of cut-up cans. He must have stared at it for several minutes. "I wonder how he did this," he said out loud.

"Your guess is as good as mine. At least we can watch the other artists at work. Jimmy does his in private, then puts them on display."

"Interesting. The honor system." Gaines nodded in the direction of the sign. The tag on the bat was $150. "Wow, that's steep for recycling." But he seemed incapable of putting it down. "It's well balanced, and the weight feels right. About two pounds." He looked around to make sure nothing was in the way. He planted his feet several inches apart, pulled the bat over his right shoulder, and took a swing. "Impressive. It's remarkable that he was able to spell out the word *BASEBALL* along the side. Maybe from Budweiser, Stella Artois? Very cool." He turned the bat over in his hand. "Carter would get such a kick out of this."

Luna chuckled. "Oh, *Carter* would get a kick out of it? I think Carter's dad is getting a huge kick out of it."

Gaines smiled. "You are so observant."

"Nah. I got the vibe." She laughed.

Gaines opened his wallet and took out a pen and one of his business cards. He wrote "baseball bat" on the back and placed it in the honor system box. "I guess this can't be gift wrapped," he said jokingly.

"Not here, but my friend Chi-Chi can probably help you out." Luna gestured to the sign that said SILVER & STONE. "Follow me."

They walked past the other galleries. Gaines stopped in front of the Clay-More pottery studio. "I could use a set of dishes." He peered inside.

"Who knew I was taking you on a shopping spree?" Luna laughed.

"Honestly, I hate to shop, and when I do, I have little time. This is a much better way to do it. And I'm supporting local artists." Gaines was very matter-of-fact.

"Well, I am happy to see you supporting Ellie's project. She worked extremely hard to make all of this possible." Luna followed Gaines into the pottery shop, where he was immediately drawn to a set of cobalt-blue dishes.

He picked up a dinner plate. "Very *wabi-sabi*," he said casually.

"OK. Now I'm really impressed. You know what *wabi-sabi* means." She was truly taken aback.

"Japanese for simplicity and taking pleasure in imperfections." He said it quite casually while inspecting the matching pieces. He reached into the shopping bag that contained the glasses he had purchased from Hot Sand. The colors were a perfect combination of blues.

"You are a very interesting dude," Luna said with admiration.

"Why, thank you, Miss Bodhi. Don't tell anyone, but sometimes I think of myself as a Renaissance man."

"Bodhi?" Luna stopped in her tracks. She wasn't sure what was more shocking, his knowing her nom de plume or that he considered himself a Renaissance man.

"I am in the law-enforcement business. I know someone who knows someone . . ." His voice trailed off as Luna finished his sentence.

". . . who knows someone." She put her hands on her hips and pursed her lips. "I guess I'd better be on my best behavior around you."

"I think I can handle it." Gaines looked her straight in the eye. It sent a little shiver down Luna's spine. But in a good way.

Jennine, the potter, walked over to them. "Hi, Luna. Who do we have here?" She eyed the handsome gentleman who was handling her workmanship.

"This is my friend Christopher Gaines." Luna put a protective hand on his arm. *Protective or possessive? Watch that body language, girl.* But Gaines didn't flinch or seem to mind.

Jennine held out her hand. "Nice to meet you, Christopher Gaines. I'm Jennine May. I'm the shopkeeper and potter." She held on to his hand a few seconds too long as far as Luna was concerned.

"I like your style." Gaines eyed the dish, being complimentary without being flirtatious.

"Why, thank you."

Luna was starting to get annoyed. She checked her own body language and tone. "Christopher? What do you think?"

He turned over the plate and saw that it was marked at twenty dollars. He did some quick calculations in his head.

"Do you have matching cereal bowls?" He had a budget of $300 for tableware in mind.

"I do. I also have salad plates and mugs."

"I'm looking for service for four. Do you sell them in sets?"

"For you? Of course." Jennine batted her eyes.

Jennine pulled out her pocket calculator. "Four dinner plates, salad, bowls, and mugs. "That would be $260 for the set. How does that sound?"

"Sounds good to me." Gaines was pleased that he didn't have to go over his budget, and he was getting exactly what he had been looking for. Something cool-looking yet masculine.

"I'll wrap these up for you." Jennine began to stack the dishes.

"Let me help," Gaines offered.

"Me too," Luna chimed in, and picked up the four mugs, two in each hand. "While Jennine is packing these, let's head over to Chi-Chi's."

"Good idea. I'm going to have to hit the road soon," Gaines agreed.

"We'll be back in a bit." Luna put her arm through his and steered him toward the doorway.

Gaines was laughing softly. "What was that all about? I sensed a little bit of tension between the two of you."

Luna was totally forthright. "She's a vampire."

Gaines burst out laughing. "But it's daylight." He nodded up at the skylights with the bright sunlight streaming in.

"Ha. That's what makes her a really good vampire," Luna replied.

Gaines snorted. "You are a funny girl."

"I come from a family of comedians," she retorted. As they walked toward Silver & Stone, she stopped short.

"What?" Gaines asked.

"The Bodhi thing." Luna looked up at him. "Why? How?"

Gaines cleared his voice. "Before we could hire you as a consultant, we had to do a background check. Strictly routine."

"But I only use Bodhi for . . ." She wondered how she was going to explain her side job.

"I know. Your paranormal psychology studies." Gaines didn't flinch.

"So you know about that, too?" Luna hoped it wasn't going to make any relationship impossible.

"I do."

"And?" Luna held her breath as she awaited his response.

"I don't judge. That's for the courts. I only uphold the law." Gaines smiled. "So as long as you aren't doing anything illegal, I really can't do much about it."

"You don't think it's weird or spooky?"

"Remember what I said to you the first day we met? I've seen and heard a lot doing my job. I don't disavow anything without proof or from my personal experience."

"Hmmm." Luna wasn't sure how to answer. "So you don't think I'm kooky?"

"I didn't say *that*." Gaines chuckled. "You're an interesting person. Enough said."

"Deal." Luna was relieved he didn't think less of her or worse of her.

They finally came upon Silver & Stone. "This is my friend Chi-Chi's place." Luna peered around. "Chi-Chi? You have company."

"Be right there!" A melodious voice with a subtle Nigerian accent floated from the back room. Chi-Chi moved with the supple flow of her caftan. "*Sannu*," she said in the Hausa language of Nigeria, placing her palms in a prayer position and bowing slightly.

Gaines responded in kind. "*Sannu*."

"Ah, a man of many languages, yes?" Chi-Chi remarked.

"Not really. I know a few ways to say hello and good-bye. Believe me, I am no linguist," Gaines replied.

"This is Christopher Gaines. Marshal Christopher Gaines. We've worked together on a few projects," Luna explained.

"Ah, yes, you have told me about him." Chi-Chi extended her hand. "Nice to meet you, Marshal Gaines."

"Please, call me Christopher." He smiled. "I hope Luna has only told you good things about me."

"But of course." Chi-Chi wasn't about to reveal Luna's secret crush, which wasn't much of a secret anymore. Nonetheless, Chi-Chi was keeping a lid on it. "I see you've been shopping." She pointed gracefully at the shopping bag and the baseball bat.

"Yes, and Jennine is wrapping a set of dishes for him."

Luna gave Chi-Chi an eye roll when Gaines wasn't looking. He was busy gawking at the finely polished silver jewelry. "Chi-Chi, do you think you could wrap the bat in something? It's a gift for his son. Or so he says." Luna gave him a sideward look.

"I most certainly can do that for your son." Chi-Chi emphasized the word "son."

"Your pieces are stunning." Gaines was looking at a bib necklace adorned in tourmaline.

"This is one of my favorites. I brought the stones back from Nigeria," Chi-Chi said proudly. "I am working on a festoon with the same gems, for a customer who was here last night."

"I arrived late, so I missed most of the festivities, but Luna was kind enough to offer me a tour this morning."

Luna almost corrected him. Wasn't *he* the one who *asked her* to take him on a tour? She was starting to get jumpy again. He would have to leave soon. How would that wind down? Or would it wind up? *Darn it. Why couldn't she "see things" for herself?*

"Right, Luna?" Gaines had said something, but she was daydreaming about how they were going to part that day.

"Sorry. I was mesmerized by that stone over there." She was half telling the truth. It was an exceptionally large piece of raw amethyst, the stone for intuition, psychic abilities, relieving stress and anxiety. Luna was hoping it would activate all those properties in her at that very moment.

"Ah, yes. You have admired that before." Chi-Chi gracefully swept her hand in the direction of the quartz, with its brilliant shades of purple. "It calls to you."

"Uh, we better not get too deep with Marshal Gaines here. He already thinks I'm a little quirky," Luna quipped.

Gaines cleared his throat in an amusing way. He pinched his forefinger and thumb together, measuring about an inch. "Yes, this much."

"Ha. Ha. If this marshal thing doesn't work out for you, you should consider being a stand-up comic," Luna mocked. "You and my brother can take it on the road. Steve Martin and Martin Short, look out!"

Chi-Chi let out a big hoot. "You two are both very funny. It is nice to hear people laugh. Sometimes, the seriousness of the world can be heavy on one's shoulders. We must lighten the load as much as we can for each other, if not in deed, then in word. It is important to have a sense of humor."

"I couldn't agree with you more," Gaines said. "I seem to have been doing a lot of laughing since I got here."

"It's particularly good for the soul. It gives it nourishment." Chi-Chi was on a roll.

Gaines smiled and nodded. "Very true." He was thinking about his own load of raising a son half the time but trying to be accessible all the time. There was always a lot of stress with his job, plus he was in the process of moving, with a huge renovation job ahead of him. He hadn't felt this relaxed in he couldn't remember when. Must be the endorphins and serotonin the brain releases when you're laughing. That, he knew, was a scientific fact.

Luna was getting conscious of the time. "We should head back over to Jennine's. She should be finished wrapping your dishes by now." She gave Chi-Chi another eye roll.

"Ah, let me see the bat. I have tissue and a large tote bag." Gaines handed it over to Chi-Chi.

"We'll go pick up the dishes and swing back here," Luna suggested.

"Very good." Chi-Chi went to the back room, and Luna and Gaines proceeded to Jennine's.

Jennine was pacing the floor. "Oh, there you are." Luna could feel her vibe gushing out of every pore.

"Yes. Is everything ready to go?" Gaines asked, noticing that there were no shopping bags awaiting him.

"Oh yes. But I thought I'd give you a tour of my workshop before you go."

Luna was about to lose it, but Gaines immediately responded.

"Thanks, but I really have to get going. I have an appointment at the Biltmore in a half hour."

"Perhaps when you're done?" Luna couldn't believe Jennine was *so* pushy.

"I'm afraid I'll be tied up until I have to return to Charlotte." He was beginning to get impatient. Luna could see his body language. He was moving his toe up and down slowly. Not quite tapping it, but the sentiment was there. Luna almost laughed out loud.

Jennine stiffened. She knew when she was being rebuffed. It wouldn't be the first time. Luna wished she could tell Jennine not to try so hard. Especially with *her* friend.

"Well, I do hope you come back to our art haven. It would

be lovely to see you again." Jennine just couldn't help herself. She reminded Luna of Samantha from *Sex and the City*. Jennine went behind the counter and produced three shopping bags holding several boxes in which his dishes were carefully packed in bubble wrap.

Luna took the shopping bag that held the hand-blown glasses and Gaines took the bags from Jennine.

"Bye, now!" She waved as if she were saying "bon voyage" to a lover.

They quickly walked back to Chi-Chi's to pick up the bat. "I think you're going to need a hand with all this stuff."

"You're probably right," Gaines agreed, when Chi-Chi handed him the bag.

"I'll take the bat and the glasses," Luna offered.

"My car is parked on the other side. Near your place," Gaines noted. "Can we swing by and see Cullen?"

"Sure!" Luna was more than happy to have one last kumbaya moment with her two favorite men.

"I want to talk to him about that old table in the back."

Luna froze. "Really?"

"Yes. Why? You weren't serious when you said . . . oh, wait. You *were* serious. Something about that table, eh?" Gaines was getting some of what made Luna tick. Then he let out a guffaw.

"What's so funny?" Luna was about to stomp her feet in protest.

He had to tell her. It was too funny to keep to himself.

"So I was thinking, 'I wonder what makes Luna tick?' Luna-tick? Get it?"

It wasn't the first time she had heard it, but coming from Gaines, it was rather hilarious.

"Like I said, if this marshal thing doesn't work out . . ."

"Yeah. Yeah. I'll work on a stand-up routine."

Luna stuck her head into the café. "Sabrina? Hey! I'll be back in about ten minutes. I'll take Wylie with me now."

"No problem," Sabrina called back, as she was frothing someone's mocha latte. "He's been very good while you were gone."

Cullen was taking down one of the ceiling fixtures some-one had purchased the night before. "Hey, guys." He looked at all the shopping bags. "What's all this, Luna?"

"Ha. Not mine." She broke into a hillbilly accent. "This here marshal done himself some shoppin'. Got hiz-self some purdy dishes and glasses. Real kinda glasses. Not them jelly jars, and guess what? They all match! Yes indeedy . . . bought hiz-self some fine things, he did."

Gaines hooted. "You people are too much fun."

Luna smiled her biggest smile. "And so are you, Marshal."

"Nah. I'm just a good audience." He blushed. "Hey man, let me give you a hand." He set the shopping bags down and grabbed the bottom of the chandelier.

"Thanks," Cullen said.

"So I was going to ask you about that table. The one that your sister has grown attached to, but I fear she will cross me off her Christmas-card list if I try to buy it from you."

"What makes you think you're on any list of mine?" she huffed, enjoying the banter.

"Could I have one more look at it? Maybe you'll be able to find something like it for me?" Gaines asked.

"Sure. Come on back." He carried the chandelier to the workshop and set it down.

The three of them approached the table as if it were about to come alive. Gaines didn't want to usurp Luna's claim to it, Cullen didn't want either of them to be disappointed, and Luna was getting some kind of vibe. Almost like a cry for help.

She was the first to reach the table. She pulled her maxi dress to her knees and crawled under it.

"Now that's no way to claim it. Make it your fort?" Gaines teased.

Luna surveyed the underside of the table. She felt that there was something.

"You all right under there?" Gaines leaned over to take a look.

Luna was feeling the seams that joined the side trim to the tabletop. Then she felt something. "Cul? You got a flashlight handy?"

"Coming up." He pulled one off the pegged wall that held dozens of hand tools.

He handed it to Gaines, who handed it to Luna. "What is it?" Gaines asked.

"Looks like a piece of paper. Maybe the corner of an envelope. I don't want to pull on it. It might rip. Got a tweezer? Or needle-nose pliers?"

"Yep." Cullen grabbed a small tool with a slanted point he used to peel off leftover veneer.

Another hand-over to Gaines to Luna. "Looks like there are a few pieces stuck together. I'm not going to get them out this way. There appears to be a drawer that's jammed. You're going to have to take the table apart."

"OK. But not today. I have to pack the light fixture and finish Mrs. Lowery's mantel."

Luna crawled out from underneath. Gaines put his hands up as if she were pointing a gun at him. "Not me. I have places I need to be, and pronto."

"I know. I know. But see? I told you there was something about this table. Na-na na-na na. Na."

"Cute. Isn't she?" Cullen shook his head.

"Rightly charming." Gaines folded his arms in satisfaction, not as in shielding.

"Oh boy. I'm outnumbered." Luna sighed cheerfully.

"Listen, I've gotta hit the road. This has been a lot of fun. Thanks for inviting me, Luna. I very much enjoyed hanging out with both of you."

"Great spending time." Cullen held out his hand. "Hope to see you again. Maybe when you have your think tank, or whatever. Remember, dinner is on us."

"Will do. And put out a BOLO, be on the lookout, for a similar table."

"You got it."

Luna helped gather his bags and walked him out to his Jeep.

"I'm glad you were able to make it out here."

He flipped the tailgate open with his key fob. "Me too."

"And you have souvenirs from your adventure." Luna handed him the bag with the baseball bat. He lowered the tailgate and leaned in. At first Luna thought he might kiss her. Instead, he pulled her close and gave her a warm embrace and kissed her on the forehead. "Thanks again. I truly enjoyed myself."

"So did I." She smiled back.

Luna thought she was six inches off the ground as Marshal Gaines's Jeep pulled out of the parking lot. He gave her a final wave. She resisted the temptation to blow him a kiss. Maybe she should have. Maybe next time. She still felt the warmth from his embrace, the ripple of muscles through his shirt.

Wylie gave a woof. "You like him, too, dontcha, fella?" She bent over to give him a hug. Wylie rubbed the back of his neck against the back of hers.

The sun was bright, and the sky was deep blue. Almost the color of Gaines's eyes. She looked down at Wylie. "You know something, buddy? I think I have a crush on that guy." Wylie yapped in agreement. "I'm glad you approve. So, do you think he likes me?" she asked her pooch. Wylie yapped again. *Animal instincts*. She hoped.

Luna knew that the odds of anything serious happening between them were very long. He hadn't even kissed her yet, and she was already thinking ahead. *Take it easy. Go with the flow.* Charlotte isn't *that* far away. Two hours. People made that commute every day in some areas, especially large urban sprawls. Sometimes it can take an hour to drive fifteen miles. She was simply calculating. Maybe weekends? *OK. Stop.* She smiled at herself. *At least I still have a pulse!*

Chapter Nine

North Carolina
Stillwell Art Center

Luna cut through Cullen's workshop on her way back to the café. When she entered the workshop, she was once again pulled toward the table. "Hey, Cul? Ya think you could start on that table sooner than later?"

"Oh, Luna. I am really backed up right now. Can you give me a few days, at least?"

Luna stroked the top of the table and lowered her voice. "Don't you worry. We'll figure it out."

"What did you say?" Cullen called out.

"Nothing. Just mumbling to Wylie." The dog gave a funny whine, knowing Luna was fibbing. "Whose side are you on?" She shushed him.

Cullen appeared from behind an armoire he was working on.

"Why are you so obsessed with that table?"

"Because there is something hidden in it," Luna reminded her brother.

"It's probably an old piece of newspaper. Or a grocery list," Cullen said while he was polishing the new hinges.

Luna walked to where Cullen was standing. "That looks fantastic," Luna noted.

"Hard to imagine it was sitting along the side of the road. It took a bit of sanding to get all the years of paint off it. There had to be over an inch of it. I can't believe someone actually used automobile paint at one point." Cullen chuckled. "The bones of the piece were in good shape, but I had to replace the door panels."

"Oh, I like the caning you used for the panels. Gives it an updated look. Are you going to stain it?"

Cullen pointed to a few imperfections. "You see right here?"

Luna could barely notice the tiny flecks of leftover paint. "Hardly."

"Some of those flecks are in pretty deep. I need to sand it down just a bit more. I'm thinking of leaving it a light natural color and maybe paint the cane gray."

"I'd leave all of it natural. In case someone wants a different color." Luna tilted her head.

"And this is why I ask your opinion." Cullen smiled through his acrylic face shield.

"Glad to help."

"So how was the tour with Marshal Gaines?" Cullen continued to work on the armoire.

"It was great. He supported a few of our artist colleagues. I must say he has excellent taste."

"Do tell," Cullen pressed.

"He bought glasses at Hot Sand, dishes at Clay-More, and a baseball bat from Jimmy Can-Do." Luna ticked off the items.

"He bought the baseball bat?" Cullen seemed surprised. "That's a bit whimsical, don't ya think?"

"He said it's for his son. Apparently, Christopher and his son are into baseball."

Cullen gave her a sideways look.

"What?" Luna asked.

"I think you like him." Cullen kept working.

Luna feigned surprise. "What are you talking about?"

Cullen stopped and pulled off the face shield. "You're not the only one around here with good instincts. I could see the way you looked at him. All googly-eyed."

"Oh stop. I did not." Luna crossed her arms in protest.

Cullen nodded at her stance. "Even *I* know what your body language is saying right now."

"OK. So what if I find him attractive? And fun? And interesting?" Luna had a faraway look in her eyes.

"See. And that look on your face." Cullen wasn't letting up.

"All right. That's enough about the marshal. What about my table?"

"*Your* table?" Cullen mocked her. "I thought you and the marshal were going to duke it out."

"Nope. He said it's mine if I want it," Luna stated with emphasis.

"What are you going to do with it? You don't have enough space in your house. Unless you want to put it in your yoga room." Cullen reminded Luna of the small two-bedroom cottage she was renting.

Luna furrowed her brow. "Maybe I can put it in the café."

"I'll tell you what. Tomorrow, I will move it away from the wall and we can see what's inside the drawer. Once your curiosity is satisfied, will you leave me alone, so I can get down to real business?"

"OK. Fine. But tomorrow. I am going to hold you to it."

Luna was about to exit when Cullen stopped her.

"So, you really like him, don't you?" He wasn't going to let it go.

"Look. He lives over a hundred miles away. He has a son

and a very demanding job. Not exactly dating material," Luna said with resignation.

"Oh, that's not the Luna I know." Cullen gave her a warm smile. "You are one of the most determined people I have ever met. Or been related to," he said with a grin.

"So what am I supposed to do about it?"

"You asked him to come to the opening, and he did. Maybe a few more invitations down the road?" Cullen encouraged her. "It's pretty obvious he enjoys your company."

"I guess." Luna sighed.

"Listen, young lady, I am not going to have you pining away over this. We'll come up with another excuse for him to come out here," Cullen encouraged her.

"This is why I love you." Luna pecked him on the cheek. Wylie whimpered. "And I love you, too." She leaned over and gave him a hug around the neck. "How about this? You finish the table and call him. Tell him it's his if he wants it." Luna was getting excited about this new plan she and her brother were conjuring.

Cullen groaned. "OK. Good plan, but not for a couple of weeks. I am really backed up. Plus, you don't want to sound too anxious, now do you?" Cullen had to buy more time. He didn't want to disappoint clients at such an early stage of his business.

"Deal. But you will move it so we can see what that paper is all about? Right?" Luna pressed him again.

"Yes. Fine. Now skedaddle. I was only working on the armoire until the finish on the desk dried. Should be ready for a second coat now. So scram."

Luna chuckled. "Come on, Wylie. I know where we're not wanted." Wylie let out a woof. "Right, pal. Let's blow this Popsicle stand."

"See you for dinner?" Cullen called out.

"I'm having dinner with Ellie and Chi-Chi. Want to join us?"

"Possibly. Depends on how grimy I am later."

"Okeydokey." Luna made her way into the café. Sabrina had everything under control. "Thanks so much for covering for me."

"He was kinda cute. For an older guy," Sabrina said.

"Huh?" Luna thought, *An older guy? Is she serious?* Then she realized for a twentysomething-year-old, anyone over thirty was ancient. "He's not *that* old," Luna disputed. "Sure, he has a couple of gray hairs, but he's just a little older than Cullen."

"Right." Sabrina realized her faux pas. "Sorry. I'm used to younger, gangly, scruffy guys. Most of them are a mess. Which is probably why I thought he was cute. I bet he was really handsome when he was younger."

Again with the age difference. Just wait until you cross the thirty-year-old mile-marker zone.

"You do realize you will be thirtysomething at some point? Do you want to be considered old when you get there?" Luna asked simply.

Sabrina stopped for a moment. "Yeah, but no. I mean yeah, I'll be thirtysomething, but no, I don't want people to think I'm old. But won't I be?"

Luna wasn't sure how to deal with that question. "Yes, you will be older, but how you age is up to you. Look at me, for instance. I'm ten years older than you are. Cullen is twelve years older, and Ellie is a few decades older. Do you consider any of us old? As in decrepit? Haggard?"

"Of course not!" Sabrina was sputtering. "I would never call you old. Or Ellie for that matter."

"Good. Let's try to keep that word out of our vocabulary." Luna was surprised at how sensitive she was about the subject. She hadn't given it much thought, but Sabrina had inadvertently reminded her that her biological clock was ticking.

Sabrina gave her a thumbs-up. "Good idea! No more talk about age."

Luna locked her arm around Sabrina's shoulder. "And I agree. Marshal Gaines is kinda cute."

"Are you going to see him again?" Sabrina asked innocently.

"I hope so, but when? That's a question for the Ouija board." Luna laughed. She never used one, but considering her propensity for the paranormal, she thought it was a good joke.

The mention of a Ouija board grabbed Sabrina's attention.

"Do you have one? Do you know how to use it?"

"No, I don't. Frankly, I'm not a fan. It can draw in unwanted energies. I prefer psychometry."

"What's that?" Sabrina asked.

Luna explained it's when you get vibrations from personal objects.

"Ooh . . . can you psycho me?"

Luna guffawed. "It's not psycho. It's psychometry. Psychometrics."

"Whatever. Can you do it for me?" Sabrina urged.

Luna looked around the art center. It was getting busy. "Maybe later or tomorrow. I think we're in for a big crowd today. The foot traffic is already on the upswing."

Sabrina checked out the courtyard. "I think you're right. I better get back to my station. Thanks for letting me be your barista."

"No. Thank *you* for helping out. I promise I'll do the 'psycho' thing for you when things slow down." She laughed, and Sabrina giggled.

Luna checked the old retro clock on the wall. It was almost two. The morning had flown by. She remembered the old adage "Time flies when you're having fun." The more she thought about it, the more she realized how much fun she had had in the past fifteen-plus hours.

Within a few minutes of Luna's daydreaming, an announcement came over the PA system: "May I have your attention, please. The drawing for the Lincoln Corsair will be taking place in ten minutes. If you haven't purchased your ticket, please do so now. Pages in green smocks can assist you. Thank you."

The excitement was palpable. Ellie was right about waiting until after the gala. Many more people were interested in the new center and the chance of winning a $55,000 car. Tickets were priced at ten dollars, encouraging multiple entries. There was a flood of people around each of the pages. Luna asked Ellie about giving the buyers a few more minutes. Ellie agreed to extend it until two thirty and made another announcement. "For your convenience, we have extended the time of the drawing to two thirty. And we thank you for your generosity." Ellie looked at Luna. "How was that?"

"Perfect. I think you're going to make a lot of money on this."

"I hope you're right." Ellie smiled. During the next few minutes, there was another surge of raffle-ticket purchases.

"I better give Sabrina a hand." Luna swiftly made her way over to where two of the pages were being barraged with people. Having to fill out the ticket with a name and phone number slowed down the process. Luna gave Ellie a wave for her to come over to where they were hustling with tickets, pencils, and people using each other's backs to write on the ticket.

Ellie put her hands up to calm some of the people. They

were almost in frenzy mode. "Everyone? Don't panic." She smiled. "You will all have an opportunity to finish writing down your names." Ellie reorganized the mob scene. "Purchase your tickets from Sabrina and Yvonne." She pointed to the two dazed pages. "Fill it out and then give half of it to Luna." Luna waved and stepped several feet away from the crowd. Organized chaos. You would have thought they were giving the car away, not raffling it off. When they were down to the last hopeful, Luna took his ticket and put it in the big spinning barrel that looked like a giant hamster wheel.

Ellie walked over to the cage of hopeful entries. "Is everybody ready?"

A huge roar came from the crowd. "Yes!" "You bet!" "Let's go!"

Ellie grabbed the crank of the cage and gave it a huge spin. She pointed to a small girl holding two fuzzy-looking things in one hand and her mother's hand with the other.

"Hey, sweetie. Would you like to help me pick a winner?"

The child looked up at her mother with a pleading expression. "Please, Mommy?"

Luna recognized the little girl. She was Avery. The missing child from a couple of years ago. Luna approached the mother and child. The mother recognized Luna immediately. "Oh, Miss Luna! So nice to see you! I pray for you every night and thank God you were there to help find Avery."

Luna's eyes began to mist. She squatted down to speak to the little girl. "Hi, Avery. Do you remember me?"

The little girl nodded enthusiastically. She held up both bunnies by their ears. The one from Luna and the one from Gaines.

Her mother smiled. "She is rarely without them at home, but I never let her take them anywhere. They could get lost, and that would be tragic. It's all I can do to wrestle them from her so I can put them in the wash. It's odd, but today she insisted on bringing them. She put up quite a fuss, too. She wanted them to see all the pretty things. I figured I could keep an eye on her and her bunnies."

Luna smiled. "I'm glad you still have your bunnies." Avery nodded again, even more excited.

Avery held up the bunny Luna gave her. "This is Miss Boo."

"Nice to meet you, Miss Boo." Luna gave the now-tatty-looking bunny a pat on the head. "And who is this?" She pointed to the other bunny, the one Gaines had given Avery at the hospital.

"This is Marshal," Avery said with confidence.

Luna let out a laugh. "I didn't realize she knew he was a marshal." Luna remembered Gaines's telling Avery he was a policeman.

"She saw the news coverage. She thinks Marshal is his first name. Marshal Gaines." Both Avery's mother and Luna got a kick out of that.

"Wait till I tell him. I am sure he'll be pleased." Luna was jazzed she had an excuse to contact him. She was also taken aback by the coincidence. Or was it?

Luna looked at Avery's mother, Lori Tucker. "Shall we have her do the drawing?"

"Avery, you want to help these nice ladies?" Mrs. Tucker looked at her excited daughter.

"Yes, Mommy, please! Please! Please!" Avery was jumping up and down. Ellie gave the drum another turn.

Luna lifted Avery onto the platform with the big spinning cage. Luna gave her instructions. "When the wheel stops, I am going to open the little door." Avery was just tall enough to reach it. "You are going to pick just one of the cards. OK?" Avery nodded that she understood.

"Ready?" Ellie asked. "One, two, three!"

Avery jammed her little hand into the pile of cards, fished around a little, then pulled one out from the middle. She handed it to Luna, who handed it to Ellie.

"And the winner is Tony Bandiera!" Everyone cheered. Tony was a local musician who was a favorite among the locals. He drove a classic 1950s Chevy Bel Air he had restored himself over the years, but getting his equipment into the trunk was problematic. Now he could get to his gigs in one trip. Luna looked through the crowd but didn't see him. He was probably getting ready to do a few sets at the Proving Ground, where he normally played every Saturday.

Avery was still excited about being a helper. She kept bouncing up and down, her mother trying to get her to stand still for a photo. It then dawned on Luna to take a photo of her and Avery and send it to Gaines. Luna bent over to Avery. "How would you like to take a picture with me, and we can send it to Marshal?"

"Yippee!" Avery was bouncing even higher.

Luna looked over at Avery's mom. "Is it all right?"

"Of course!" Mrs. Tucker angled the camera toward her daughter and Luna. She snapped a few photos. Luna gave Mrs. Tucker her phone number and the photos were instantaneously sent via text to Luna's phone. Now all she had to do was forward them to Gaines with a note.

Look who I found. Again!

Seconds later, her phone beeped.

Wow. Such a cutie. Are those bunnies?

Luna had to admit that their condition could lead to that question.

Luna tapped back.

Yes. Meet Miss Boo and Marshal!

And Marshal!

Miss Boo?

Adding a smiley face, Luna replied:

And Marshal. Don't know where Miss Boo came from but she thinks your first name is Marshal.

Gaines replied with:

LOL.

Then Luna worried if she should write back, but before she could decide, another text arrived.

Hope you're having a good day.

He also added a smiley face. Luna got goose bumps. *Are we texting buddies now?* She didn't know where this was going and thought she should continue to play it safe.

Yes, a great day. You too.

After adding another smiley face, she put her phone back in her pocket. If he sent another text, she didn't want to know. And if he didn't send another text, she didn't want to know that either. At least not at that moment.

She squatted down to speak to Avery. "So nice to see you. I'm very happy you came today. You were a big help." Luna stroked the bunnies, then gave Avery and Mrs. Tucker a hug. "You take good care of them, OK?"

Avery nodded like a bobblehead and gave Luna the biggest hug she could muster. "Bye-bye!" She waved before she latched on to her mother's hand.

Ellie had calculated the profits from the raffle. Another

$12,000 to add to the previous night's proceedings. It was more than she could ever have hoped for. She was thankful that the center was a big hit with the local community. The generosity of spirit was incredible, and coupled with the generosity of their donations, Ellie was walking on air.

As she checked with the vendors and artists, she discovered that the Blonde Shallot had sold all fifty of their boxed lunches and salads. The Flakey Tart had also sold every crumb. There were SOLD signs on several of the pieces of art on display. She could not be more pleased. It was like a dream, and she had to pinch herself.

The large group began to disperse, and Luna noticed a line forming outside her café. She waved at Sabrina and motioned to ask if she wanted another round of being a barista. Sabrina nodded and gave her a thumbs-up.

Ellie was thinking out loud. "I should probably contact the college and see if any other art students want to volunteer on the weekends. If things continue like this, we will be very busy. Especially during the holidays, which aren't that far away."

Luna suddenly felt guilty. "Oh, Ellie, I didn't mean to monopolize Sabrina today."

"Don't be silly. It's our first weekend. We didn't know what to expect. And believe me, this is beyond my wildest expectations. Beyond my wildest dreams." Ellie paused. "Well, to be honest, it *is* what I had dreamed. Hoped." She put her arm around Luna. "And you? You validated some particularly important matters for me."

"Really?" Luna had a rather good idea as to what Ellie was referring. The little quickie reading she had done earlier that day.

Ellie linked her arm through Luna's. "Oh, as if you don't know what I'm talking about." They picked up the pace, moving through the crowd with a lot of "excuse me" and "pardon me" coming from the two of them. Luna crept past the line and quickly moved to help Sabrina serve up lattes, cappuccinos, and tea, while Ellie did her best to pitch in. It took about a half hour to serve everyone, but no one seemed to mind. There were good vibes all around. "Now you know why I wanted to call this the Namaste Café, right?"

Sabrina shrugged.

"Not only is it a greeting, but it's the spiritual connection of oneness with mind and heart," Luna explained.

"Wow. Cool," Sabrina replied. "Is it like that psycho-thing you mentioned earlier?"

"Psychometry. Psychometrics. Drawing on the energy from an object." Luna repeated the information she had shared earlier.

"Oh. Sorry." Sabrina shrugged. "But is it? Similar?"

"Being spiritual, yes." Normally, Luna would leap at the opportunity to discuss theology, spirituality, psychology, and astrophysics, but not at the moment. It had been an extremely emotional two days. At that moment, all she wanted was to finish up, go to the Proving Ground, and have a relaxing dinner.

Luna and Ellie decided to drive the prized Lincoln to the restaurant where Tony was playing and hand the keys over to him during one of his sets. The food happened to be good, and they could have a celebratory drink with him. Luna saw Chi-Chi in the crowd and flagged her over. "We're going to deliver the car to Tony later and grab a bite there. Sound good to you?"

"It is very fine with me." Chi-Chi had a bright smile. Her English was impeccable, but the hint of her heritage was punctuated with her words. Perhaps it was the cadence or lilt to her voice. She could probably curse from here to Kalamazoo, and it would still sound lovely.

They quickly cleaned up the café. Luna slid the big glass

doors together and locked up. She and Ellie slowly moved through the dwindling crowd, taking it all in. It was truly what Ellie had in mind. A place for people to share their art and share their community. Even the dog park had been busy, with half a dozen dogs running about, some catching Frisbees while others playfully chased each other. Ziggy and Marley were waiting patiently next to Wylie and Cullen.

"I can't remember when I saw so many people in one spot. Not since the Christmas tree lighting last year."

"Oh, Cullen, you gave me a superb idea. Not that it hadn't crossed my mind, but I was so busy with the opening I hadn't put much else on the calendar. It will be a holiday art village. We shall have a Christmas tree, a menorah, and Kwanzaa candles! I'll ask the artists to make an ornament for the tree with a sign indicating decorations can be purchased. Brilliant! Thank you, Cullen!"

Cullen stood dumbfounded. It *was* a brilliant idea. Too bad he hadn't really thought of it, but mentioning it? He'd take credit for that!

Chapter Ten

Boston, Massachusetts
Millstone Manor
Breakfast

Arthur and Rowena were sitting in silence at the breakfast table, waiting for Amber. It was a little unnerving for Rowena. Arthur was usually bloviating about something. Work. Politics. Money. The club. But that morning, he was stewing. Time was running out for him to locate Colette Petrov and the missing will. Granted, the estate's attorney was concerned about the alleged new will, but as long as he couldn't locate it, Arthur would continue to have total access to the company's finances. Unless Clive put a stop to it. But that, too, could take some time. At least until the next board meeting.

The chime rang on the Howard Miller grandfather clock in the foyer. Family legend said that the established manufacturer of superb clocks was a distant relative of Arthur's family. According to Arthur, his great-great-grandfather Malcolm added the word *stone* to their surname when he bought a local quarry. He thought it gave the name more distinction.

When guests would arrive, Arthur would brag, "Oh yes. We like to keep it in the family."

His boasting made Rowena choke. Arthur had no proof there was any blood relationship between the Millers of Michigan and the Millstones of Massachusetts. Even the truth of the story about adding the word "stone" had never been established. At least not to Rowena's knowledge. As far back as the family tree went, there was no mention of any Millers. And she couldn't recall ever seeing a Christmas card from a Miller postmarked from Zeeland, Michigan.

Arthur instinctively looked down at his watch. It read 8:00. Amber would be arriving any minute. Maybe they could call off this housekeeper goose chase if Amber could shed some light on where the furniture had gone. But there was still that loose end, Petrov. Did she know anything? Did she have anything?

He thought about it. *If the document was in her possession, why would she hold on to it? Blackmail?* It had been two months since Randolph's death. Surely, she would have asked for money by now if she intended blackmail. Or maybe she was waiting to blow through the $50,000 of severance pay they gave her. It was a year's salary plus moving costs. She was planning to stay with her sister and brother-in-law until she got settled with her five-year-old son. For all intents and purposes, she should be doing all right.

Arthur stood up and poured himself another cup of coffee from the silver coffee urn and went back to his chair, not bothering to ask Rowena if she wanted a refill.

"Oh, no, don't bother. I'll get it myself," she snarled.

"Rowena, can you just zip it?" He picked up the newspaper and put up a paper shield between them while waiting for the doorbell to ring.

Rowena took her coffee into the kitchen. She had to take the scones from the boxes that were delivered earlier and put them on a platter and pretend to be a doting wife. It made her skin crawl. At the moment, she couldn't even stand to hear him breathe. The burner phone rang in the other room. Arthur had placed it on the buffet before they sat down for breakfast. "Yes? What is it?" he roared.

Rowena had noticed that Arthur had two volumes lately. Loud or bellowing. Neither was incredibly attractive. He even began to yell at the staff over everything. Even the mashed potatoes. If that missing will wasn't so important, she would book a flight to Paris. A one-way ticket. She pondered for a moment. Maybe that would be the best idea for her. Get out while she could. She couldn't file for a divorce. Not yet. She would simply be taking an extended vacation. But then she thought about it again. If she took off now, Arthur would go nuclear and cut off her credit cards. That could be extremely embarrassing. No. She had to think of something else. Perhaps being an ally and helping Arthur would be the best move. Once they found and destroyed the new will, she and Arthur could go back to their superficial marriage and her extravagant spending. She heaved a big sigh and returned to the dining room, where Arthur was finishing up his conversation.

"That's excellent news. How soon do you think you can get on a plane to Buffalo? Of course, I'll pay for the ticket. No, I don't think those flights have first class. It's only an hour, Jerry. I think you can handle it." Arthur had a much happier look on his face than he had had a few minutes ago. He ended the call with "I'll expect to hear from you in two days."

Rowena leaned against the doorjamb. "Good news, darling?" She feigned interest.

"Yes, indeed." Arthur pulled out one of his cigars.

Rowena thought it was a bit gross to be smoking something like that at the breakfast table, especially with a guest arriving at any moment, but she was in no mood to argue. Besides, this was the first time she had seen Arthur in a decent mood. "Do tell." She slithered over to the table.

"Thompson seems to think he's located our Miss Petrov. From what he gathered, she is working as a housekeeper at the Curtiss. A luxury hotel in Buffalo."

"At least she's not blowing the money we gave her." Rowena pulled a cigarette from her case. "I mean, she has a job."

"Well, let's hope this is the same Colette Petrov who worked here." Arthur sat back down and folded the newspaper.

"How many could there be in Buffalo?"

He ignored her question. Rowena freshened her cup of coffee and returned to her seat at the table. "When will you know?"

"Two, three days."

"Then what?" Rowena was genuinely intrigued. Did Arthur think Colette would easily hand anything over to him? If there *was* something she actually had in her possession?

"Rowena, must you be so relentlessly curious?"

"Well, darling, since we seem to be in this doodie pile together, yes. I am curious. What is your plan?" Rowena had had enough of being the doormat for the day.

Arthur slammed his hand down on the table, causing Rowena to jump. "Can you please stop interrogating me? I don't know what the plan is yet. First of all, Thompson has to confirm it's her."

"And?" Rowena wasn't about to stop.

"And I will fly out there and talk to her myself if necessary. Face-to-face. If she has anything, I'll be able to tell."

"So, what? Walk up to her, and say, 'Hey, remember me? I'm the guy who fired you? Gotta will you want to share?' " Rowena was tiring of Arthur and his attitude toward her.

"Don't be ridiculous," Arthur boomed.

"I was being facetious. And I am not the problem here, Arthur. I was not the one who wanted the furniture sold to generate ready cash."

"Well, you'll be the recipient of any indictments should it come to that." The vein in his neck was pulsating.

"Arthur, please try to calm down. You have a lead. Let's take it one step at a time. When Jerry confirms she's working at the hotel, why don't you and I fly out together? We can say you're on a business trip, and I tagged along. It's better if there are two of us hunting her down, don't you think?" Rowena was trying to be levelheaded.

Arthur looked up. "You may be on to something. As soon as I hear from him, we'll take the company jet. Yes, my dear. There *is* something going on in that pretty little head of yours."

She batted her eyes at him, thinking, *He's such a blow-hard. He probably thinks I married him out of love and his good looks. Jerk. Two more years, and the prenup will be updated to reflect inflation.* It would also give her a good amount of time to spend whatever she could of the Millstone fortune. *Only two more years. I can do it.*

The doorbell chimed Westminster bells. Rowena put out her cigarette and headed over to answer the door.

Rowena made a grand gesture opening the solid, hand-carved oak door. "Amber! How lovely to see you. Please come in." Rowena thought she might choke on her own saliva. She knew that Arthur and Amber had had a few rolls in the hay a year or so ago. Maybe the affair was ongoing. It didn't matter. Between the two women, Rowena had the upper hand. She had access to the money, the manor house, the yacht, the five-thousand-square-foot beachfront villa in St. Kitts, and the summer home in Bar Harbor, Maine. At least for the time being.

Amber was in her midtwenties. Overbleached blond hair with extensions, fake blue-contact-lens eyes, and a bosom that could knock someone over from three feet away. Amber was wearing a very tight-fitting knit skirt and a low-cut cardigan. As the two women walked toward the dining room, Rowena noted that it was a good thing Amber had a big butt; otherwise, she would topple over and fall on her face. Not that Rowena hadn't had her fair share of body enhancements, but Amber was over the top. So to speak. One more cliché to add to Rowena's list. And the list was getting longer and more tiresome.

Arthur got up from his chair. "Amber, dear. So nice to see you." He took her hand and gave her a kiss on the cheek. "Please sit. Rowena? Get Amber a cup of coffee."

Rowena bit her upper lip. It was all she could do to stop herself from pouring it over Arthur's head. *Such an ass.* "Of course, darling." She turned and smiled at the bimbo sitting at her table. "How do you like it?"

"Light cream, if you have it," Amber replied.

"Of course, dear." Rowena wanted to spit on both of them. She poured the coffee into a Royal Doulton cup. "Scone?"

Amber gave an annoying giggle. "Oh no, thank you. I'm watching my weight."

Rowena suppressed a groan. "You have a lovely figure, Amber. Doesn't she, Arthur?" said the spider to the fly.

Arthur tried to answer that in the most nonincriminating way. "You're a lovely young woman."

Rowena swore there were beads of sweat forming on Arthur's forehead. Amber was only twelve years younger than Rowena, but Rowena felt as if Arthur and Amber saw her as middle-aged. Once again, Rowena reminded herself that she was still the lady of the house. And as of now, Arthur was in deep. He couldn't afford another divorce. Besides, the prenup was specific about adulterous behavior by either party. Poor Arthur. He was trying to have his cake and eat it, too, but he was currently choking on all the pieces he had bitten off.

Amber put on an innocent face. "So what can I do for you? You said something about the estate sale?"

"Yes. We have reason to believe that one of the pieces contained a family heirloom. Apparently it was in a hidden compartment." Arthur made up the story, at least part of it.

"Really?" Amber's eyes widened. "What kind of heirloom? Where did it come from?"

Already, she was asking too many questions. It was Rowena's turn. "There was a note in one of the notebooks we found that said, *Please take care of the sapphire broach. It was smuggled from Belgium just before the war.* Or something of that nature. All we know is that there is an important piece of jewelry that we want to find, and it had to be hidden in one of the pieces from the estate sale."

"Wow." Amber sighed. "And you don't know which piece?"

Rowena wanted to say "Duh. No, we're just here for farts and giggles." But instead she calmly replied, "That is correct. Do you have the inventory list from the estate sale?"

"Yes, I brought everything with me." Amber pulled out a file from her bag. "But I don't know where to start. Do you have any idea what piece it *might* be in?"

Arthur was losing patience as well. "No, dear. We have no idea. What I think we need to do is track down all the buyers and check with them."

"It was sold in several groupings to a number of dealers. I can give you an inventory of all the items and who purchased them, but for anything sold to a distributor or agent, they would have to track down the pieces sold to their customers."

"I realize it's a laborious and tedious job, but I will use the resources of Millstone Enterprises to contact everyone."

Amber handed over the file. Arthur thumbed through the pages. There had to be well over a hundred entries; many of those listed were agents who were spread across the country.

"Thank you, dear. I am sure this will be extremely helpful." Rowena hoped that was a hint for Amber to scram. She and Arthur had a lot of work ahead of them.

There was an uncomfortable silence in the room. Arthur stood, followed by Rowena. Amber was still a bit slow on the uptake. She knew it was time to go, but getting the bum's rush was a little surprising. She was expecting a slower, more congenial exit. "Let me know if you have any questions." Rowena was so close on her heels that Amber thought Rowena was going to lift her from the floor and toss her out the door.

Rowena couldn't open the door fast enough. "Thank you for coming, Amber. Always nice to see you." She thought she would vomit.

Chapter Eleven

Buffalo, New York

Jerry Thompson got off the plane at Buffalo Niagara International Airport. He remembered the last time he was there. He had been chasing someone who was trying to cross into Canada pretending to be a tourist at Niagara Falls. It was almost pathetic. The guy he had been chasing showed up at one of the observation areas at the Falls, wearing a yellow slicker and carrying a suitcase. Who brings a suitcase to Niagara Falls? Unless you're on a honeymoon and checking in at a hotel, it looks a bit conspicuous.

Now, back in Buffalo, he was on a mission for his boss. As Thompson saw things, the whole world was spinning out of control. Bad for the world, but good for his business. A lot of his colleagues had moved into cybersecurity, but as long as there were human beings on the planet, there would be embezzlement, extramarital affairs, and assorted other reasons why people would hire a private detective to investigate something or other.

His first stop was the car-rental agency, after which he would head to the Curtiss. Arthur had been good enough to book him a room charged to Millstone Enterprises. It would be far easier to find Colette Petrov if they were under the same roof. Before Jerry left for Buffalo, Arthur sent him a photo of Colette, making his job even easier. He simply needed to be cagey, a talent that any good private detective had to have. Jerry had an excellent record of finding difficult-to-locate individuals.

He pulled in front of the hotel, and a young man bounced out of the front door. "Checking in, sir?"

"Yes. Thanks." Jerry hit the lift button that opened the hatch of the SUV. "Bag is in the back." He left the key in the ignition and shut the door, handing the valet a five-dollar bill in exchange for a ticket. A bellman arrived with a cart and followed him to the registration desk.

Jerry signed in under his real name. No point in hiding his identity. As far as anyone was concerned, he worked for Millstone Enterprises and was there on business. But when he was scouting for information, he would use one of his aliases, John Tatum or Jacob Taylor. He even had business cards in each of those names, which included a cell number to a burner phone just in case someone had to get in touch with him, perhaps because they remembered something, saw something, or heard something.

He eyed the type of name tags the employees were wearing. He could have one made with his name and one for Co lette Petrov. His scheme was to impersonate an employee of the hotel and claim he found her badge in one of the elevators. It was an idea in progress. It would depend on what working attire or uniforms were at his disposal. In most hotels, there is a closet of uniforms for staff to change into should one get dirty or ripped during working hours. For the most part, employees were responsible for the care and cleaning of their uniforms, but sometimes a backup was necessary. He figured it would take him a little over a day to get acquainted with the hotel and its inner workings. That would be relatively simple. If the assumption that this was the same Colette he was seeking was true, finding her at the hotel should not prove all that difficult.

He phoned Arthur. "Landed. Will be scoping out the place tomorrow. I have a guy working on some fake employee badges."

"What do you mean?" Arthur wondered what that had to do with anything.

"I sneaked a photo of the bellman's employee badge when I was checking in. My guy in Queens said he can have them to me by tomorrow afternoon. If all goes well, I should have something for you tomorrow. Provided she is the one you are looking for."

Arthur listened intently. "Look, I don't care how you get the job done. But it sounds like you have things under control."

"Don't I always, boss?" Jerry was testing out the comfort level of the bed.

"Right. Let me know as soon as you hear or find anything." Arthur hung up in his usual manner—blunt.

Jerry grabbed the remote and turned on the TV. Then he ordered a club sandwich from room service. He was bushed and wanted to get a fresh start in the morning.

As promised, the fake name tags were delivered by noon via FedEx. One said COLETTE PETROV and the other JOHN TATUM. He pulled out a black hairpiece that would fit perfectly over his well-waxed skull and a pair of lightly tinted aviator sunglasses. With two-inch lifts for his shoes, he doubted that anyone would recognize him from the day before. He stuffed his disguise and a duffel bag in an attaché case and left his room, making sure the cameras would spot him as himself. He walked to the end of the hallway and went into the stairwell, where he donned his hairpiece and glasses and inserted the lifts in his shoes. Then he turned his jacket inside out and put the attaché case in the duffel bag. He had already scoped out the security cameras. One per floor. Easy enough to avoid a straight-on look at him. He also planned to fake a slight limp.

After his transformation, he exited two floors down and proceeded to the lower level, where the supplies, the kitchen, and housekeeping were situated. There was so much hustle and bustle that no one took notice of him. He walked up to what appeared to be the youngest, most junior person around. "Hey, fella, can you tell me where I can pick up my uniform? First day on the job."

The young, pimple-faced kid said, "Sure." He pointed. "Down this side, through those doors, and on your left."

"Thanks."

"Sure. No problem." The kid kept stacking dishes.

Thompson made sure no one got a good look at his face even though it was well hidden under the glasses. He found the room marked UNIFORMS and knocked. No answer. Good news. He tried the knob, and it opened. More good news. He scanned the space, looking for an associate's blazer and found one in a size large.

He snickered. *I guess they don't have custom-made uniforms.* He took a sniff. He hoped he wouldn't break out in a rash.

Thompson quickly changed, checked that his head rug was in place and his shoes tied well enough that they wouldn't slip off his feet. Depending on what type of socks he wore, they could slip when he was wearing the lifts. He stuffed his golf jacket along with the attaché case back into the duffel bag and stowed it behind the uniforms hanging on the rack. He clipped the ID tag on his breast pocket above the hotel logo and glanced in the mirror. He was confident he would blend in.

He strode through the bustling service area, back to the elevator, and took it to the lobby level. The hotel was booked solid with a convention of dog groomers. There were hundreds of people milling about. Fortunately, Millstone Enterprises had a special deal with the hotel and was able to get him a room. Heck, Millstone Enterprises had a deal with almost everyone.

Thompson strode over to a bank of house phones and lifted one from its cradle.

"Operator. How may I direct your call?"

"Good morning. I would like to speak with Colette Petrov. Do you know if she is available?"

"Good morning, sir. Let me check the schedule." She put him on hold for a moment. "I'm sorry, sir, but she is doing her rounds right now. May I take a message for her?"

"Yes, please tell her I found her name tag in my room, and I am going to leave it at the front desk for her."

"Thank you, Mr. . . . ?" the operator asked.

"Goodrich." It was the first thing he could think of.

"Yes, Mr. Goodrich. I will let her know."

Thompson walked over to the front desk and left the name tag on the counter. He went back to the house phone and waited. And waited. It was almost an hour before Colette appeared at the front desk. He pulled out his phone and snapped a photo. Millstone would be pleased to see it. From a distance, he watched the exchange between the desk clerk and Colette. Colette was shaking her head in confusion, tapping her real name tag with her fingers. Both women shrugged, and Colette took the extra, fake one and put it in her pocket. She had a very puzzled look on her face as she walked away.

Thompson meandered through the lobby and took the wide staircase to the ballroom level, enjoying his anonymity. In an hour, he would go back to the service area, return the jacket, and retrieve his belongings. The service area was in a state of pandemonium. Perfect for him. No one paid any attention as to who was coming or going. There were two other people in the uniform-storage area, but they were too busy having a very gossipy conversation to notice him. He hung up the jacket and put his golf jacket on inside out. Hairpiece and glasses were still on his head. He nodded to a few people he had to slide past on his way out, keeping his head down as much as possible. He took the elevator to the top floor, skirted the camera, and entered the stairwell. He took the wig off his head, removed the lifts and glasses, folded the duffel bag, and placed everything in the attaché case. He took the stairs down to his floor, this time making sure the camera saw the real Jerry Thompson enter his room.

He phoned Millstone right away. "It's her, boss."

"Good," Millstone said. "What's your plan now?" he asked Thompson.

"What do you mean?" Thompson thought he was supposed to locate her, which he had.

"Now you need to find out how much she knows." Millstone was tapping his pen anxiously on his desk.

"Gee, boss, I thought I was supposed to locate her, not interrogate her." Thompson was trying not to whine. He had thought this was going to be an easy one.

"When I sent you out there, I didn't need a positive ID. I needed information. That is what I'm paying you for." Millstone was steamed that Thompson hadn't thought ahead.

"OK. OK. But now I'm going to have to find out where she lives."

"That shouldn't be so hard. Follow her, you idiot." Millstone slammed the phone.

Thompson stared at the dead air. "Guess I'll be here for a while." He knew Colette was working that day, so he would have to keep an eye out and follow her home. *Then what?* He wasn't used to interrogating people. Maybe ask a few questions. Spying on them, yes. Beating them with a rubber hose? Definitely not. He had to come up with some ruse. But what? He couldn't just knock on her door and say, "Hey, lady, fork over the document." No, he had to be more subtle. He could say he was inquiring for the estate lawyer. They wanted a full accounting from her, since she had left abruptly after she found Randolph in the garage. She was the one who had called 911. "Yeah. That's it!"

He changed into a suit, went back to the lobby, and asked the bellman where the employees parked. There was a parking garage on the lower level; the street entrance was on the next block. He gave the valet the ticket for his car and it arrived in a few minutes. Thompson pulled his car around the block and waited on the side street across from the garage exit. This was going to be a little difficult. He didn't know what kind of car she drove. He decided to call Millstone. Big mistake. "How the hell should I know what she drives?" He sounded like a madman. "Just find her!" Again, Thompson's phone went dead. He didn't know how long he would be able to keep his car where he was parked, so he decided to wait until someone told him to move on. After several hours, he was getting hungry and had to go to the bathroom. Two things he hated about a stakeout: lousy food and no facilities.

Around five, several cars exited through the underground garage. Colette was not driving any of them. He was getting cranky and extremely uncomfortable. Finally, a Chevy Spark edged its way up the exit ramp. The woman put her ticket into the slot, and the gate went up. He was able to get a good look at her face and breathed a sigh of relief. His plan was to follow her home but wait until the next day to talk to her. Early. Daylight. He figured if he rang her doorbell at this hour, it might spook her. She would surmise that she had been followed. Too creepy. He thought about returning later in the evening and leaving a note at her door. Also probably creepy, but how else was he to connect with her without jumping out from behind the hedges. Then he had another brilliant idea. Send a note via a messenger service. Granted, it showed that someone knew where she lived. On the other hand, he was pretty sure that she hadn't kept her home address a secret.

Thompson thought it was odd that the Millstones never asked her for forwarding information. What Thompson did not know is that the Millstones had simply given her a big pile of cash in an envelope and delivered a short exit speech. "Colette, we thank you for your service, but since Randolph is no longer with us, we need to reevaluate our needs. Here is a year's severance in cash. We will not be informing the government about the payment. What you do is strictly up to you. We wish you the best."

He shrugged and squirmed. He hoped she didn't live too far away. He desperately needed to find a bathroom.

For the next twenty minutes, they dodged in and out of rush-hour traffic. Finally, Colette pulled into the driveway of a split-level house. As she was getting out of the car, a young boy flung the front door open and hurried down the front steps. He ran up to Colette and wrapped his arms around her knees.

Thompson watched from a few yards away. Careful not to look like a stalker, he pretended to look in his glove compartment. Once the two went inside, Thompson noted the address. His plan was to have a messenger deliver an official-looking letter and business card requesting she get in touch with Jacob Taylor. The card would indicate he was from Dunbar, Wilson & Chase, Attorneys-at-Law, Boston. He knew that if Colette had one ounce of intelligence, she would recognize that it was Randolph Millstone's law firm. She had been constantly at his side.

He dialed the hotel and inquired about when the business

center closed. They told him that it was open until nine. He had plenty of time.

On his way back to the hotel, Thompson stopped at Target, used their bathroom facilities, and purchased a small package of linen paper with matching envelopes and card stock. He hustled to his room, pulled out his laptop, and opened the Publisher program. He began to create a heading that looked official:

DUNBAR, WILSON & CHASE, ATTORNEYS-AT-LAW.

He included their address but used his burner phone number.

He typed out a letter introducing himself as Jacob Taylor.

Ms. Petrov:
This is to inform you that Mr. Jacob Taylor, represent-
ing Dunbar, Wilson & Chase, Attorneys-at-Law, needs
to speak with you in order to ascertain Mr. Randolph
Millstone's state of mind prior to his heart attack. We
are asking in order to have the final reading of the will,
blah . . . blah . . . blah. *Mr. Taylor will be in town for*
two days; please contact him as soon as possible. Thank
you for your cooperation . . . yada . . . yada . . . yada.

Thompson saved the letter to his flash drive. Then he created business cards using the same font and information and put that on the flash drive as well.

He grabbed the bag with the paper, envelopes, and cardstock, and left his room. The hotel was a flurry of dog groomers coming and going to meetings, dinners, cocktail parties. He inched his way to the business center, which was also crowded with people. All he could do was wait his turn. He recognized the pimply-faced kid from the kitchen busing tables strewn with discarded glasses and plates. This would be a test of how well Thompson had disguised himself. The kid walked right past him. Not a blink. Not a second look. Thompson was happy he hadn't lost his touch. It had been a long time since he had gone on a job that required a wig and glasses. Mostly, he had to meet people face-to-face, ask a few questions, and was done. But this Millstone thing was a little dicey. Thompson thought about how wound up Millstone had been the last few times on the phone. *What did he have to be so freaked-out about? Heck, the old dude had beaucoup bucks and a hot young wife.*

Then it hit him. *Maybe Millstone was being blackmailed. But for what?* In spite of his predilection for mystery, Thompson decided this was one he'd better stay clear of. He would do his job. Period. The real reason behind Millstone's wanting to locate Colette Petrov and have her interrogated was none of his business.

By the time he had finished his project and gotten back to his room, it was after ten. He called the concierge and asked for a messenger service first thing in the morning. The letter needed to be delivered between seven and seven thirty. If the messenger missed her, it would have to wait another day unless someone from Colette's house would phone Colette at work and tell her that a messenger had delivered something. It was a chance he had to take. It had to look legit. Not desperate. Let Millstone steam if he had to. This assignment was getting a bit shady. Shadier than usual.

His normal routine was tracking down disgruntled ex-employees who had sticky fingers when they had left the employ of Millstone Enterprises. One numbskull didn't think anyone would notice a missing tractor from one of their home-improvement supply centers. He simply drove it off into the sunset. He was pretty crafty, though. Two days before, he rented a U-Haul and parked it on a side street. He pulled the tractor up the planks, into the truck, closed the back, jumped in the cab, and drove from Arlington, Texas, to Boise, Idaho, where he met up with a man who fenced stolen goods. He had heard of jewelry fences before, but tractors? That was a new one on Thompson. When he caught up with the tractor bandit, he discovered that the FBI had been looking into a black-market farm-machine ring operating in the Midwest. *Who knew?*

Thompson folded the phony letter, placed the card inside the official-looking envelope, and brought it down to the concierge.

Identified subject. Check. Informed employer. Check. Found residence. Check. Initiated contact. Check. It had been a long but productive day. He was about to call Millstone, but he knew that Arthur would probably be in a foul mood. Nope. The yelling could wait until morning.

Chapter Twelve

Buffalo, New York

Colette Petrov had been born in New York City, specifically in the Howard Beach section of Queens, thirty years earlier. Her parents were originally from Moldova. Her father worked in fiberglass manufacturing and her mother was a nurse. When Colette was in high school, the family moved to a small town outside Boston. They wanted to be closer to other family members, but the main reason for moving was to escape from the crime that was spreading throughout all the boroughs of New York City. With his experience in working in fiberglass, Colette's father found work at a boatyard, and nurses were in high demand everywhere.

When Colette graduated from high school, she went to a state college and studied business management. She hoped to work her way up as an executive at a big company in one of the big, beautiful, shiny new buildings in Boston. She dreamed of meeting a nice guy, not the kind who hung around in Howard Beach. Many of them were thugs or wannabe wiseguys.

After she graduated, she took a job at a small printing

company, though she realized from the start that it was not where she wanted to spend her career. While working there, she met a sweet-talking handsome salesman who swept her off her feet. Two years later, they were married and she became pregnant. She took the year off after Max was born, but they needed money, and she had to go back to work. And soon. Colette didn't want her college studies to go to waste and continued her search for a good job with a good company in which she had the opportunity for career advancement.

Every week, she scanned the newspapers and social-media sites, paying special attention to a few companies in which she was interested. All the companies were huge and had their fingers in a lot of things. Big box stores, and a heavy-machine-manufacturing plant with government contracts. Like a giant squid, they had their tentacles everywhere. Millstone Enterprises was one of them.

She continued to check their websites for job postings and spotted one for manor concierge. It was at Millstone Manor. Her education and experience matched the job description. It entailed maintaining the household schedule, coordinating the staff, ordering groceries and supplies, and helping to organize dinner parties and other social/business events.

When she interviewed for the job, there appeared to be a big difference as to what was expected. When Randolph saw her qualifications, he thought Colette could serve as his personal assistant at home. She could be his girl Friday. His heart condition had slowed him down, and he no longer wanted to make daily trips to the office. There was no reason why he had to, either. With all the technology available, it would be relatively easy to set up a working office in the house.

Until his health began to deteriorate, he had been vehemently opposed to bringing work home, let alone having to work *in* the home. Things were stressful enough, and his doctors cautioned him to take life a little bit easier. He finally acquiesced and turned the library into his personal office. With an assistant at home, he could easily handle the day-to-day management of Millstone Enterprises.

On the other hand, Rowena had a different opinion of what this person's job should be. Rowena's take on the position was that its occupant should report to her, since she was married to Randolph's son and Randolph was a widower. To her way of thinking, that made Rowena the lady of the house, charged with its running. But Randolph reminded her, in no uncertain terms, that he, not she, was still the head of the house, the family, and the business. It was his way or the highway.

Colette had no way to know that Randolph did not approve of the way Rowena treated the household employees. In point of fact, Randolph didn't like Rowena at all. To be perfectly honest about it, Randolph considered Rowena, who had only been married to Arthur for a few months, a stuck-up, first-class bitch. And that relatively benign assessment was only because of her wardrobe. Without that, he thought, she would have been no different than most of the women you could pick up on certain downtown Boston street corners.

It wasn't until Colette had been working at Millstone Manor for three months that Randolph began dropping hints about his feelings about Rowena. Over the next two years, Colette had gotten an earful. The staff secretly referred to her as "Rowena de Vil" after Cruella de Vil from *A Hundred and One Dalmatians*. She felt bad for Mr. Millstone. He was a kind man, yet his family was insufferable. She was deeply saddened when he passed away. Another good man gone.

After he died, Colette thought it odd that she was dismissed so abruptly, but one thing she had learned after working at the manor for almost three years was that one does not question Rowena. She could try to ignore her, but with Mr. Randolph, as she called him, gone, no one had her back. When Arthur handed her the envelope of cash, it included a glowing letter of recommendation. It was a curious scene, but she knew not to ask any questions. She also didn't know what to do with the small notebook Randolph had handed to her when she found him on the floor of the garage. He was trying to say something. Something about the notebook. And Clive.

As Randolph was gasping for air, Colette saw terror in his eyes. Not fear of dying, but fear of the person behind her who had entered the garage. It was Arthur, who pushed past her, practically knocking her over. At first, she thought that Arthur was going to give Randolph CPR. But instead, he did no more than lean over his father and watch him struggle to breathe and clench his chest. She held her cell phone in one hand speaking to 911, while her other hand slipped the spiral notebook behind her. Whatever was in it, she was certain that it was something Randolph didn't want Arthur to know about.

Arthur made a contrived effort to check Randolph's pulse. An excruciating ten minutes went by before the paramedics arrived. They placed an oxygen mask on Randolph's face and gently lifted him onto the gurney. As they wheeled him out, he looked at Colette with a pleading look in his eyes and made a waving motion with his hand as if to say, "Hide it."

When Arthur bumped into Colette, an envelope fell out of the notebook. She didn't notice it until they shut the ambulance doors. She bent down to pick it up as Arthur came back into the garage, yelling all sorts of expletives at her, finishing with, "Get out! Meet me in the drawing room tomorrow morning." She backed away from him and banged into an old, dilapidated table. She knew she couldn't put the envelope in the notebook without Arthur's seeing her. She felt around her back. There was a drawer slightly ajar. Just wide enough for her to stuff the envelope in it and close it shut with her hips. She sidled her way out and moved swiftly to her car. Then she remembered that she didn't have her purse. She had to go back into the main house. She shoved the notebook under the passenger seat and thought she might be able to return to the garage and retrieve the envelope. But when she got inside the house, the staff was a hot mess. Crying, questions, more crying.

"Everyone. Listen. Please. Mr. Randolph is on his way to the hospital. I don't have any more information than that. We've been dismissed for the day except for Chef and Kate. I do not know where Mr. and Mrs. Millstone will be having dinner, so I suggest you stand by. Please. Everyone else, go home, be with your families, and say a prayer for Mr. Randolph." Colette always referred to the senior member of the family as Mr. Randolph. He wanted her to call him by his first name, but she didn't think it respectful enough, so they both settled on a combination of the two, something they do in the South. Arthur and Rowena were Mr. and Mrs. Millstone to everyone. There was nothing casual when it came to the two of them. Though they earned no respect from the staff, they insisted on the outward trappings of it.

When Colette got to her car, she noticed the garage door had been closed and latched. It wouldn't be feasible for her to get in there now, and she had promised her son, Max, that she would be home in time for an early dinner.

Later that evening, she brought the notebook into her house and began flipping through the pages. There were lists with dates and amounts. Nothing else. She wondered what it meant, but she wasn't about to investigate either. She decided to keep it safe until someone came asking for it. Maybe that would happen when Mr. Randolph awakened. She hoped it would be soon.

The next day, she obediently arrived in the drawing room.

She was anxious to hear how Randolph was doing. Arthur entered the room, Rowena on his heels, and without showing an ounce of grief, blankly announced that his father had died in the hospital during the night. Not a tear. Not a quiver. They say people grieve in their own way. Colette doubted that Arthur was capable of grieving. Nor was he capable of feeling. Before Colette could express her condolences, Arthur and Rowena dismissed her. Permanently. He handed her an envelope, giving her more or less explicit instructions to take the money and run. They practically carried her out the door. She knew then that getting back into the garage would be impossible. She fretted about not being able to recover the envelope she had stashed in the drawer of the table in the garage. But she certainly wasn't about to announce that she had a notebook that Mr. Randolph had given her, much less that she had stuck an envelope with some sort of document in it in a piece of furniture. She knew for sure she had to keep it safe. But for how long? She had no idea, maybe forever.

As she pulled into the driveway of the house she rented, Colette wondered how she was going to break the news to Max. They had to move away. Though $50,000 was a lot of money, it wouldn't last long.

Colette needed to find another job somewhere and soon. She phoned her sister in Buffalo and explained that her boss had died and she had been fired. Her sister, Irina, gladly extended an invitation for Colette and Max to come live with her. Irina had a large split-level. Plenty of room. Much more than they had experienced when they were small children and shared their bed with their grandmother. Or was it the other way around? When they moved to Massachusetts, the family was able to afford a house with more space and a bath and a half. They thought they were living in the lap of luxury. Now, her sister had really gone up in the world. Colette's brother-in-law was employed by a large electronics company, and Irina worked at a day-care center a few blocks from her home.

Colette was determined to make this work for her and Max. Colette had divorced his father soon after he had gone to jail for armed robbery. Her worst fear, of marrying a thug, had been realized right after their first anniversary. Apparently, certain parts of Boston have their fair share of hoodlums. Handsome, charming hoodlums. Colette credited her mistake to being young and foolish, and much too anxious to have a family. She loved Max, and thought having him was well worth the cost of her misguided marriage.

She knew that Max's father wasn't getting out of prison anytime soon, and the more remote she and Max were from him, the better. She had avoided bringing her five-year-old to visit his father in the penitentiary. She argued that he was too young. Now she had the perfect excuse. Thankfully, Max never asked about his father. Max had still been a toddler when his father was hauled away. Moving to Buffalo would be a fresh start for both him and Colette.

Within a few weeks of her abrupt departure from the Millstone household, she and Max were unpacking boxes in the lower level of Irina's house in Williamsville, around fifteen miles outside Buffalo. Colette quickly found a job as head of housekeeping at the Curtiss, a five-star hotel. The letter of recommendation worked like a charm. It was a glowing reference from the Millstone family, and the hotel knew exactly what sort of company Millstone Enterprises was. They were renowned throughout New York State as well as New England. Colette thought that perhaps Randolph was watching over her from the other side.

The hours were from eight thirty to four thirty. She mostly sat at her desk, arranging schedules and making sure the guests were well accommodated. *Extra towels? No problem. A robe? Absolutely.* She kept track of all the supplies and orders. It was a well-oiled operation, and everyone seemed nice. Nice enough that she enjoyed going to work each and every morning. Not having to cope with Rowena was like drawing a breath of fresh air after escaping a smoke-filled room.

About six weeks after they had settled in, Colette was helping Max get ready for school when the doorbell rang. It was a messenger with an envelope for Colette Petrov. She signed for it and eyed it suspiciously. "Open it up, Mama," Max exclaimed.

"OK. OK." Colette walked back into the kitchen, where she found a letter opener in the designated junk drawer. She stared at the piece of paper. Her hands began to tremble.

"What is it, Mama?" Max looked inquisitively at her.

"Nothing, sweetheart. Someone sent a special letter, that's all."

"But what is it?" Max was becoming insistent.

"Nothing important. Work stuff. Now you go with Aunt Rini. I'll see you after school." She kissed him on the head, picked up her keys, and walked to her car. She started the engine and reread the letter. She didn't recognize the name Jacob Taylor. She knew Clive Dunbar and David Wilson, but not Jacob Taylor. Maybe he was new. But what should she tell him? She was worried about the notebook. What if he asked for it? If so, she would only speak directly to Clive. Colette wasn't a suspicious person by nature, but she had seen a great deal of nastiness in the Millstone house. Arthur and Rowena were not nice people. She decided that she would call Mr. Taylor during her break at work and find out what he wanted from her.

Meanwhile, Thompson, aka Taylor, was waiting in his hotel room to get the call. Hours went by. Nothing. He called the messenger service, and the person who answered confirmed that the letter had been hand-delivered to Ms. Petrov. *What was taking her so long?* He knew he would get a major tongue-lashing from Arthur if he didn't have any information soon. He was certain that Arthur was wearing out the carpet in his office, huffing and puffing.

During her break, Colette looked into her tote bag to get the letter and make the call. She dug around and couldn't find it. Then she dumped the contents onto her desk. No letter. Then she remembered that she had left it stuck to the visor of her car. It would take too long to go to her car, so she decided to phone the law office instead. Perhaps they could give her Mr. Taylor's cell-phone number. She still had the main number in her contact list. Things had been hectic since Mr. Randolph's passing and her swift dismissal. Then there was the packing. Through the transition, it hadn't occurred to her to delete phone numbers she no longer had any reason to use. At that moment, she was grateful.

She pressed the green "call" dot on her phone. As the phone rang on the other end, she thought about how upset she was that Arthur and Rowena hadn't had a proper funeral for Randolph. They were going to plan a memorial sometime in the future. It was obvious to Colette she was not going to be invited, and knowing Rowena, the memorial service would be by invitation only.

She snapped out of her reverie when the receptionist answered. "Dunbar, Wilson and Chase. How may I direct your call?"

"Hello. This is Colette Petrov."

"Hello, Colette. How are you?" The receptionist remembered that Colette had worked for Randolph Millstone for three years and phoned often to speak to Clive.

"I'm very well, thank you. May I speak to Jacob Taylor?"

"I'm sorry. Who did you ask for?" the receptionist queried.

"Jacob Taylor?" Colette hesitated.

"There's no Jacob Taylor here, Colette. Are you sure you have the right number?"

"I'm sure. The card said Dunbar, Wilson and Chase, but I

left it in my car, and I still had your office number in my contact list. What about Mr. Dunbar? Is he available?"

"No, I'm sorry, he's away on business; and then he's going to take a short vacation. Can I take a message for you?"

Colette gave the phone an odd look. *No Jacob Taylor?* "No, that's all right. I'll try again next week. Thank you. Bye."

"Bye, Colette."

Colette had a bad feeling about this. Yesterday, someone had said they found her employee badge which wasn't missing, and now a letter from someone who doesn't exist. Her fight-or-flight instinct was firing off signals. Again. The first time was when she had been dismissed from her position with Millstone Enterprises. Arthur and Rowena had made it abundantly clear that Colette should disappear as soon as possible.

Now she was wondering if it was time to disappear again.

Chapter Thirteen

Boston, Massachusetts
Millstone Manor

If someone had taken Arthur's blood pressure at that moment, they would have called the paramedics. He was shrieking at the top of his lungs. "What do you mean you haven't made contact?" He snapped his fingers at Rowena to pour him another scotch.

Rowena stretched her long legs and sashayed to the console where Arthur kept his single-malt scotches, bourbons, and cognac. He held up three fingers indicating how much liquor to pour. The equivalent of three fingers wrapped around the glass. Rowena laughed to herself. *If he means his, I'll have to use four of mine.*

Arthur could barely control his rage. "You are supposed to find out if she signed it, does she know what was in it, and where it might be! It shouldn't be this hard! You had better speak to her in person by tomorrow, or I'll be on my way out there and you'll be on your way out. Do I make myself clear?"

Rowena handed him the tumbler of scotch. Maybe that

would calm him down. Rowena couldn't understand why Arthur was so exasperated of late. Yes, several months before Randolph died, he had told Arthur to "start making other plans." What Randolph meant was that they were going to have to move out of the mansion into a place of their own, for one. The other, Rowena suspected, was that Arthur might find himself no longer a part of Millstone Enterprises. If Randolph decided to cut Arthur out of his will, or at least to leave him something much smaller than the family fortune, something both she and Arthur feared he might do, Arthur would be left up the proverbial creek without a paddle.

Rowena knew that Randolph had been aware of Arthur's past gambling problems and that they were possibly becoming a problem once more. Perhaps Randolph had been planning to put Arthur on a tight leash. Rowena figured that Arthur was probably seriously in debt. Just how seriously was the question. Judging from how Arthur was behaving, he probably owed a staggering amount, requiring that he inherit more than a token amount if he were to avoid serious repercussions. One thing she knew for certain, the people Arthur was dealing with were not nice people.

On more than one occasion, Rowena walked into Arthur's study as he was writing out checks to himself. One evening, before he got home from the office, she went through the drawers of his desk and found the checkbook. Rowena was surprised he hadn't locked it away. Perhaps he thought no one would be rummaging around in his desk or he had simply forgotten to lock it. Lately, he had been hitting the booze in large quantities, so it wasn't totally surprising that he might have forgotten. But there it was for her to get a good peek. It appeared he was siphoning off money in dribs and drabs. Checks for a few thousand dollars every other week or so. Nothing that would set off any alarms. Heck, a few thousand dollars would just about cover one day of Rowena's purchases. But now things seemed to be escalating to disturbing heights.

Rowena watched Arthur guzzle the scotch. That's when she started putting it together. She figured Arthur had gotten deep into debt and that Randolph had found out. Randolph had bailed him out once. But he had warned him that it was the first, last, and only time it would happen. For a while it appeared that Arthur had kicked his habit, but Rowena was sure that appearances were deceptive, especially after she got a glimpse of the checkbook.

No one else realized that he had gone back to gambling. It seems that after placing a few small bets, he started winning. The more he won, the more he gambled, until he started to lose. Then the more he lost, the more he gambled. She couldn't comprehend how much he might owe, but his behavior screamed *a lot.*

Arthur slammed down the phone again. "I don't know what I pay him for."

"He was supposed to confirm where she lived." Rowena almost felt sorry for Thompson. Almost.

"Well, now he needs to confirm whether or not she signed the will."

"But you don't know whether or not she knows anything. She was only supposed to witness his signature. That doesn't mean she was supposed to read the whole thing. She may know absolutely nothing." Rowena refilled both their glasses.

"But that's the point, Rowena. There are several pieces to this puzzle. Are you dense? We need to know. Did she witness his signature? Did she know what she was signing? Does she know where it is? Three simple questions. That's all he has to ask her." Arthur took a big pull of his drink. "She shouldn't have any objections to answering them."

"I suppose you're right. They are simple questions." She

took a swig of her drink. "So, do you think he'll make contact with her tomorrow?"

"He'd better. Or you will be making a lot of phone calls to people who bought the furniture."

"Me? Why me?" Rowena protested.

"Because you are in this as much as I am," Arthur huffed.

The following morning, Rowena knew she had a lot of paperwork ahead of her. She went through all the pages in the file Amber had provided, matching the material there with the data in the Excel computer file. She didn't want to take either at face value. Begrudgingly, she painstakingly crossed off the names on paper if they were in the computer. If not, she would add them to the Excel data file. It was tedious work and wreaked havoc on her manicure. Her long nails kept getting caught between the keys, causing her to curse every few minutes. She had been working on the task for hours, but it was the only way to consolidate and organize the information. She also cursed Amber because much of the information had not been entered into the computer file as it should have been, creating more work for Rowena. She understood why Arthur didn't want anyone from his office getting involved. There were already too many loose ends. They didn't need curious eyes producing problems should they decide to do some sleuthing on their own. The Millstone estate was too visible. They couldn't take any chances.

Rowena highlighted the columns and sorted the data by state. There were three major antique dealers who had bought several pieces each, but she didn't know if any of the items had been sold to consumers. How could she find out quickly? And what excuse would she use? "Hey, did you happen to find a will that would blow our lifestyle?" Nah. She got up and poured herself some brandy. Then it came to her. She could say, "My husband has been very depressed over his father's death. Everything happened so quickly, and a few items from the estate were mistakenly sold." OK.

That sounded good. Now the big question was would she have to go to each dealer and check every piece on her own? That could be problematic. Some of the furniture might have to be broken apart. *Buy back everything?* That was an option. But Arthur would have to come up with a lot of money to do it that way. And then where would they put the pieces? They'd have to find a storage unit. If Arthur was in as dire straits as she thought, she might have to sell some of her jewelry. Scratch that. If they were going to lose everything, she was at least going to get out with her diamonds and gold. She figured she could raise well over $300,000 on her own. But only if it was necessary to get away. And if it came to that, then screw Arthur. If it came to that, he was on his own.

Rowena culled the lists. There was one dealer outside Boston, one in New York, another in Kentucky, who collectively had purchased the largest number of pieces. Then there were a few smaller dealers in New Jersey, Connecticut, Vermont, and Pennsylvania. It could take weeks, perhaps months, to track everything down. She picked up the phone and called Arthur's office.

When he answered, without even acknowledging her, he said, "I hope you have a solution."

"And hello to you, too, darling." Rowena gave the phone an annoyed look. "I have an idea, but I don't think you're going to like it."

"Why am I not surprised?" Arthur growled.

Rowena ignored his tone. "There are too many pieces scattered over seven states. I can't see how we could go to each place and try to scrutinize everything without drawing suspicion. We can't very well go into a shop with crowbars and start tearing the furniture apart. Because that's what it's going to take. Crowbars. We inspected every piece before the sale and could not find a thing. Which means we will have to dismantle each and every piece. And that means you and I, Arthur. We can't trust anyone else."

"Aren't you the astute one?" Arthur continued to bully her.

"Listen, Arthur. I've been working on this all morning. We need to contact all the dealers and buy everything back, put it in a large storage unit, and take every piece apart."

Silence. She could hear the clinking of a glass. Arthur was probably pouring himself a drink. "Arthur. Did you hear me?"

"Yes, dear. Buy it all back. Put it in storage. Pry each piece apart." His voice was unusually calm.

"Well? What do you think?" Rowena was getting impatient.

"Do it. Let's just get this over with."

"Really? You want me to go ahead?" Rowena wasn't sure if Arthur was of sound mind and wanted to be absolutely sure she had heard what she had heard.

"Yes. Do it! I'm still waiting to hear from Thompson. If he doesn't make contact with that woman today, I am going to have someone else take care of it."

"OK, Arthur. Just be careful." Rowena actually sounded like she cared. Well, sort of. But only to the extent that it would affect her if the plan went horribly wrong.

Arthur hung up without saying another word. In point of fact, they could have everything sent back to the estate. There surely was enough room in one of the outer buildings, but that would draw attention. No. It had to be off the property. She checked for nearby facilities and found a storage facility with enough space several miles away. Close enough to be convenient, far enough for no one to notice. They had to be careful.

Rowena made a list of the dealers she would contact first.

Arthur didn't mention how they would pay for any of it, so she assumed it would be covered by Millstone Enterprises. And that is what she would tell the dealers. Let everyone fight for payment later. Right now, that was not her concern and quite likely never would be. Paying people, that is. Getting the furniture was the only thing she cared about. With that in mind, she began making phone calls.

The first dealer, in Kentucky, would be open later that day. The second one was in New York. She made the plea that *her husband was very depressed over losing his father and regretted selling everything in haste, and would it be possible to purchase them back?* She actually got some sympathy from her little boo-hoo story. Fortunately, it had only been a matter of weeks since the dealer had actually received the pieces, so the pieces were still in the original crates. They hadn't begun to process them, so returning them shouldn't be an issue. One down. To expedite the transfer, Rowena planned to rent a truck or two to pick up the items. She tried to make the transaction and shipping as seamless as possible. They would have enough to deal with once all the furniture was in the storage unit.

The next call she made was to the dealer in Kentucky. If she could reach the others quickly, she could do one big sweep and have the furniture back in less than a week. She would also give the truck drivers a cash incentive. It occurred to her to give the dealers a cash incentive also. After another dozen phone calls, she had secured almost every piece.

The financial inducement made the dealers quite amenable. The transactions were swift. She was rather pleased with her display of business savvy. There was only one piece that had found its way to a consumer, the Louis XVI sideboard. She thought she could probably persuade the new owners to sell it back to her, but the dealer wasn't keen on giving Rowena the buyer's personal information. She'd deal with that later. Besides, she had personally checked that particular item before the estate sale. She was certain the will was not hidden there. Of course, Arthur would have a conniption fit, but he would have to give her credit. She had done a remarkable job. At least for the moment, Arthur should be in a better frame of mind.

Chapter Fourteen

Buffalo, New York

Thompson was getting nervous. Why hadn't she called him? It was lunchtime. Surely, she would have taken a break. Maybe he should just go downstairs to the housekeeping office? He snapped his fingers. He'd call her from the house phone and ask if she had gotten his letter. Then he would ask if he could stop by and ask her a few questions. She wouldn't be able to run away, and she might feel safer in her own environment. The question was should he be dressed as himself? Why not? He really wasn't doing anything illegal. He was simply seeking information for his employer. But why was this job giving him a creepy feeling? There was a tense undercurrent in his communications with Arthur. *Anger and desperation*, Thompson thought.

His job was to find out whether or not Ms. Petrov had witnessed a signature. And to find out whether she saw where Randolph Millstone had put the document. There was nothing truly shady about finding out about those two things. But the subterfuge he had used involved more deceit than was usual in his investigations, and therefore seemed shadier.

Thompson took the elevator to the lobby, went to the phone banks, and asked to be connected to housekeeping. A woman answered. "Housekeeping, Colette speaking. How may I help you?"

"Hello, Colette, this is Jacob Taylor from Dunbar, Wilson and Chase. I believe a letter was delivered to your home this morning," he half asked.

Colette's heart started to pound. She didn't know who it was who was pretending to be from Dunbar, Wilson & Chase, but she was going to find out. She might be naïve when it came to men, but when it came to life in general, she was pretty savvy. "Yes, Mr. Taylor. My apologies for not calling you sooner. We have had a busy day this morning. A lot of people checking out. And in. You mentioned something about Mr. Millstone? What is it that you need from me?"

"Do you have a few moments to sit down with me? If it isn't any trouble, I could come to your office. I won't take up much of your time."

Colette put him on mute and looked over her cubicle. There was a lull in the confusion, and she had a lunch break coming up.

"Are you close to the Curtiss?" Colette thought she heard familiar music in the background. The music they played in the hotel lobby. Then she checked the caller ID and saw the call was coming from an internal line. It was not from the cell number on the card.

"Yes, actually. I'm right down the street. I could meet you in ten minutes." He'd stop in the men's room to kill some time.

"There is an employee cafeteria on the mezzanine level, but you have to take the service elevator from the kitchen."

"I'll figure it out."

"How will I recognize you?" Colette asked.

Thompson stopped for a moment. *He* knew what *she*

looked like, but *she* didn't know what *he* looked like. And he wasn't about to tell her, either.

Conversely, he didn't know that she knew he was a fraud. They each thought they had the upper hand.

He gathered himself. "I'm wearing a gray jacket with black pants. I'm bald, with black-framed glasses."

"All right, Mr. Taylor. I will sit close to the elevator door."

"See you soon."

Colette called the front desk immediately. It was the same music she had heard in the background when she was on the phone with Taylor. Or whatever his name really was. She was taken aback that he was already in the building. Now she was really on her guard.

She stood and leaned over the barricade that separated her desk area from her coworker. "Dottie? Got a few minutes?"

"What do you need?" Dottie answered.

"I need for someone to come with me to the cafeteria."

Dottie chuckled. "Can't find your way?"

"No. Just come with me, and I'll tell you. Like now!" She yanked her head in the direction of the elevator.

"OK. OK." Dottie grabbed her purse and met up with Colette at the elevator. "What's going on?"

"I don't know yet. But someone who claims to be with my previous employer's law firm wants to talk to me."

"What do you mean, *claims*?" Dottie asked.

"Someone sent a letter to my sister's house, where I'm staying with my son. The letter said he was from the law firm and had some questions for me. But I left his card in my car, so I phoned the law office directly. When I asked for him, they told me there was no one by that name working there." Colette was almost out of breath.

"Jeez. So?"

"So, he just called me. From a house phone. He wants to meet me in the cafeteria to ask me some questions."

"Sounds a little nefarious, dontcha think?"

"Very." Colette exited the elevator and walked to the nearest table that was empty. "Go sit at another table and just keep an eye on us without looking like you're on a stakeout." Growing up, Colette had watched a lot of crime dramas and used the jargon often.

"Roger that," Dottie joked. "I'll be right over there. With my camera."

Colette gave her a look.

"Relax. I am a primo stealth photographer." Dottie gave her a wink.

"Please. I'm nervous enough. I don't want to know about any of your dark secrets. At least not right now."

The elevator door opened, and the self-described bald, black-rimmed glasses man stepped out. He recognized Colette immediately, but he pretended to look around. Colette seemed to cringe when he approached her. Was it her imagination, or was she being paranoid?

"Colette?" the man asked.

"Yes. Hello," she replied evenly.

"Did you have the opportunity to read my letter?"

"Yes, briefly. As I mentioned, we were terribly busy this morning. I glanced at it in my car but didn't have time to read it carefully. And, unfortunately, I left it in the visor." Her thought trailed off to *and I called the office and you don't exist.* Even though she didn't say it, the words were floating in her head.

Taylor, or whatever his real name was, shook her hand and sat down across from her at the small, square table.

Colette laced her fingers together and placed them on the table. She sat up tall. "What can I help you with, Mr. Taylor?"

"You were present when Mr. Randolph Millstone passed away, correct?"

"Yes. That is correct."

"Did Mr. Millstone ask you to witness papers at some time before he died?"

Colette sat up even taller. "Yes, he did. About two, maybe three weeks earlier."

"And what was on those papers? Did you read them?"

"No. I was only told to witness his signature. And that I be present when he signed it. That's all he instructed me to do. There was no reason for me to read the document."

"Do you know where that document was kept?"

"I do not. But I would think it would be in his safe. That was where he kept all the important documents." Colette remained calm. But her mind flashed to the envelope. The envelope she had not been able to retrieve from the drawer in which she had hidden it. Then to the small spiral book under her passenger seat. She cocked her head. She had to pay attention and not give him too much information. She wanted to find out who this man really was and why he was asking her these questions.

"Apparently the document in question was not in his safe."

"I really don't know what to tell you, Mr. Taylor." This time, she couldn't help but emphasize "Taylor." It occurred to her that he hadn't asked about the notebook, and she was not about to offer any information about it either.

"Just so I can close this case, you affirm that you did, in fact, witness a signature of Mr. Randolph Millstone on a document, but you do not know the nature of said document?"

"That is correct." Colette looked him straight in the eye. Something wasn't right with any of this.

"Well, thank you for your time, Ms. Petrov. If you should think of anything, please call me. Have a good afternoon." Taylor got up, extended his hand for a shake, turned, and waited for the elevator. To Colette, it seemed like an eternity.

As soon as Taylor, or whatever his name was, disappeared into the elevator, she nodded at Dottie. The two women hurried to catch the next car. Colette wanted to follow him as far as she could without being noticed. She and Dottie entered the lobby and watched Taylor walk to the guest elevators. Colette thought he might be staying at the hotel. Colette told Dottie to watch the elevator light and see if she could tell on which floor he got off. Meanwhile, Colette walked over to the front desk. "Hi, Eddie. Do we have a Jacob Taylor registered here?"

Eddie scrolled through the database. "No. No Jacob Taylor." Colette stood there, thinking for a moment, when Dottie dashed over. "The elevator stopped at the fourth floor, then continued up to eight."

"Eddie, can you check who is registered on those two floors?"

Eddie ran down several names that didn't sound familiar. Then Eddie came to a Jerry Thompson, who was with the Millstone Group. Colette gripped the counter. Why would that man lie to her? Something was terribly wrong. She needed to find Clive Dunbar.

"Dottie, can you cover for me?" Colette asked in haste, not waiting for an answer. She sped back to her cubicle and dialed Clive's office number again. Again, the same cordial receptionist answered.

"Dunbar, Wilson and Chase. How may I direct your call?"

"Hi, it's Colette again. You said Mr. Dunbar was out of town on business? Do you know where?"

"Let me put you through to his assistant."

"Clive Dunbar's office. How can I help you?" A familiar voice was on the other side.

"Hi, it's Colette Petrov." She could barely breathe.

"Colette. Nice to hear from you. What can I help you with?"

"I need to find Mr. Dunbar. It's particularly important." Colette slowed down.

"He went to Toronto on business and was going to meet up with his son at their cabin on Cranberry Lake in upstate New York."

"Do you know when he'll be back?" Colette tried not to sound desperate.

"Not until the end of next week. Is there something I can help you with?"

"I don't think so. But thank you. Please tell him I called. I have the same cell number." Colette gave it to the assistant just in case. "Thanks very much."

Colette grabbed her purse and made a beeline to the employee parking garage. She zoomed out and proceeded to Max's school. The imposter knew where she lived and where she worked. Colette tried to keep her wits about her, not knowing what kind of danger they were in. She phoned the school to let them know she was picking him up. Family emergency was her reason.

Colette remained calm when she arrived at Max's school. She explained that they were going on another adventure. "For how long?" Max was curious.

"Just a few days." Colette hoped it would only be a few days before she tracked Clive Dunbar down. If memory served her, she had a rough idea as to where his cabin was located. She had certainly helped Randolph plan a few trips there, but she didn't have Clive's cell number. She thought about calling the office again and asking for it, but right now, she wasn't sure whom to trust. That could have saved her a lot of trouble, but she had to move, and move fast. *Think. Think. How many cabins could there be on Cranberry Lake?* She would soon find out.

When they got back to Irina's house, Colette helped Max pack a small bag with three days' worth of clothing and a few games. She threw a few things together for herself and left her sister a note:

> *Had an emergency to deal with. Nothing terrible but had to leave town for a couple of days. Will call later. Love, C.*

Confident she had not been followed, she packed up the car with a small cooler filled with water and juice boxes. On her way out of town, she stopped at a large bookstore and purchased a spiral-bound road atlas. She also let Max pick out a book. Since she wasn't sure of the exact location of the cabin, once she got there she would need something that showed the area and the terrain. Sitting in the car, she opened the atlas and saw it would take the better part of five hours to get to Cranberry Lake. She would have to wing it the rest of the way.

Colette and Max had been on the road for almost four hours. It was getting late, and they were both hungry. Colette decided to stop for the night and get a fresh start in the morning. She pulled out her phone and searched for a decent motel. There were several national chains outside Watertown. From there, it would be another hour to Cranberry Lake. They would get up early, have breakfast, and get back on the road. It would be much better to navigate in daylight. Plus, she needed to rest and regroup. The last twenty-four hours had been alarming.

They pulled into the parking lot of a Courtyard by Marriott and dragged their bags into the lobby. Checking in was no problem, and there was a nice family restaurant several yards across the parking lot. Colette took it as a good sign.

Max was always excited when they would go out for a meal. It wasn't that often, so it was a big treat when it happened. Colette was happy that Max was in good spirits. She had been concerned he wouldn't do well with another shuffle. He had been quite fine with the move to Buffalo. His aunt, uncle, and cousin were a loving family and welcomed them with open arms. Colette thought Max was a well-adjusted boy with a positive temperament. He was happy and bright, with a kind, sweet disposition. Colette thanked her lucky stars for that. And today he was all in for an adventure. As long as she could remain calm and make it appear that this was totally normal, Max would respond to her mood. She prayed she had the strength and asked St. Jude, the saint of hopeless causes and miracles, to intervene. And anyone else who might be listening. She smiled, thinking about her former employer. *And you, too, Mr. Randolph.*

"What kind of adventure are we doing?"

"Remember Mr. Randolph, my former boss?"

"The one who went to heaven?" He looked at her with puppy-dog eyes.

Colette smiled. "Yes, that's right. Well, he has a friend named Mr. Dunbar, and I have something I need to give him."

"Like a present?" Max asked with wonder.

"Sorta. Like a present." Colette hoped it would be a welcome gift. It was certainly an unexpected one.

The waitress came by to take their order. "What can I get for you?"

Max was bobbing in his seat. "I would like a cheeseburger, please."

Colette said, "I'll have the same. Medium rare for him and rare for me. Lettuce and tomato on both, please."

Max made a face. Colette gave him a sideways look. "You know the drill."

"Always have greens at dinner." Max heaved a huge sigh of resignation.

The waitress chuckled. "Wish my kid were that smart."

Max sat up straight, realizing that this nice lady thought he was smart.

"They come with fries. Is that OK?" She looked at Colette.

Max was mimicking a plea. Colette couldn't resist how cute her kid was, and said, "Yes! Fries for both of us."

Max clapped his hands gleefully. "Thanks, Mom."

Colette noticed that he had stopped calling her "Mommy" lately; she was now "Mom." Occasionally, he'd call her "Mama," but only if he wanted something really badly. It made her feel old, but she understood the need for a kid not to be thought of as a mommy's boy, especially around new friends.

"Anything to drink?" the waitress asked. Water for both of them. As she was about to turn away, she pointed to the container of washable crayons on the table. "Feel free to use them on the place mats. If you turn it over, there are drawings on the other side and you can color or draw however you like."

"Thank you!" Max whooped with delight.

"So what kinda present are you giving Mr. Millstone's friend?" Max went back to their original conversation.

Colette wondered how she should answer. Be honest. He doesn't need details. "It's a book."

"What kinda book?" Max started to draw on the place mat.

"It's a surprise." Colette didn't know what else to say, but it wasn't far from the truth.

"What kind of surprise?" Max kept making circles on the paper.

"Well, now, if we knew, then it wouldn't be a surprise, would it?" Colette was relieved that Max accepted that answer.

Max nodded in agreement. "So what else are we going to do?"

"I'm not sure yet. Maybe that will be a surprise, too!"

"Goody!" Max was content with the plans for surprises.

Several minutes later, the waitress brought their food. Colette was so hungry that she thought she would inhale all of it at once. Max dived straight into the fries. "Easy now." Colette was speaking to him, and to herself.

Max proceeded to tell his mother about some kids at his new school who play in the Pee Wee League. "We can talk about it after your next birthday. Then you'll be old enough."

"When is my next birthday?" Max still wasn't old enough to grasp lengths of time very well. Something months away might as well be a decade for a kid his age.

"You have four more months to go."

"How long is that?" he asked innocently.

"It's a little while. Not too long. Now finish your dinner before it gets cold."

They ate in a comfortable silence, listening to the music playing in the background. It was Ed Sheeran followed by Sam Smith. *Men in love.* She hoped one day someone would feel that way about her.

"Mom?" Max broke the spell.

"Yes, love?"

"Can we watch some TV when we get back to the hotel?"

Colette checked her watch. "OK. But not too long. We both need to get a good night's sleep." She hoped she would be able to sleep. As exhausted as she felt, her mind was racing at a hundred miles a minute.

The waitress returned to collect their plates. "Anyone for dessert?"

"Ice cream, please?"

"Sure. Why not. We're on an adventure." Colette smiled. "A scoop of chocolate for me, and a scoop of vanilla for Max."

"Very good. I'll be right back." She was about to remove the place mat but Max stopped her. "Please, can I keep it?"

She looked at Colette.

Colette saw that it hadn't been soiled too much. Just a few dribbles. "Of course."

"A suberneer." He meant souvenir, but his mispronunciation was endearing. Neither corrected him. It was the sentiment that was important.

They finished their ice cream, Colette paid the check, and they walked back to the motel, Max skipping a few feet ahead. Colette stopped at her car before they went to the room. She wanted to get the notebook and the road atlas. She opened the trunk, retrieved the books and then closed the trunk. They walked from the parking lot into the motel lobby. Max pushed the button to bring the elevator to the first floor. On the ride up to their room, Colette thought she'd study one book and try to unravel the meaning of what was written in the other while Max watched a movie.

"Go put on your pajamas and brush your teeth." Colette ruffled Max's hair.

"OK, Mom." He opened his backpack and pulled out his pj's and toothbrush. "Toothpaste?"

Colette handed him the tube. "Remember the rules?"

"Don't squeeze hard."

"And?" she urged.

"And put the top back on!" Max grinned.

"Right-o."

Max marched into the bathroom. He could barely reach the sink, but he wasn't going to say anything to his mother. He wanted her to think he was a big boy. He struggled to reach the faucet, but he was determined. Much like his mother.

He climbed onto the lid of the toilet seat and reached over. One twist, and a big splash of water came out and hit the sink with so much force, it splashed all over his pajama shirt. He tried not to panic. He didn't want to upset his mother, but he knew that if he tried anything less than the truth, it would make her sad. "Mom!" Max yelled.

Colette ran to the bathroom. "What? What happened?"

He turned to face her. His eyes welled up in tears. "I'm sorry, Mommy."

He called her "Mommy." Colette's eyes also welled up in tears. She gave him a big hug. "It's OK, sweetie. Come on, let's put a dry shirt on you." Colette knew it had been a stressful day for both of them.

Colette picked out one of the *Toy Story* movies for him to watch. He had probably seen it a half dozen times, but he always wanted more. Colette tucked him into the bed next to hers. She was glad they had a double room. She knew she would be up for at least another hour mapping out her route for the next day. Once she got to Cranberry Lake, she would stop at a local market or gas station and ask if someone could direct her to Clive Dunbar's cabin.

She thought about her approach and did a personal inventory. She was a slender, attractive woman in her late twenties. She was dressed well and had a small son with her. Truly, no one would think she was menacing in any way. She would also explain she had something from her former employer, who died recently, to give to Mr. Dunbar. She wasn't sure how much information she would have to give away to get his address, so she rehearsed what she would say. "Hello, my name is Colette Petrov. I am looking for Mr. Clive Dunbar. My former employer, Mr. Randolph Millstone, was one of his clients. He died recently, and I have something Mr. Millstone wanted to pass along to Mr. Dunbar." That was a perfectly reasonable explanation for the request. If she were really lucky, they might have met Mr. Randolph on one of his trips to the cabin.

She looked over at Max. His eyes were fluttering, and he soon drifted off to sleep. Colette lowered the volume of the television and pulled out the road atlas. There was an entire page devoted to the Cranberry Lake area. How she was going to find one cabin in the entire area would be a challenge. She pulled out her laptop and put *Cranberry Lake/ Food* into Google. Several results popped up with virtual pushpins. She wrote down the names and addresses of a few of them. She would plug the information into her GPS when they got in the car in the morning. Colette got up, turned on the light in the bathroom, and closed the door halfway in case one of them had to get up during the night. After a day like the one she just had, waking up in a strange place could be quite disorienting. She switched off the television and the lamp next to her bed, and hoped she would be able to get some sleep. She had to be on her best game for the next part of this "adventure."

Chapter Fifteen

Stillwell Art Center
Two weeks after the grand opening

The ebb and flow of attendance was still hard to predict. There was a huge turnout on the opening weekend, which is normally the case. And the following weekend was also bustling. New place. New stuff to see. New stuff to buy. The center hours were eleven to seven Wednesday and Thursday; ten to ten Friday and Saturday; and noon to five on Sunday. The shops were at liberty to make their own hours, but Ellie encouraged them to be open when there was a regular flow of people. She knew she had to find more support staff for the busier hours, but they hadn't been open long enough to figure out exactly what hours those would be.

The local university had a community-credit program that allowed students to earn credits for working at certain non-profits in a number of disciplines. Ellie Stillwell was delighted when they assigned her one student for each artist, and four as pages. Having an apprentice or student would enable the artists to continue to work while someone minded the store, so to speak.

It would be a wonderful opportunity to learn about art and business. A delicate combination. Many artists have no interest in the business end of things.

It was early Friday morning. Luna was unlocking the doors to the café when she spotted Ziggy and Marley coming over to greet Wylie. Luna was thrilled that Wylie had others to play with during the day. The dog-park idea was genius, and made working at the center especially convenient. Luna looked at the calendar. They had been open for a week, and she was checking her inventory. She was pleasantly surprised to discover that she had sold out of most of the espresso blend. She wasn't sure if such a robust cup of coffee would be popular, but it was. People especially liked the lattes, so she was sure to have more milk on hand as well. Good thing Cullen had a refrigerator in his shop. She might have to take up some of the space with her supplies. It was a good problem to have.

Luna checked the calendar again. It had been almost two full weeks since she and Gaines had communicated. She wasn't sure how to take it. Was he interested in her? Or was he not? *Shake it off, girl.* She stood still for a moment and put her thumbs and middle fingers together to form a small circle with each hand. She closed her eyes and took a long, deep breath and released it slowly. When she opened her eyes, it occurred to her Cullen still hadn't moved the table. That was going to be next on her list. The past couple of weeks had gone by so quickly that she hadn't had time to bug him about it.

After she finished her list, she walked over to the Flakey Tart to place her order for the next day. "Hello, Heidi! Looks like everyone has been busy this week."

"You ain't kiddin'," Heidi called back from behind the counter. "What can I do for you?"

"I'm going to need more scones for tomorrow. At least

two dozen, a dozen blueberry muffins, and a dozen crumb-cake muffins." Luna smiled at Heidi.

"Can you believe it?" Heidi checked off the items on her pad. "I'm going to have to rethink my menu. Have a few different things but have a daily special. The oven is getting a workout!" They both chuckled.

"I'm still amazed at how Ellie pulled off this Herculean task," Luna said with admiration.

"Right. And it was really smart to have a small selection of food. Keeps people here longer."

"Good thinkin'," Luna replied. "I'll be by to pick everything up around eight thirty. Thanks for offering to bring it with you. Saves me a trip."

"I have to come here anyway, plus I borrowed a van, so I don't have to make more than one trip. Unless we sell out, in which case I'm going to have to wing it!" Heidi laughed.

"Do you have backup in your kitchen?" Luna had never thought to ask before.

"I keep some of the cakes in the freezer, but I don't like to sell them. I usually save those for my son and his friends. They're not very fussy. You know how adolescents can be," Heidi noted.

Luna thought back for a second. "Sure do. My brother, Cullen, would bring a bunch of guys over after practice, and they would scour the kitchen for anything edible."

"Must be in their genes," Heidi joked.

"For sure. Gotta run. Have a groovy day." Luna smiled.

"Groovy. Cool, man." Heidi laughed at her own response.

Luna checked the time. Cullen should be opening his shop shortly. She was preparing to pounce on him about the table when he walked in with his hands in the air. "I know, I know, I know."

Luna snickered. "You promised, and I have been a very good sister not nagging you about it." She pouted in fun.

"You are correct." Cullen gave her a kiss on the cheek. Luna returned the gesture they had long established since they were in college. "Want to give a look now?"

"We have about an hour before the center opens. Let's do it!" Luna clapped her hands in excitement. "I'll go turn on the coffee machine and be right back."

Luna buzzed into the café and checked the machine. Full. Clicked the switches to the ON position. Everything was ready for the first customer. But just in case someone came looking for her while she was next door, she put up a tie-dyed sign with an arrow pointing to Cullen's shop. The café was also on the honor system.

Luna scurried back to Cullen's workshop. She was excited and anxious at the same time. She knew there was something about that table, and now she was about to prove it. She began to slip on a pair of cotton gloves.

Cullen gave her an odd look. "What are those for?"

"I don't want to leave any fingerprints," she said slyly.

"You're kidding, right?" Cullen gave her another odd look.

"Kinda. I was hoping I could get one more week out of this manicure. I get them so rarely." Luna held up her fingers. "See? Pretty, eh?"

"Very." Cullen never noticed things like that on his sister. Other women, yes. Luna, not so much. He figured if she wanted him to notice something, she would be quick to bring it to his attention. Not that he wasn't aware of his sister's good looks. But it was more her aura that he appreciated and took notice of. He had to admit she had looked stunning the night of the opening. Maybe it was the marshal who had inspired that glow. He smiled.

"What?" Luna eyed him.

"Nothing."

"Yeah. Right. Spill." Luna nudged him.

"When you mentioned your manicure, I recalled how pretty you looked at the opening." He gave her a sideways glance.

"Well thank you, Cullen. You looked rather handsome yourself. Us Bodmans clean up real good!" Luna snickered.

Cullen wondered if he should ask her about Gaines and if she had heard from him. Then he thought she would have told him if she had. But then, maybe not. He took a chance. "Have you heard from the marshal?"

Luna didn't bat an eye. "Nope." She went to one end of the table. "Come on. Move your heinie."

"All right. All right." Cullen made a face and went to the opposite side of the table. "Ready?"

"Yes!" She was practically screaming. "One, two, three!"

They slid the table far enough away for Cullen to get around to the side where the drawer was jammed. He tried to pull it loose but it didn't budge. "Hand me that putty knife." He pointed to the wall where all the tools were neatly stored.

Luna grabbed the smallest one and passed it across the table to Cullen. He began to wriggle it between the drawer and the table. "Whoever closed this the last time gave it quite a shove." Cullen bent down and peeked under the table. "I think maybe you should get underneath so when I can get this blasted knife in the slat, you can push while I pull."

Luna twisted the bottom of her skirt and tied it in a knot. She grabbed a shop towel and put it on the floor and clambered to the spot. "Glad you swept," she muttered mockingly from under the table.

Cullen kept trying to wedge the knife. "I need a hammer."

"Get it yourself," Luna grumbled. "I'm not budging."

Cullen slithered between the table and the wall until he was free. He grabbed the nearest hammer and slithered back. He jammed the knife with one hand and gave it a bang with the hammer. A few pieces of old paint flew off. Still, it wasn't moving. He let out a big sigh.

"What?" Luna mumbled from her position.

"Nothing. I need a crowbar." Cullen already knew he wasn't going to get any cooperation from his sister and slithered once again to the tool rack. And back again to the stubborn drawer. "OK. I'm going to pull it out with this. Better get out from under there just in case this whole thing falls apart."

Luna made disgruntled sounds as her head reappeared. She stood and brushed the dust off her hair.

"I'm going to push the table toward you, so move away from it," Cullen instructed her. "I need some room to get leverage." He shook his head. "I've never had this much trouble with a piece of furniture, ever. This had better be worth it."

"Maybe it's a treasure map!" Luna's eyes lit up like those of a child whose favorite uncle had just walked in holding a package.

"Just as I said, it's probably an old grocery list." Cullen put one foot on the leg of the table and began to pull at the drawer with the crowbar. With a loud crack, the front of the drawer came off, but it still left the rest of the drawer stuck to the table. "Hand me a flashlight, please?"

"Aren't you Mr. Bossy today?" Luna kidded, as she reached for the torch.

Cullen shot a beam into the dark space. He peered inside, then reached inside. He gently tugged at the paper he had seen. It was an envelope with a name written in cursive on the front.

"Huh," Cullen muttered. "An envelope. It just says 'Clive.' Wonder who he is." He turned it over in his hand.

"Give me that thing!" Luna reached halfway across the

table, practically climbing on top of it. She snatched it out of Cullen's hand. "We have to open it."

"Wait. Maybe we should try to find out who Clive is first."

"Oh yeah. That will be a breeze. I'm sure there are only a couple million of them in the United States."

"You're the psychic. Maybe *you* can figure it out." Cullen was really razzing his sister by then.

"Oh shut it, you. I told you there was something about this table. See?" She waved the envelope at him. "Maybe the name of the owner is within the contents of this envelope," she mused.

"Maybe. Maybe we should have someone other than us open it," Cullen suggested.

"Why?" Luna asked with a smirk. "Finders keepers."

"Oh no, missy. That's *my* table."

She reached in her pocket and pulled out two single dollar bills and placed them on the table. "Here you go. The table now belongs to me." She folded her arms to indicate the conversation on the subject was over. It was technically hers.

Cullen looked pensive. "I bought this table at an auction with a few other pieces."

Luna acknowledged him. "Yeah. It was a bulk sale. You had to buy the entire contents of the container."

"Correct. But I bought it from a dealer who bought it from someone else."

"So, the real owner of this envelope may be looking for it," Luna insisted. "We may very well be doing someone a favor.

"I seriously doubt it. If they shoved it in this junky old piece of furniture, chances are they aren't missing it."

"OK. But I'm still opening it. Aren't you the least bit curious?" Luna looked at him wide-eyed.

"Of course I am," Cullen admitted.

Luna tilted her head to the side. "I'm going to go get Chi-Chi. Then there will be three of us witnessing the 'unveiling' . . ."

Cullen finished her sentence. ". . . of the secret grocery shopping list."

"Ha!" Luna barked. Wylie echoed her. "Come on, pal. Let's go get Chi-Chi." Luna placed the envelope on the table. "Don't go away."

Cullen smiled. He had to hand it to her. She was right. There was something about that table. And now they would soon find out what it was.

A short time later, Luna reappeared with Chi-Chi, Wylie wagging his tail. He was as fond of Chi-Chi as she was of him. In her melodious voice, she asked, "And what is the big commotion all about?"

Luna pointed to the table and the envelope. "We found this. It was inside a drawer that was jammed shut."

"Why don't you open it? Maybe it is important," Chi-Chi offered.

"See? I told you," Luna teased her brother. She took the putty knife and used it as a letter opener. Her hands were shaking as she unfolded the paper and began reading out loud.

" 'I, Randolph Millstone, of Millstone Manor, in the state of Massachusetts, do hereby declare this is my last will and testament and revoke all previous wills and codicils.' " She stopped abruptly and handed it to Cullen. "Do you think it's real?"

Cullen looked at the last sheet where a signature appeared as well as a witness to his signature. "The signature is legible." He placed the letter on the table. The room went quiet.

"Randolph Millstone, the bazillionaire?" Luna said softly. "Huh. Didn't he pass away a couple of months ago?" She pulled out her phone and entered his name in the search bar of her Internet browser. Within a few seconds, several news websites appeared with headlines, BILLIONAIRE MILLSTONE OF MILLSTONE ENTERPRISES DEAD AT 87. Luna leaned against the table.

Chi-Chi was the next to speak. "Do you suppose this is the *real* last one and that there may have been others before?" She pointed to the sentence about revoking all previous wills.

"What should we do?" Luna looked at Chi-Chi and Cullen.

"Contact the family?" Cullen suggested.

Luna picked up the will and began to read it. "I'm not so sure about that." She continued to scan the pages. "It looks like Mr. Millstone is leaving his fortune to various charities. There is nothing in here indicating that any money goes to family members."

"So what do we do?" Cullen asked.

Luna's face lit up. "I just happen to know someone in law enforcement. Perhaps he can advise us." Her impish grin was amusing.

"Oh, girl. I think that's a splendid idea." Chi-Chi was right there with encouragement.

Cullen grinned. "It really is a good idea."

Luna took a few long inhales. She needed to center herself. Then she asked, "Text or call?"

Chi-Chi did not hesitate. "Call."

Cullen gave a "Text!" rapid-fire response.

"I think a phone call would be better. We may not want a trail of messages," Luna said wisely.

"You're not going undercover, for heaven's sake," Cullen stated.

Chi-Chi folded her arms and stared down at Luna. "Call him." Luna's phone was sitting on the table. Chi-Chi picked it up and handed it to her. "Now."

Luna started wiggling her shoulders and hips as if she were

about to step into a boxing ring. Cullen burst out laughing. "What are you doing? Some kind of woo-woo jig?"

Chi-Chi stifled a laugh. She knew Luna was getting her own chi energy aligned. Shaking off the cosmic dust, so to speak.

Luna made a face at him. "Never you mind." She scrolled through her contact list and found Marshal Christopher Gaines. She pressed her finger on his name.

"Marshal Gaines." He knew it was Luna, but he didn't want to seem too excited to hear from her. Even though he was.

"Hey, Marshal. Luna-tic here." She paused.

He chuckled. "Well, hello, Ms. Bodhi. And to what do I owe this pleasure? I trust all is well in your world."

"Marshal Gaines. I am doing well, thank you. And you?"

"Well. Busy, but well. Trying to make the house habitable has been a challenge, but I'm fine. What's on your mind?"

"Remember the table you saw in Cullen's workshop? The one we were both vying for? The one that I thought was special?"

Gaines couldn't help but smile. "I do indeed. Are you ready to give it up?"

"Oh no, sir. But I do have an interesting situation about which I could use some advice."

"Shoot." Gaines knew that wasn't always a good expression, but he was in a playful mood. He was elated that Luna had called. No matter the reason.

As if reading his mind, Luna broke in with, "That's not a very good word for a marshal to be using, is it?"

Gaines laughed out loud. "I was thinking the same thing." *How does she do that?*

I knew that, Luna thought to herself, and smiled.

Chi-Chi gave her a long wink. She could feel the warm energy coming off Luna from her end of the conversation.

"OK. So. Cullen finally moved the table to get to the drawer. He had to use a crowbar. Anyway, we found an envelope with what appears to be the last will and testament of Mr. Randolph Millstone."

"As in Millstone-everything?" Gaines was genuinely stunned.

"Seems that way," Luna continued. "But we don't want to notify the family."

"Why not?" Gaines asked.

"Because if this document is legit, his family is going to have a cow. Several. A herd of cows." Luna's level of excitement was increasing.

"I'm going to be in your area, not this weekend but next, for our think tank. Mind if I stop by and take a look?" Gaines's voice was even.

"That would be great. Which day and what time?" Luna replied, giving a thumbs-up.

Cullen offered, "Tell him we'll take him out to dinner."

"Oh, my brother offered to take you to dinner."

"That should work out well. The session is over at four thirty. I can come by and take a look at the document and that table," he joked. "I have dibs on it, too, if you remember."

"I do remember. We'll have to arm wrestle for it."

"Before or after dinner?" Gaines was getting more comfortable flirting with Luna.

"Ha. Well, when you see the condition it's in now, you may change your mind. Cullen had to rip the drawer off with a crowbar."

"Is the document dated?" Gaines asked.

"Yes. It was dated eleven weeks ago," Luna replied, checking the document once again.

"When did Millstone die?" Gaines asked.

"A little over two months ago, I think," Luna replied.

"I'll check on it," Gaines said. "Is there a witness to his signature?"

"Yep. Someone named Colette Petrov."

"OK. That gives me enough to go on," Gaines said. "See you a week from Saturday. Five-o'clockish."

"Deal! Thanks a bunch," Luna said, waiting for another response.

"Meanwhile, try to stay out of trouble," Gaines teased.

"I'll do my best. Bye now." Luna ended the call. She was swimming with delight.

Chapter Sixteen

Boston, Massachusetts
American Storage Center

It had taken only ten days before the final delivery of the estate furniture Rowena had managed to track down from
the dealers had arrived. The cash incentives to the dealers
and the drivers had paid off handsomely. She was not eager
to rip apart a few hundred thousand dollars' worth of antiques, but could not see any other way forward. However,
she was not about to do it alone. Arthur was just going to
have to get his hands dirty. For real.

Rowena pulled out the files and began to check off each
piece that had come back. Everything was there except the
Louis XVI sideboard. She felt a sense of relief knowing that
virtually all the items were back in their possession. She
thought about the missing buffet but consoled herself once
again with the knowledge that she had personally checked its
every nook and cranny. Unless there was a secret compartment, she was certain it wasn't hidden there.

She looked around the space. She knew she would need
Arthur to remove the furniture from the packing crates. The

question was the process. Should they uncrate everything first or should they do one at a time? She'd let Arthur decide how to use his atrophied muscles. Too bad he was so out of shape, but she wasn't about to hurt any of her own body parts yanking off the wood that protected the contents. There were over forty pieces of furniture that needed to be dismantled. Doing it all could take days. Too bad for Arthur. He wouldn't be able to spend so much time at his club in the days and weeks ahead. Not if he wanted to secure his future—and hers, of course.

Rowena was satisfied that they had completed stage two of their plan by getting the furniture back. Phase one had been locating it. Phase three would be tearing it apart. If they were lucky, they would find the will right away and be able to sell the pieces that had remained intact. She took one last look at the project that lay ahead, shook her head, pulled down the overhead door, padlocked the unit, and drove back to the mansion.

The first thing that came to mind was that she had absolutely nothing to wear for the job at hand. She certainly wasn't going to ruin any of her Gucci jogging outfits. Not that she ever jogged, but that was beside the point. She dreaded having to go to a big-box store to purchase sweatpants. She might be recognized. Heaven forfend. Then she thought about buying the outfit online. It might take a day or two to arrive, but she couldn't risk the embarrassment of being seen shopping for such plebeian things. The thought made her skin crawl.

When she got back to the house, she immediately went to Arthur's study and opened the cabinet where he kept his computer. She logged in and started her shopping spree. She laughed, thinking she could buy an entire season's wardrobe for the same amount of money one of her outfits had cost. But then a little voice in her head reminded her that if they didn't rectify the predicament they were in, she might be shopping at these stores for the rest of her life. That is, if they didn't go to prison. Clothing would no longer be an issue. God, how she hated the color orange.

She purchased five pairs of sweatpants, T-shirts, and sweatshirts; two pairs of sneakers and a half dozen work gloves. She groaned, thinking about her hair, so she added two baseball caps to her online shopping cart. When she checked out, it said that the items would be delivered the day after next. Good enough. She felt safe now that the goods were back in her and Arthur's possession.

As the website promised, Rowena's new wardrobe arrived in two days. It was time she and Arthur got down to the next phase.

Two days later, her pedestrian outfits having arrived, Rowena sat in Arthur's study chain-smoking again, waiting for him to return from his office. She could never figure out exactly what he did when he was there. Except perhaps some creative accounting.

She was fidgeting, nervously waiting for his reaction. Finally, she got up and poured herself a drink. She glanced at the antique clock, the position of whose hands indicated that it was three thirty. *Who cares.* She knew he would have a fit when he saw the job that lay ahead of them. Well, too bad. He was the one who had got himself into this mess in the first place. She had warned him to stay on his father's good side. To be nicer to the staff and Colette. Arthur had taken for granted that his father would continue to look fondly upon him no matter how often he screwed up. Since he hadn't asked his father to bail him out in a long time, Arthur assumed that his father had no idea that Arthur had found other means by which to access the family fortune. His arrogance was incomprehensible. But then again, Arthur had been spoiled and entitled his entire life, an arrogant child who had never been forced to grow up.

Rowena settled back into one of the large, overstuffed leather chairs and waited for the eruption that would soon follow. As things turned out, she wasn't very far off in her prediction. Arthur clomped into the room and slammed the door behind him. "You counted everything? Are they all there?" he asked in his most obnoxious voice.

"Yes, darling. All but the Louis XVI. And I told you I practically picked that piece apart before it was sold. So let's please not get into any squabbles. We need to get to work." Rowena felt the effects of the scotch and was feeling a little more relaxed. She truly didn't want to get into it with him just then.

"When do you propose we begin your resolution to our issue?"

"As soon as you change your clothes." Rowena eyed him up and down.

"What do you mean?" Obviously, it hadn't occurred to Arthur that he might be getting his hands dirty, much less his expensive clothes.

"Arthur, do you have any idea how dusty and filthy those places are? And the work involved?" Rowena thought he truly had no clue.

Arthur took in a big breath, walked to the console, and poured himself a drink. Instead of sitting behind his massive desk, he took the chair next to where Rowena was sitting. He took a few sips. "Look, I know I've been a bit of a jerk, but this could kill us."

"Do you know for sure that he changed his will?" Rowena kept hoping all of this was just an overreaction from Arthur, and that maybe Randolph had simply made a few adjustments, added a few bequests, and the like. Not the total disinheriting that Arthur feared.

Arthur kept his temper. "Rowena, we need to know exactly what he changed. Remember, he more than hinted we were going to have to move. He wanted to sell this place." Arthur made a grand sweep with the hand holding the tumbler.

Rowena sighed. "OK. Let's get this show on the road. You're going to have to pick out something else besides that Brioni suit you're wearing. Maybe there is something in the gardening shed." Rowena got up. "I'll go check. Meet you upstairs."

Rowena left Arthur to finish his drink and ponder what was ahead. She went through the rear kitchen door that led to the outside facility area where the garden shed stood. It contained all of the equipment necessary to maintain the twenty acres of land on which the manor sat. She stepped around a small tractor and a few different lawn and leaf machines and reached the built-in cabinets on the far wall. She opened the doors one by one. Fertilizer. Gravel. Weed killer. Mulch. Finally, overalls. She plucked a pair from the hook. They looked a little the worse for wear. She held them up and took a sniff. At least they were clean. Not that it mattered. They looked large enough for Arthur's growing girth.

She folded them up and put them in a plastic bag. She didn't want any of the remaining staff to see what she was carrying.

As she returned to the kitchen, one of the maids stopped her. "Hello, Mrs. Millstone. Is there something I can help you with?"

Rowena resisted the temptation to scream at her. Instead, she smiled, and said, "No, thank you," and kept on walking, hoping she didn't pique anyone's curiosity. It was a rare occasion for Rowena to enter the kitchen, let alone use the rear door. "Just checking to see what herbs were left over."

"Is there something in particular you were in need of?"

The maid kept pushing, but not with any agenda. She simply wanted to be sure Rowena's needs were being handled. Heaven forfend if they weren't.

Rowena decided to expand on the ruse. "I saw a wonderful cocktail with fresh mint. I was hoping there was some left." Such bull.

"Oh, I could have taken care of that for you, Mrs. Millstone."

"It's fine. I needed a breath of fresh air anyway." Rowena lied her way out of the kitchen.

She hurried up to Arthur's bedroom suite. He was standing in the dressing room in his boxers. Rowena almost gagged. Not a pretty sight. *What the heck has happened to him in the past three years?* He turned sixty and went to pot. She thought about all the men his age and older who looked terrific. Denzel Washington, Kevin Costner, Richard Gere. And then there was Bruce Springsteen. He was older than Arthur and could play a three-hour concert. *How did I go so wrong? Duh. The money, of course.*

"Here. Try this on." She handed him the overalls. He took them cautiously, as if they were contaminated.

"What am I supposed to wear underneath?" He sounded like a child.

"For heaven's sake, Arthur. A shirt. I'm sure you have one that you won't mind tossing into the trash later."

"How cold or warm is it in that place?" Arthur was referring to the storage unit.

"I'm sure we'll both be working up a sweat, so find something lightweight." She started opening drawers, hoping to find something appropriate. The only thing she came up with were his golf shirts. "Pick one of these."

Arthur grabbed the first one he put his hands on. Rowena knew he wasn't happy about any of this. "I told the kitchen we wouldn't be having dinner here tonight."

"Well, what are we supposed to eat then?" Arthur struggled with the brass buttons on the side of the overalls.

Rowena wanted to say, "Doesn't look like you need to eat anything for a long time." But she suggested picking up sandwiches at the Gourmet Kitchen instead.

"Call them so we don't have to wait. I'll have pastrami with Swiss cheese and mustard on rye." Arthur tried to suck in his stomach. "And don't forget the pickles."

Rowena dialed the local shop and placed their order. *A big fat sandwich for the blowhard,* ". . . and a spinach salad for me."

Arthur looked at himself in the mirror. He looked like the guy in that show from the 1960s, *Green Acres.* He didn't know what to think except that *this was going to be a long night.*

Rowena excused herself to change into her polyester blend of who knows what that was labeled MADE IN CHINA. She was surprised it didn't have a warning sign saying to keep away from an open flame. With the number of cigarettes she was smoking lately, that could be a problem. She remembered there was a fire extinguisher at the storage unit. She pulled on a pair of baggy pants and a T-shirt and tied a sweatshirt around her waist. She pulled a brush through her hair, lamenting the $150 she had spent on a blow-out a few days before. She pulled it back behind her ears and slapped on one of the baseball caps. She wanted to cry. It was odd. She couldn't remember the last time she had actually cried.

Rowena appeared in Arthur's doorway. "Well, aren't we the pair? You look like you're about to milk a cow, and I look like a soccer mom who just rolled out of bed. Nice." Rowena frowned. "I hope we don't run into anyone we know. Oh, heck. The Gourmet Kitchen. I'll have to wear a raincoat over this. Ugh. My hair. No one has ever seen me in a baseball cap."

"Rowena, will you please stop chattering. I'll call them and ask them to deliver it to the car. I'll give the guy a big enough tip, he won't notice you're a Red Sox fan. At least you didn't buy a Yankees cap."

"What are you talking about?" Rowena had no idea the Yankees and Red Sox were sworn rivals.

"Nothing." Arthur didn't want to talk anymore. What he really wanted was a stiff drink and a cigar, but he was driving. It would be horrible if he got pulled over, especially looking the way the two of them did. "Ready?" He looked at Rowena.

"No, but I'll do it anyway." The cheap sneaker squeaked when she turned around. She was sorry she hadn't sprung for the $1,200 pair of Dior high-tops.

Chapter Seventeen

Cranberry Lake—Cobblestone Hill

Colette and Max got up early and went to a local diner for breakfast. Max was in his glory. Two restaurant meals in a row! He couldn't decide between waffles and French toast. Colette could barely think of food. Max decided on the French toast, so Colette opted for the waffles. Maybe she could choke them down. The day before, she had had so much resolve. That day, she was a nervous wreck.

"Mom? Are you OK?" Max looked at her impishly.

"Yes, honey. I'm OK. Just a little tired. I didn't sleep all that well."

"Aren't you having fun on our adventure?"

"As long as we're together, for sure." Colette reached across the table and stroked his small hand. The waitress brought their breakfast, and Max dug in. Colette was pleased that her son was taking this organized chaos so well. She kept reminding herself that he would take his cues from her, so it was important that she keep a smile on her face.

"Where are we going today?" Max swirled his food in the maple syrup.

"We're going to try to find Mr. Dunbar and give him his surprise."

Max kept chomping on his breakfast and nodded. "Oh yeah. I remember. You're going to give him a book, right?"

"That's right." Colette was impressed with her son's recall.

When they were finished, she paid the check and made Max go to the bathroom. "Don't forget . . ."

"I know. Wash my hands!" Max marched into the small bathroom while Colette waited outside the door.

A few minutes later, Max appeared, holding his hands up, palms out. "All clean."

Colette tousled his hair. "OK. Let's get this show on the road!"

They had another hour of driving ahead. Colette typed a few destinations into her GPS, hoping that someone at one of them would be able to direct her to Dunbar's cabin. She racked her brain to remember the name of the cabin. It seemed like everyone of them had a name rather than an address. Then it hit her—Cobblestone Hill. She breathed a sigh of relief. Surely someone would know where the cabin was. From the photos she had seen, it wasn't exactly what a regular person would consider a cabin, unless a five-bedroom, four-thousand-square-foot home on lakefront property counted as a cabin.

Max was pointing out the various trees and plants from the child's car seat in the back. "Mom, look at that big tree. And that one." He even commented on how good the air smelled and asked if all the windows could roll down. "For just a little while." Colette was pleased he was in a happy mood. They played the I-Spy game for the duration. They also passed several campsites along the way and included them in their game. It was Max's job to count them.

Colette smiled, hoping the rest of the day would be productive. Her nerves had settled as soon as she remembered the name of the cabin. It was as if Randolph had whispered it in her ear. Within the hour, they pulled in front of a small general store.

"I'll be right back." She turned off the engine and locked the car. The place was much more rural than she was used to. It almost spooked her. She had to admit, she was pretty much a city girl. A revelation.

She went inside the very old building. It looked like something out of *The Andy Griffith Show*. A table in the front had a pile of denim jeans and flannel shirts. Another table had local honey. One wall was filled with fishing rods and tackle, a pile of coolers was against the far wall next to a large freezer filled with bags of ice.

A skinny man with leathery skin and wearing a straw cowboy hat was hunched over the counter. "Can I help ya, miss?"

"Hello. I am looking for Cobblestone Hill. Mr. Clive Dunbar's place? Can you direct me?"

"Sure can. I have a delivery I have to make there in a bit. I can show you."

"Oh, I don't want to put you out of your way."

"No trouble, miss. I'll be heading over as soon as I pack up my truck."

"Thank you. I have my son in the car, so I'll wait outside."

"Sure thing, miss." He tipped his hat and handed her two apples. "Be right out."

"What do I owe you?"

"Nothin'. I grow 'em myself." He disappeared into the back of the store and returned with a carton filled with eggs, milk, bread, and produce.

Colette was feeling better with each minute. The man didn't act surprised or suspicious, and he knew exactly where she needed to go. She got back in the car and watched the man close the door of the store and pin a sign on it:

DON'T YOU GO AWAY. BE RIGHT BACK.

So this is what country living is like? she thought to herself. She wondered if he even locked the door.

He placed the goods in the back of his pickup and waved her to follow. She pulled up alongside and lowered both her window and the one in the back so Max could thank the nice man for the apple. "Thank you, sir!" He waved the apple.

The man tipped his hat again and hopped into the cab of the truck.

They tore through the gravel and back onto the highway. Cobblestone Hill was less than ten minutes away. She followed the pickup down the long driveway and parked her car next to the truck. A man, maybe mid to late thirties, came out of the house. He was lanky and wore black-rimmed glasses. His hair was cut short. He could almost pass for a geek.

"Hey, Elmer!" The man waved.

"Logan," Elmer acknowledged in return.

"Here, let me get that." Logan took the big box from the man and looked over at Colette. "Hello?"

Colette got out of the car. "Hello. I'm Colette Petrov. I used to work for Mr. Randolph Millstone. I'm looking for Clive Dunbar. He was Mr. Millstone's lawyer."

"Yes, of course. Is he expecting you?" Logan asked.

"No, I'm afraid not."

Logan smiled. "I'm sure it's fine. There isn't a whole lot to do up here except scare the fish. Dad is on the porch pretending to tie flies." He had a nice, easy manner about him. Much like his father from what Colette remembered.

Elmer jumped back into his truck without saying another word. He tipped his hat to Colette.

"Thank you very much!" She waved at him and turned toward Logan. "I have my son with me." She nodded toward the back seat of the car.

Logan bent over to look inside. "Hey, dude!"

Max looked at his mother for approval before he said anything. She nodded.

"Hey. I'm Max."

"I'm Logan. Nice to meet you."

Colette opened the rear passenger door, unbuckled Max, and helped him out. He took her hand.

"Right this way." Logan walked to the side of the massive house. Calling it a cabin was just short of absurd. It looked more like a lodge with vertical, gray wood siding and colossal stonework. No wonder they called it Cobblestone Hill. The entry area had a large walk-in pantry on one side and a big laundry room on the other. Another door led to the patio in the rear of the house. A private outdoor bathroom facility, including a shower and dressing room, was in an alcove. Two sliding doors opened into the kitchen area.

Logan placed the box on the island counter. "Hey, Dad! We have company."

"What? What company?" Clive Dunbar meandered into the large kitchen and stopped short. "Colette?" He said it as if he were seeing a ghost.

"Yes, sir. It's me." Colette smiled weakly. "This is my son, Max."

"This is a pleasant surprise, I must say," Clive said. "I've been trying to locate you, but the Millstones said you had left no forwarding information. I was actually thinking of hiring a private detective agency." He chuckled. "Seriously."

"But why?" Colette asked.

"Come in. Come in. Logan, why don't you take Max down to the lake and show him how to skim some rocks. Feed the ducks. Would you like that, Max?" He squatted to speak to the boy face-to-face.

Max looked up at his mother.

"That sounds like fun. Doesn't it?" Colette encouraged him.

Max was nodding so fast she thought his head might bounce off. She mouthed the words, "Thank you," to Logan. He gave her a sly thumbs-up.

"Come on, Max, before the fish run away."

"Fish can run?" Max asked quizzically. "Don't they swim?"

Logan laughed. "Let's go find out." Max skipped behind Logan as they made their way down the back lawn to the dock.

"Nice kid," Dunbar said.

"He's a good boy. Smart, too. But I have to say that. I'm his mother." Colette laughed nervously.

"I think we have a lot to talk about, Colette. Can I get you something to drink? Water? Coffee? Tea?"

"A coffee would be very nice." She hesitated a moment. "I have something in the car I need to show you. That's why I'm here."

"Sounds intriguing." He smiled at her.

"That is a good way to put it. I'll be right back." Colette moved quickly to the car and retrieved her tote bag, where she kept the spiral booklet. Her hands were shaking uncontrollably. She steadied herself. She had made it this far. She was safe. She had always liked Clive Dunbar. He wasn't arrogant or dismissive the way Arthur was. He had always been polite to Colette. He didn't treat her as if she was just a servant. Dunbar was smart and loyal. She could understand why Randolph trusted him to protect his interests. She stood tall and walked back into the house through the side door. Clive was making a carafe of coffee in a French press.

"I hope you like your coffee on the strong side?" Clive smiled at her as he pushed the plunger down.

"I do. Thank you."

Dunbar pulled out a small tray and placed the coffee urn, two cups, cream, and sugar on it. He walked back into the massive pantry and brought out a crumb cake. "I just love this stuff. I probably shouldn't eat it, but my niece is a great baker, and she makes dozens of these at a time. I usually bring three or four up here with me. Don't tell my wife. She'd kill me." Dunbar was acting like a granduncle toward her. He was making a great effort to make Colette feel comfortable. He could only imagine what she had felt when Randolph died and Rowena tossed her to the curb. He did not believe for one minute that Colette would steal anything from the Millstones. Randolph had trusted her, and that was enough for Clive to trust her as well. Randolph did not suffer fools gladly. He was sharp as a tack. Clive thought about his friend and had a moment of melancholy.

"Come, let's go out to the porch. We can talk and watch Max and Logan skip stones."

Colette followed Dunbar to the porch area. It was expansive, reaching from one side of the house to the other. And it was large enough to hold several dozen people. She wondered how many people came to visit at the same time. There surely was enough room for many. Clive indicated for her to sit at one of the teak tables. He put the tray down and pulled out a chair for her. He took his place opposite from where she was sitting.

"So, tell me what brings you to this neck of the woods?" Clive poured the coffee and cut several slices of the coffee cake.

"Mr. Dunbar, I don't know where to begin."

"Let's start with the day you found Randolph in the garage."

Colette's eyes welled up. "It was a terrible day, Mr. Dunbar."

"First, please call me Clive. I feel as if I've known you long enough, if not in person, at least through Randolph."

"OK. Clive." Colette nodded. "Mr. Randolph was on his way to the garage to meet you for your appointment. I realized he had forgotten his cell phone, so I went after him. When I got into the garage, he had already fallen down. I ran over to see what I could do, and he handed me this." Colette reached into her bag and produced the spiral notebook. She slid it across the table.

Clive looked down at it. "Do you know what it is?"

"I have no idea. But there was an envelope inside. It fell out when Arthur came bounding into the garage. I could tell from the look on Mr. Randolph's face that it was something he did not want Arthur to see. He looked terrified." She paused and took a sip of her coffee and a bite of the cake. "This is delicious. I understand why you like it. And I won't tell your wife." She smiled.

"What happened to the envelope?" Clive asked easily.

"Well, when Mr. Millstone came barging in, I hid the notebook behind my back. When he followed the paramedics to the ambulance, I picked up the envelope, but before I could put it back in the notebook, he barked at me to leave." She took another pause. "I knew I couldn't keep the notebook secret if I tried to put the letter back in, so I shoved it into an old table. I thought I would be able to go back to retrieve it, but they sacked me before I could." She took a few deep breaths. "I feel terrible that I couldn't get it back."

"OK. We'll take this one step at a time." Clive patted her

hand. "So as far as you know, the envelope is still in that table?"

"I suppose."

"What else can you tell me?" Clive gently nudged her.

"A very strange thing happened the other day when I was at work. A man claiming to be a Jacob Taylor got in touch with me. He sent me a letter with your law firm's name on it, with a business card."

"Jacob Taylor?" Clive asked curiously.

"Yes. A letter was delivered to my sister's house asking that I call him to set up an appointment. The thing is, I left his letter in my car, and it was going to take too long to get it. I still had your office number on my cell phone, so I called it directly, and Abigail told me there was no Jacob Taylor at your firm."

"That much I know is true," Clive assured her.

"So who is he?" Colette asked.

"I don't know. Did you meet with him?"

"Yes, after I knew he wasn't who he said he was, I was curious. Plus he called me at work and said he was nearby and asked if we could talk. I agreed, and he met me in the hotel employees' cafeteria." Colette took a break. "I had a friend sit at another table. She took a photo." Colette pulled out her phone and pulled up the photo Dottie had forwarded to her. She handed the phone to Clive.

"Huh. That's a man named Jerry Thompson. He's a private detective who often works for Arthur Millstone."

Colette's hands started to shake again. "But why was he looking for me? And lying to me?"

"What did he want?"

"He wanted to know if I had, in fact, witnessed Mr. Randolph's signature and if I had read the document. I told him that I did witness it but did not read it."

"What did he have to say about that?"

"Not much, really. I don't know if he was satisfied, but I wasn't about to give him any more information."

"Smart," Clive encouraged her.

"Then I thought about this notebook. I surely wasn't going to tell him about it, and that's when I thought I should bring it to you. Mr. Randolph trusted you very much."

"And he trusted you as well," Clive said kindly. "So, let's take a look at that book." Clive spun it around and began to peruse the pages. Columns of dates and amounts and initials. The dates ranged over the course of a year. The amounts varied from $3,000 to $7,000 at a time. The initials were always the same: A.M. Clive stared down at what appeared to be a journal of cash disbursements to Arthur Millstone. There was no other person with those initials.

Now the question was where had this information come from? The family household expenses, or one of the many bank accounts Millstone Enterprises had? Clive noted that the checks were not for huge amounts according to the expenses the family household incurred. But there had to have been over $100,000 recorded from where the journal began and ended. Clive closed the binder. "I cannot thank you enough for bringing this to me."

"I didn't know what else to do." Colette was finally feeling calm. Safe.

"When I spoke to Arthur recently, he claimed that they couldn't find the missing mysterious will."

"If that's what the document in the envelope was, how did they know about it?" Colette was certain she had hidden it well.

"I told Arthur that I had a meeting scheduled with his father the day he had his heart attack and it had something to do with his will." Clive poured another coffee for both of them. "Randolph told me he had changed it, but he never had the opportunity to share the changes with me. But he did say you witnessed his signature. That's why I was trying to get hold of you."

"No wonder people are looking for me." Colette slumped in her chair.

"I don't want you to worry about anything. For the time being, you and Max will stay here. Until we can sort this out."

"Oh, but I wouldn't think of imposing."

"Look around, dear girl. There is plenty of room for all of us. Besides, it will be nice to have some fresh faces here. I know Logan is probably sick of looking at mine." Clive was genuine in his invitation.

"But I just started a new job recently, and I can't take off any more time. I'm lucky I was able to have someone cover for me for two days." Colette was trying not to fret.

"Who is your current employer?" Clive got up to get a pad and pen.

"The Curtiss Hotel. I'm the housekeeping manager."

Clive sat down at the table and started taking notes. "For one, we can handle the Curtiss. I'll have someone from my office call them and explain you were called away on legal business. Most employers don't dare ask or protest if a law firm is involved."

Colette sighed, relieved and happy to have Clive act on her behalf. "Well, it is the weekend tomorrow, so Max doesn't have school. He's in kindergarten."

"Then it's settled. This should only take a couple of days to sort out, but I must warn you, you will be at the mercy of my cooking, or worse, Logan's!"

Colette finally relaxed and laughed. "Not to worry, Mr. Dunbar. I'll be the chef while we're here."

"And you must call me Clive, please." He knocked on the table.

"OK. Clive. I called Mr. Millstone, Mr. Randolph. He wanted me to call him Randolph, but out of respect, I couldn't. So it became Mr. Randolph. Sometimes people got confused, but he was the only person I really had to please."

They sat in silence for a few minutes. Max was laughing and jumping up and down. Colette couldn't hear what he and Logan were talking about, but it warmed her heart that Max was having fun. Max had a sensitive soul and was always in tune with his mother. He had been through a lot of upheaval, and it was nice to see him act like a kid. Colette did her absolute best to shield him from any angst and worry, but she knew he had to be bewildered and disoriented. She smiled again. She was proud of her son.

As if he read her mind, Clive said, "You have a fine young man there."

Colette was taken by Logan's kindness and patience. "It appears that you also have a fine young man." She reached over the table and squeezed Dunbar's hand. "I cannot thank you enough. Ever since Mr. Randolph died, things have been tumultuous, to say the least."

"I can only imagine. It must have been very disturbing to have Jerry Thompson, or whatever he called himself, show up and interrogate you." Clive shook his head, wondering what Arthur was up to. Judging from what he could glean from the notebook, it could be any number of desperate things.

Clive looked at the clock. "It's getting close to lunchtime. Shall we call the boys in?"

Colette chuckled at Clive referring to his son as a boy. Maybe that's something all parents do no matter what age. When Logan and Max returned to the large porch, Clive announced that Colette and Max would be joining them for two or three days. Max shrieked in delight! "Goody! Now Logan can show me how to moon fish."

Colette looked at Logan and furrowed her brow. "Moon fishing?"

"We hang a lantern off the dock and see if any fish will come and take the bait. We're not usually very successful, but it's something to do." Logan smiled at her. "Let me get your things." Colette handed him the keys to her car. "Please move it if it's in the way."

"I don't think we'll be getting any more visitors." Logan smiled again and headed out the door.

Max went over to Colette and rested his head on her shoulder. "Mom? I'm liking this adventure."

"Me too." She kissed him on the top of his head. She got up from her chair. "All right, Mr. Clive Dunbar. Show me the way around the kitchen, and I'll see what I can come up with for lunch!"

There was some cold roasted chicken in the refrigerator, along with mustard, mayonnaise, celery, and sweet pickles. "Chicken salad OK with everyone?"

She got a round of approval. "While you're doing that," said Clive, "I'm going to make a phone call from the landline in the den. Cell service is rather sketchy up here." He excused himself while Colette, Logan, and Max worked together in the kitchen. Logan dragged a stool over to the counter where Colette was chopping celery and the chicken. Once she had put everything together in a large bowl, she handed Max a spatula. "Remember how I taught you to mix?"

Max pursed his lips and nodded. "Who is going to hold the bowl?"

Logan jumped in. "I guess that's my job." He held the bowl with both hands while Max attempted to mix the ingredients together. Logan noted that the kid wasn't doing a bad job.

"Bread?" Colette asked.

"In the pantry. Second shelf on the left."

Colette entered a pantry the size of Max's bedroom. Everything was meticulously arranged. "White? Rye? Whole grain?" she called out.

Max was the first to reply. "Rye!"

"Make that two!" Logan added.

"What will Clive have?" Colette asked.

"He's on a gluten-free kick." Logan chuckled. "Next week it will be keto. He's always looking for ways to improve himself."

Colette laughed. "That's not such a bad thing." She went back to the refrigerator and pulled out some lettuce to go with the chicken salad. She was struck by how comfortable she had become in just over an hour. But it made sense. She knew that Clive Dunbar was a good, honest man. And she was gratified to have relieved herself of the notebook. It was too bad about the document, presumably a will, that had been in the envelope.

While Colette, Logan, and Max were preparing lunch, Clive dialed Arthur's cell phone number.

Arthur picked up immediately, wiping the dust off his hands. He and Rowena were taking apart more of the crates. So far, they had come up empty-handed.

"Hello, Clive! Good to hear from you." Arthur was overly pleasant. "Obsequious" was the word that came to Clive's mind. It was too bad Arthur was his best friend's son. Randolph and Arthur couldn't have been more different. Clive thought how sad it must have been for Randolph. He gave his son everything and every opportunity to make something of himself. But instead of living up to his father's hopes and expectations, all Arthur ever did was make a mess of things.

"Hello, Arthur. How are things?" Clive asked congenially.

"You tell me, Clive. What's the latest?" Arthur was chomping at the bit to hear the words that the will was going to be read.

"I'm putting some documents together, and I noticed the inventory from the estate sale isn't in the file." Clive waited for Arthur's reaction.

"Oh?" Arthur kept his temper under control. Another thing to slow down the process. He wanted to choke Rowena. "Didn't Rowena or Amber send copies over to you?" He shot Rowena a killer glare.

"No. There's no record of receiving it." Clive waited for a response.

"One must have thought the other did it. I'll have it taken care of right away." Arthur paused. "And then how long do you think it will be before we can hear the will?"

"I don't know exactly, but I can assure you we are working on this as quickly as possible."

"Thanks, Clive." Arthur sounded content with the answer.

"If you can have Rowena e-mail it to my assistant and copy me, I would appreciate it, Arthur."

"Absolutely. I'll take care of it right now." He hung up and looked at Rowena. "Get back to the house and e-mail Clive the inventory. Cripes, I swear I have to do everything myself."

Rowena looked around the massive storage unit with all the returned pieces from the estate. She wasn't going to be bullied. Not today. Not while she was wearing sweatpants, a T-shirt, and cheap sneakers. "Take a look around, Arthur, *darling*. None of this would be here if I hadn't arranged for it to be."

"Zip it, Rowena. Go back to the house and e-mail the information to Clive. He sounded like he was coming around. Maybe we won't have to chip away at any more Chippendales."

"Oh goody." Rowena pulled off her work gloves and tossed them on top of one of the crates. She had been dying for a cigarette but was concerned the place would go up in smoke. She slipped on her raincoat. Heaven forfend that anyone see her dressed the way she was.

Rowena made it back to the manor without seeing anyone. She went to Arthur's study and pulled up the Excel spreadsheet. That was when she noticed the second tab at the bottom of the Excel workbook. It said SALVAGE. It hadn't occurred to her to check that list. All those items had been sold to someone in bulk. It was the contents of the garage and one of the sheds. Mostly old, dilapidated items. There was only one entry. It was to a salvage company in Pennsylvania. She hesitated for a moment. Then shrugged. *Why on earth would Randolph hide something in an old piece of furniture?* Surely, he wouldn't.

Rowena pulled up her e-mail account and sent the file to Dunbar and his assistant. *That ought to speed things up. If only.*

She hurried back to the storage unit to continue with the Millstone demolition derby with Arthur. It made her sick to rip such works of art apart. Not that any of it was her style. She had to be honest. It was more the monetary value than anything else that appealed to her sense of value. Once she and Arthur were done, none of it would be worth a plugged nickel. Maybe for kindling, but that was it.

Arthur was pulling another crate apart. "Well?"

"Well what?" Rowena yapped back.

"Did you send it?"

"What do you think I did? Obviously, I wasn't getting my hair done." She shook her head in disgust and continued to pry the front off the drawers off a Hepplewhite inlaid mahogany writing desk. If Randolph were still alive, he would

surely have had a heart attack witnessing the destruction oc-
curring there.

Rowena tossed the small crowbar into the corner. "Can
we finish this later?"

Arthur gave her the stink eye. She needed no other response. She opened a bottle of Fiji water and took a gulp. It
was going to be another long haul.

Chapter Eighteen

Cranberry Lake
Saturday evening

Colette was busy preparing dinner for Clive, Logan, and Max. She felt amazingly comfortable navigating her way around the Viking appliances. There was a pork tenderloin in the freezer that she was able to defrost. Potatoes, green beans, and salad would finish off the meal.

Logan was the first to enter the kitchen. "Something smells phenomenal."

"A special blend of seasonings," Colette said over her shoulder. "Something my mother taught me, mixing the right herbs together."

Logan opened the oven door to take a peek. "And roasted potatoes?"

"Yes, and salad and green beans."

"Impressive. I don't think my dad and I have eaten this well before."

"I always try to have a well-balanced meal for Max. He knows he has to have something green at dinner."

"Looks like you have that covered." Logan nodded in the direction of the large salad bowl.

Colette smiled. "I cannot tell you how much I appreciate your father's invitation. I was getting very nervous, especially when I found out that the man claiming to be Jacob Taylor wasn't really a lawyer with your dad's firm."

"Don't worry. Dad will get to the bottom of all this."

Max came skipping into the room. "Mom! Look what Mr. Dunbar taught me!" He proudly held up a tangled fishing fly.

"He's getting the hang of it," Clive said, as he walked into the kitchen behind him. "My word. Something in here smells delicious!"

Colette smiled. "I hope you like what I prepared."

"If it tastes anything like it smells, I think we have a winner."

Colette wiped her hands on a dish towel. "I realized I need to charge my phone."

"Not that it will do you much good up here. As I mentioned, we have terrible service."

"I understand, but it's in the red zone now. I'll be right back. Don't anyone touch anything!" Colette climbed the stairs to the second floor and into the guest room she was occupying. She dug out her phone and plugged in the charger. She frowned. *No bars. They're right.* It wasn't as if she didn't trust them. Some carriers can provide better service than others, but it seemed clear they were in a cell-phone dead zone. She understood the need for a landline here. She let her phone charge up. She would need it when she headed back to Buffalo. She had a charger in the car, but she always felt more comfortable if the phone was fully charged.

Colette went back to the kitchen. The others were setting the table. Max was in charge of folding the napkins. Colette was quite pleased at how well he was getting along with Clive and Logan. The timer on the oven rang. Dinner was about to be served.

Clive pulled out a bottle of Flowers chardonnay, popped the cork, and began to pour. He hesitated for a moment. "Do you like chardonnay?"

"Oh yes. And it will go well with the pork." Colette was familiar with good wine. Mr. Randolph had enjoyed teaching her the nuances of different varietals. She sighed. She deeply missed her former boss.

Logan rigged a chair with a large book and a pillow for Max, so could be at a comfortable height at the dinner table. "How's that, buddy?"

Max gave him a tight smile and a couple of nods.

Logan went back into the kitchen to carve the meat. Colette was tossing the salad. Clive brought the green beans to the table. Once everything was in place, they each took their seats. Colette was the first to speak. "Do you mind if we say grace?"

Clive beamed. "Not at all. Please, go ahead."

Colette reached for Clive's hand, then Logan's. Both of them took Max's. Colette began. "Bless us, oh Lord, for these thy gifts which we are about to receive. Thank you for the kindness of Clive and Logan. May they be blessed. Amen."

"Amen" went around the table.

Lots of chatter as the plates were being passed around. "So, Max, you want to try fishing tomorrow?" Logan asked.

"Yes, sir!" Max's enthusiasm was over the top.

"Excellent. We have to get up early, though. Think you can manage that?" Logan asked.

Another "Yes, sir!"

"Great. Soon as the sun comes up."

"Yippee!" Max was genuinely excited. He had only been fishing once with his uncle and hadn't been allowed to do much more than hold the pole. He would be happy if they simply sat together and dangled their legs off the dock and fed the ducks. There were a bunch of them. Probably because they threw breadcrumbs in the water. He loved being by the lake.

The lights flickered as they were enjoying their meal. A

brisk wind had picked up. "Here we go," Logan said matter-of-factly.

"What?" Colette asked.

"Not only do we have lousy cell service, but the telephone and power lines are hanging by a thread. When the wind picks up, we get intermittent service. Outages usually only last for a few hours. Then they send the trucks out to fix it. Fortunately, we have a generator for the whole house," Clive explained. "You would think they'd fix the issue permanently, but they haven't. We've learned to live with it."

It occurred to Colette she should get in touch with her sister and let her know she and Max were OK. "I should try to call my sister."

Logan got up. "I'll go check the phone line." He pushed out his chair and walked to Clive's den. He called out. "Sorry. We're incommunicado for now."

Clive asked, "What about the Internet?"

"That's down, too," Logan replied.

Clive was happy that he had downloaded the file from Rowena before the service went down. It could be days before they got the Internet back up.

Colette sighed. "I hope Rini isn't worried."

"If we don't get the phone line back by tomorrow morning, I'll drive you to the general store. We can use Elmer's phone if it's working. Or we can drive to the other side of that big hill until we get cell service."

Colette felt a sense of relief. Little did she know that her sister didn't feel the same way.

Chapter Nineteen

Stillwell Art Center
That same Saturday evening

The big day finally arrived, and Luna was fretting over what she should wear. She wanted to look pretty but not over-the-top. She didn't want to give Gaines the wrong impression. Or was it the right impression? She settled on a long denim pencil skirt with a soft, flowing white blouse. A long silver necklace with chunks of lapis and matching earrings completed the look. Hair? Loose, flowing down her shoulders. She applied some makeup, blush, and lipstick. She took a good peek in the mirror. Powerfully feminine. Exactly the look she was going for. She wanted to erase from his mind his memory of her crawling under the table.

Fat chance. Little did she know he had been taking copious mental notes about her: *not exactly delicate, yet girlish at the same time*. The juxtaposition was endearing.

She packed a little makeup bag in case she needed to do any touch-ups at the end of the day. She wanted to look fresh for the evening. She dabbed a little Santal perfume on her wrists. It had a subtle woodsy fragrance. She was happy she had gotten off the patchouli kick years ago. How she had been able to stomach it was still a mystery.

She recalled the time when Cullen came into her bedroom and literally gagged. "What *is* that?" He sneezed several times. Then it dawned on her. She was drowning in patchouli. Apparently, after a while you can't smell what you're wearing. She had never touched it again after that.

Luna was counting the hours. Not only was she excited about seeing Gaines again, but she was also curious as to what they should do with the will. If it was, in fact, real.

She and Cullen decided they would bring Gaines to the Chestnut, where everything is grown locally. Even though he had the restaurants at the Biltmore at his disposal, something quaint, with crafted food and drinks, seemed appropriate. She also decided to invite Chi-Chi.

Luna had a feeling Cullen had a soft spot for her, but she knew that Cullen would never admit it. He was unusually shy when it came to women. Luna would tease him and say, "Not every girl is as nutty as I am!" Although that was a hard one to prove. As far as Cullen was concerned, women were enigmas. He'd had his fair share of broken hearts, although none seemed to haunt him like most people. He could never understand "carrying a torch" after a breakup. Sure, for a little while, but some people carried it forever, refusing to move on with their lives. Such a waste.

The day seemed endless. She must have checked the clock every five minutes. *Why is it when you're waiting for something the time seems to drag on forever?*

She was happy to see Chi-Chi's beautiful face as she moved across the courtyard. Luna wished she could move the way Chi-Chi did. She always appeared to be gliding.

"*Sannu.*" Chi-Chi bowed to Luna. Luna said, "*Sannu,*" in return.

"My, aren't you looking quite lovely this evening?" Chi-

Chi's melodious voice rang like soft, low-pitched wind chimes. "I am sure the marshal will be very impressed with your aura tonight." Chi-Chi took both of Luna's hands in hers. "Please try to keep it working this evening."

"Whatever do you mean?" Luna looked at her with a pout.

"I know you are standing on a cliff. 'Should I jump? Should I run the other way?'" Chi-Chi had hit the nail on the head.

"Oh, Chi-Chi. I do like him, very much, but he lives so far away!" Luna frowned.

"Oh, don't you be silly. It's two hours. You must learn to relax and go with it, wherever it takes you."

Luna chuckled. "You sound like me! I suppose I should take my own advice!"

"Now that is what I am talking about. You are so lovely. He seems like a genuinely nice man. Good-looking, too." Chi-Chi was still holding on to Luna's hands and started rocking them back and forth. "Good girl. Get *your* chi going. So says Chi-Chi."

They laughed and hugged. "Oh my gosh. Here he comes now!" Luna stepped back and waved him in. "Marshal! So nice to see you!"

He leaned in to kiss her on the cheek and missed, causing their noses to smash into each other. Awkward, but funny. They both laughed. Gaines was first to regroup. "Let's try this again. Aim for the right one as in opposite of left."

Luna couldn't help but giggle. "Great. Kissing instructions. How lame is that?"

Chi-Chi gave her a wide-eyed look. Luna took the cue.

"OK, Marshal. On three. Ready? One. Two. Three!" This time their lips landed in the right place. Chi-Chi clapped her hands wildly.

"That was some kind of negotiation." Gaines chortled.

"Yes. We will need to plan these things ahead of time." Luna was feeling much more confident and enjoyed being a bit flirtatious. Chi-Chi stroked the back of Luna's hand and winked at her.

"Sorry I came empty-handed this time," Gaines said sincerely.

"You brought yourself." Luna felt like a schoolgirl, but she decided to take Chi-Chi's and her own advice. *Go with it.*

"I mean you came here to do us a favor." Uh-oh. Luna was backing off again.

"I came here because you asked my advice, and I said I would help. Let's not call it a favor, OK? Friends do things for each other. Right? Chi-Chi, help me out here."

"You are most absolutely right, Marshal. This is what friends do for each other. So let us get down to business." Chi-Chi had a rascally look in her eyes. "I'm sure Cullen is waiting for us."

Luna appeared to be frozen in place. She was processing everything that had happened in the past four minutes. Chi-Chi gave her another wide-eyed look. This time Luna thought Chi-Chi's eyes would pop right out of her head.

Chi-Chi turned and gave a nod. "Come on."

Luna slid the large glass doors shut and put up her sign with an arrow saying NEXT DOOR.

The three of them followed each other to Cullen's space and made their way to the back room. Cullen was waiting with the envelope. Gaines shook his hand. "Good to see you, man."

"Same here." Cullen smiled.

"So let's see this mysterious document."

Luna removed the pages inside the envelope and spread them on the ramshackle table. "Look!"

Focusing on the first line, Gaines read the pages carefully and reread them again out loud. " 'I, Randolph Millstone, of

Millstone Manor, in the state of Massachusetts, do hereby declare this is my last will and testament and revoke all previous wills and codicils.' " Then he checked the signatures. "I'm going to have to find out who represented Millstone. That should be easy enough. I'll call the main number."

Luna was already searching for the number in the search engine on her phone. "Here it is. It's 617-555-4500."

Gaines punched the number, then realized it was Saturday. They were closed. "This might have to wait until Monday."

Luna started to pace the floor. "I guess we have no other choice, do we?"

"Doesn't appear so." Gaines looked at the signatures again. "Looks legit, but we won't know until we find the lawyer."

Luna hated waiting for anything, but she knew there was little to be done at the moment. The only thing that was under her control was enjoying dinner, and that she was sure about.

Cullen, Luna, Gaines, and Chi-Chi climbed into Cullen's SUV, everyone chatting a mile a minute about what they were going to order for dinner.

"You guys are confusing me." Gaines chuckled. "Cullen, you had me going for the lamb, but now Chi-Chi tells me the brisket is excellent."

"Let's not forget they have specials, too," Luna chimed in.

"You're killing me." Gaines groaned.

Several minutes later, they arrived at the restaurant and were greeted by the owners. "Dinner with the Bodmans! Nice to see all of you."

Gaines shot Luna a look. "Do you know every restaurateur in the county?"

"You say that as if it were a bad thing." Luna gave him an elbow.

"Just kidding," Gaines shot back.

When they were seated, a perky waitress approached them. "Good evening. Can I get y'all something to drink?"

Gaines looked at his watch.

"Going somewhere?" Luna chided him.

"No. Just a habit."

"Which is what?"

Gaines thought a moment. "Checking my watch."

"Because?" Luna prodded.

"Because I always seem to have to be somewhere," Gaines replied.

"*Everyone* has to be someplace," Chi-Chi responded in her melodious voice.

Gaines nodded toward the two women. "Ladies?"

Luna ordered a dry rosé, Chi-Chi asked for a stinger, and Cullen settled on an IPA beer. Gaines then answered the waitress. "I'll have a manhattan with Maker's Mark, please."

"Comin' right up." The waitress had a very strong Southern accent. The word *right* sounded like "raaht."

When she returned with their drinks, she began to recite the half dozen specials of the day.

Gaines faked a shiver. "I'm going to need some help deciding."

"Depends on what you are in the mood for. The catfish is excellent."

"I'm thinking more of a meat dish."

"Then the lamb. Definitely the lamb," Cullen offered.

"Luna? Got any suggestions?" Gaines asked.

She put her fingers against her temples and closed her eyes. "I'm thinking beef!" Everyone laughed.

"You're thinking correctly. The short ribs sounded great," Gaines added.

The waitress was called away before they gave their orders and disappeared into the kitchen.

"This is a cool place." Gaines looked around, then frowned.

"What is it?" Luna asked.

He pulled out his phone. "Possible AMBER alert."

"Here?" Luna sounded surprised.

"No. New York State."

"Why are they notifying you?" Luna asked.

"They alert all the field offices because they don't know what direction the missing person may be headed. Then they send updates as they get them."

Luna frowned. She felt that something wasn't right.

His phone buzzed again. He read the text and paraphrased. "A woman called in that her sister and nephew took off yesterday but did not leave any information. A man went to her house last night asking for her, but the sister did not recognize the man. They've only been gone for twenty-four hours, so she'll file a formal missing child report in the morning. This was a heads-up."

Luna tried to relax, but she couldn't. Another buzz on his phone. He furrowed his brow. "What was the name of the witness on the will? Colette Petrova?"

"Colette Petrov," Luna replied.

"Well, guess who is missing?" Gaines leaned back in his chair.

"Oh my. That is not good," Chi-Chi said softly.

"What do you mean?" Luna was aghast.

"Looks like Colette is on the run with her son. Her sister said she left yesterday but didn't say where she was going and she hasn't heard from her. It's been over twenty-four hours."

"But why would she be on the run?" Luna looked perplexed.

"Your guess is as good as mine," Gaines answered.

"Do you think it has anything to do with the will?" Luna asked.

"Beats me, but I wouldn't be surprised."

Luna bit her lower lip. "Do you think it possible that the Millstones are looking for her?"

"If they have any idea about that will, they probably are."

"Well, that can't be good," Cullen observed.

"No. That family has connections everywhere. And the resources," Gaines stated emphatically.

"I wish we had the name of the lawyer," Luna mused.

"I'll see what my resources can find out. Meanwhile, keep that document under lock and key."

"Uh, it's in my tote." Luna patted the bag hanging off her knee.

"Not such a good idea. It really should be locked up."

"Luna, let's put it in the safe in my shop," Chi-Chi offered. "And I have a lot of security."

Luna had to admit Chi-Chi was right. Chi-Chi had more security than the café. Probably more than any of the other shops. Chi-Chi had tens of thousands of dollars' worth of jewelry. Cullen had a small safe but not the camera load of Silver & Stone. Cullen didn't think it was necessary for his space since most of his work required two people, or a hand truck, to handle the merchandise. Hard to slip an armoire or a buffet table out the door without someone noticing.

"Sounds like a good plan. We'll go back after dinner," Gaines declared.

"Really? I think it will be OK until tomorrow, no?" Luna offered.

All eyes went to Luna. "What?"

"Speaking of security systems, isn't your inner alarm going off or something?" Gaines was half joking.

"Again, Comedy Central." Luna smirked. "You don't think I can keep this secure for one night? It's been in that table for over a month."

"Do I have to pull out my badge and pull rank on you?" Gaines stifled a grin.

"Oh, and now you're going to use your law enforcement on me?" Luna bit her lip, trying not to smile.

Gaines shook his head. Cullen jumped in. "See what I have to deal with every single day?"

Luna looked at Chi-Chi and pouted. "They're picking on me."

Chi-Chi patted her hand. "Now, now, lovie. We all have your best interests at heart."

"Well, it's not like I'm going anywhere with it except home." Luna slouched in her chair.

"We have to go back so everyone can pick up their cars anyway. It won't take more than a couple of minutes." Cullen became insistent. "Right, Chi-Chi?"

"That is correct, Cullen." Chi-Chi put down her fork and turned to him. "I think you and I must take charge of the situation."

Luna tried to kick Chi-Chi but hit Gaines's leg instead. "Ouch! What was that for?"

Luna gave him a blank look. "I have no idea what you're talking about, *Marshal* Gaines." As she took a sip of her wine, the waitress returned from wherever she had been, to take their orders.

There was a lot of jovial commotion going around the table, people changing their minds when they heard what the other was ordering. It was hard for the waitress to keep up. "All right, y'all. Y'all sound like my kids. I come here to get away from them." Everyone stopped suddenly and burst out laughing.

Chi-Chi looked at the waitress sympathetically. "Don't you mind them. They are allowed out only once a month." She said it with such a straight face the waitress blinked several times until it hit her. "Ha. Funny."

"See? Comedy Central." Luna gestured around the table with both of her arms, imitating the women on *Let's Make a Deal* or *The Price Is Right*.

The waitress stood there, tapping her pen. "Y'all need a few minutes? Suggestions?"

"What if we order a few salads to share?" Luna asked the others. All agreed. Pear Salad. Beet Salad. Luna placed her order. Pappardelle. Trout for Cullen. Shrimp and grits for Gaines, and squash vindaloo for Chi-Chi. It was a gastronomic adventure.

The conversation was lively: sports, recent movies, and who was binge watching what coming up. Gaines gave them updates on his renovation. The evening passed quickly, just the opposite of the excruciating wait Luna had had during the day.

They ordered a couple of desserts to share. Decaf and tea.

Cullen told the waitress in advance that he should get the bill. No matter what. "Badge or no badge."

She shrugged. "Whatever you say, chief."

The busboy cleared the table while everyone let out a few groans and did a couple of stretches. As they were getting up from the table, Gaines turned to Cullen. "That was terrific. Thanks. I really appreciate it."

"Are you kidding? You're practically family." Cullen slapped him on the back, and Luna almost fell over.

They walked to the SUV slowly, each of them moaning about how good the food was and how much they had overeaten. "But I'd do it again in a heartbeat. Although if I keep eating like this, I may not have one," Gaines joked.

"Next time you're in town," Cullen added quickly, knowing how Luna was sweet on Gaines.

"I'll be here until Monday. If we're finished early, I'll swing on by tomorrow," Gaines said casually.

Luna's legs were getting rubbery again. And it wasn't from one glass of wine. *Was it her imagination, or did she really feel a strong pull between the two of them?* Chi-Chi picked up on Luna's wobble and linked her arm through Luna's. That was something girlfriends did. Help each other stand up tall and move forward. It was more than a metaphor. That night, it was literal. Luna put her head on Chi-Chi's shoulder as they sauntered to the SUV.

Fifteen minutes later, they were pulling into Stillwell's parking lot. All four got out and headed to the rear entrance of Silver & Stone. Chi-Chi pushed a bunch of buttons that released the outer door. Then another keypad to enter the small office that opened up to the showroom. Chi-Chi walked over to her large safe, pushed a few more buttons, then a fingerprint. She unlatched it and held out her hand to Luna. Luna obediently handed Chi-Chi the envelope. "Happy now? Everyone?" Luna muttered.

It was a resounding "yes" from the others. On their way out, Chi-Chi locked everything in their path. They said their goodnights. And there it was. The awkward moment. Gaines took the lead. He placed his hands on Luna's shoulders. "Incoming. Right side." Luna thought she was going to faint. A peck on the cheek. "Mission accomplished. You OK driving home?"

"Cullen is giving me a lift. But thanks!" Luna was good at acting nonchalant, even when she wasn't feeling it.

Gaines gave her a short salute. He gave Chi-Chi a kiss on the cheek as well and shook Cullen's hand. "Thanks again, man."

"A pleasure."

Chapter Twenty

Boston—American Storage Center
Late Saturday night

Rowena slumped against the wall, covered in sawdust and splinters. Arthur looked like he had been in a brawl with a china cabinet. The storage area was piled high with shattered furniture, strips of paint, and broken hinges. It was a terribly expensive pile of kindling. Arthur wiped his brow on his sleeve. Rowena looked over at him. He, too, sagged in defeat.

"It must be in that Louis XVI," he said with resignation.

"Arthur, I really don't think so." Rowena wasn't in the mood to argue about it again. "Unless it had a very secret compartment, the will was not in there."

"So now what do you recommend?" Arthur had never looked so deflated.

"Hey." Something had just dawned on her. "Wait a minute." Rowena brushed off her pants and stood up. "Wasn't your father supposed to meet with Clive the morning of his heart attack?"

"Yes. Why?" Arthur muttered.

"And wasn't he in the garage when he fell?" Rowena's voice took on a note of excitement.

"Yes, Rowena. Everyone knows he was in the garage when he fell. What's your point?" He sounded rather weary.

"My point is, if he was in the garage, then maybe he shoved it somewhere in the pile of junk that was in there." Rowena pulled out the printed copy from the sale. "Dang."

"What is it now?" Arthur was exhausted and annoyed.

"There was another tab at the bottom of the file. I didn't pay any attention to it because all the salvaged items were listed. So I didn't print out the second page."

"Again, I ask, what's your point?"

"My point is that I am going back to the house and track down the guy who bought the contents of the garage." Rowena had a sudden burst of energy. "Come on!" She held out her hand and hoisted Arthur to his feet. He looked around at the mammoth pile of destroyed antiques. If he had had the energy, he would have cried. Not because of the sentiment. It was because of the money. Indeed, it was almost certainly the most expensive pile of firewood in all of New England, perhaps all of America.

"Now that we've ruined all of this, what do you propose we do with it?" Arthur didn't have the energy to think.

"Let's not worry about that right now. We rent on a month-to-month basis. This stuff can sit here until we find the guy who bought the contents of the garage."

"And where do you propose we put said contents if or when we locate them?" Arthur was picking flecks of paint off his pants.

"Seriously, Arthur. I wouldn't be so concerned about those pants right now," Rowena complained.

He looked at her blankly. "I suppose you're right."

"Arthur, do not fade on me now. I think we may be at the end of this wild-goose chase soon. Let's go!" She was just a few decibels from shouting.

Rowena locked the unit and broke every traffic violation on the books, hurtling past stop signs, clipping corners, driving over people's lawns. The "yee-haw" wild ride broke Arthur's spell. He started to shriek. "Rowena! Watch out! What are you doing? Are you out of your mind? Slow down! Rowena! Stop!" The final turn into the enormous driveway was coming up. Arthur buried his head in his hands as she careened past the stone lions at the gate. She missed them by millimeters. If the car had had one more coat of paint on it, it would have been scraped off by the statues. Arthur was relieved the gates were open, or they would be a tangled mess of wrought iron, sawdust, and metal.

The car came to a screeching halt. Rowena jumped out of the driver's side while Arthur sat for a moment to regain his composure. He was convinced Rowena was going to kill him. One way or another.

Rowena ran into Arthur's study and fired up the computer. She pulled up the file. There it was. The second tab. SALVAGE. There was only one name. Nelson Architectural Salvage Company. It was located in Reston, Virginia. She looked at the clock. It was past eleven. She dialed the number and planned to leave a message. A husky voice answered the phone. "Yeah?"

"Uh, hello. Is this Nelson Architectural Salvage Company?" Rowena was sure she had dialed the wrong number.

"This is George Nelson. What can I do ya fer?"

Rowena heard noise in the background. He could have been in a bar. There was honky-tonk music and voices. Men's voices. "Georgie! Yer up!"

"Hang on . . ." he said to Rowena. "Gimme a minute," he said to the guy in the background.

He turned his attention back to Rowena. "Yeah. This is Nelson."

"Hello, Mr. Nelson. I'm sorry to bother you at such a late hour. I assumed I would get an answering machine."

"You can lose cust'mers if you ain't available all the time."
His accent was thick.

"I suppose you're right. I'll be brief. My name is Rowena
Millstone. I believe you purchased the contents of our garage
several weeks ago."

"You the place up there in Boston?"

"Yes, that's us. Anyway, I was wondering if you still had
any of the items? Unbeknownst to me, my husband wanted
to have some of those things refurbished. Family mementos
and such. He is in such a state of depression, and I feel terrible that I allowed this to happen." Rowena was lying
through her teeth, hoping she'd get the answer she was looking for.

"Uh-huh. Sorry about your troubles, ma'am, but I'm sorry
to tell ya I sold them off in one big heap."

"Would it be possible for you let me know to whom you
sold them?"

"Yeah, I suppose I could, but not tonight." He turned his
head away from the phone and shouted to his friends, "Hold
yer horses, be right there."

"Of course. I completely understand." Rowena was pouring it on so thick, Arthur thought he'd go into a diabetic
coma.

"I can give ya a holler in the morning. That OK with you,
ma'am?"

"Is there any possible way you could get it to me tonight?
It could be later. I would be happy to compensate you for
your time. Say a thousand dollars?" Rowena iced the cake.

"Well, in that case, I can run back to my place and get it
for you within the hour. In the meanwhile, I'll send you a
Venmo, or if you'd rather, PayPal?"

Rowena pulled the phone from her ear and gave it a curious look. *This guy is a fast operator.* "Whichever works for
you," Rowena replied.

"PayPal is good. I'll call you in a bit. Is the number you called me a good one to reach you at?"

"Yes—617-555-1954," Rowena answered.

"Seriously? Well, I'll be darned. That's the year of my birthday. Ooo-eeee. Ain't that some kinda co-inky-dink?"

Rowena was getting impatient. "Happy birthday, Mr. Nelson."

"Well, no, it ain't my birthday today, ma'am. It's the year I was born."

Rowena's head was going to explode. Rowena started to respond, "No, I didn't mean—oh, never mind. Yes, a co—whatever you called it."

"Co-inky-dink. When two things happen at the same time. Get it?"

"I do, Mr. Nelson. I'll send that payment over to you as soon as you send the request." She was not in the mood for a game of wits, especially with someone who was totally lacking the equipment to play the game. She gave him her e-mail address to send the PayPal invoice.

"Right. I'll get that info to you A-SAP!" Just before he ended the call Rowena heard him say to his friends, "Gotta run, guys. I'm about to make myself a sweet grand. Drinks on me!" There was cheering, then the line went dead.

Rowena looked up at the weary Arthur. "How do you like me now?"

"Better than I did ten minutes ago." He walked over to the credenza and poured two triple shots of scotch. He downed half of his before he turned to Rowena. "Here. You earned this."

It was Arthur's most expensive scotch. The richness of chocolate-covered oranges, malt, and oak fetched a mere $5,000 a bottle for the Macallan thirty-year-old elixir.

"Yes, I certainly did. Let's hope it will get us what we want." She raised her glass in the air. "Cheers!"

Arthur finished his in one more gulp. Such a waste of good scotch. Not the slightest opportunity for the palate to enjoy the smoothness of the blend.

Rowena sipped hers. "I'm going to take a shower. This guy is going to be a while. Although I'll bet there is a PayPal invoice waiting for me to deal with." She set the glass down and went back to the computer. "Bingo. And there it is. You think he doesn't trust us?"

"Do you think we should trust *him*?" Arthur asked in return.

"It's a gamble I'm willing to take." She hesitated but couldn't resist. "Come on, Arthur, since when did you ever walk away from a sure thing?"

He shot her a vile look. "Don't start, Rowena. I was close to being in a better mood."

"Fine. I'm going upstairs. I'll leave my phone here in case he calls while I'm cleaning up my act."

"I might want to do the same. I'm not exactly tidy myself."

Cranberry Lake—Cobblestone Hill
Saturday Night

After dinner was over, everyone helped clear the dishes and wash and dry the pots and pans. The kitchen was spotless by the time they were done.

"Not only haven't we eaten this well, but I don't remember the last time the place looked this good." Clive glanced around the room. "Let's go sit out on the porch for a bit."

"I will have to get Max ready for bed," Colette said.

"All right. Then after he's tucked in. We have kind of a tradition here. Every night after dinner, Logan and I sit on the back porch and listen to crickets. Not because they sound good, but because there isn't much else to do up here at night."

"Oh, but it's so beautiful. Tranquil," Colette replied.

"And that's the point. It's beautiful, tranquil, and there is absolutely nothing else you can do in the evening except read a book or watch TV. But you can do that anywhere. It's not often you can simply sit and listen to crickets." Clive poured himself a glass of port. "Would you like one?"

"Yes, thank you." Colette felt the weight of the world lifting off her shoulders. "I'll be right back."

She motioned for Max. "Say good night to Mr. Dunbar and Logan."

Max put out his hand. "Very nice to meet you, Mr. Dunbar. Thank you for inviting us." He turned to Logan. "And it is very nice to meet you, too." Such a grown-up. Colette put her hands on his shoulders. She was proud of her little man.

When they went into Max's guest room, he sat on the bed and eyed the space. It wasn't a typical cabin. The walls were paneled in wood, as expected, but with a more updated spin. The planks were three inches high and four feet long, alternating colors from light gray to tans, and charcoal. The planks started at the floor and ran halfway up the wall. The effect was a rustic look without the heaviness. The rest of the walls were painted white, with light gray wood beams spanning the ceiling. Max lay down with his hands folded behind his head. "Mom?"

"Yes, Max."

"I think this is the most beautiful room I have ever slept in. In my whole life!" He sat up and bounced a little on the bed.

"I know. It's a beautiful place." Colette pulled out a pair of pajamas for him, his little dopp kit, and a pair of sleeper socks, the kind that had the antiskid bottoms. Sometimes they'd get stuck on the sheets, but it was better to have something on your feet when you got out of bed, and kids and slippers don't usually find each other. The slippers end up having a lonely life under the bed, until a stray sock or another slipper gets abandoned.

"Mom?"

"Yes."

"Do you think we could stay here a while longer?" Max rolled over and propped himself on his elbows.

"Oh, sweetie, I think Mr. Dunbar has been a most gracious host. I do not want to overstay our welcome. And I will have to get back to work, and you have to go to school."

He heaved a dramatic sigh. "I know." Then he jumped up. "But do you think we could come back and visit?"

Colette appreciated her son's enthusiasm and didn't want to ruin his mood. But she had no expectations of a future invitation. "That would be nice, wouldn't it?" And she thought to herself, it *would* be nice. *Logan seems like a very nice man.* She laughed a little to herself. A girl can dream.

Colette pulled down the neutral-toned comforter. "It's like a marshmallow." Max brushed the fine bedcovering.

"OK. Say your prayers."

Instead of the traditional kneeling on the floor, Max's routine was to get into bed first, sit up, say his prayers, then fall backward onto his pillow and get a kiss on his forehead from his mother.

Tonight was no different. Except the people, the place, and pretty much everything else.

"Good night, Max," Colette whispered. There was an en suite bathroom between their bedrooms. Max was comfortable knowing his mother was only a few feet away. She left the door ajar, creating a stream of light on the floor in case he woke up during the night.

Colette went back downstairs and through the great room that served as the living room. To one side was the large dining area. A ten-foot-wide granite-topped island cabinet separated the kitchen from the dining area. A stone fireplace was on the opposite wall. Vaulted ceilings and skylights brought the wonderful natural surroundings inside. It was a grand open-floor plan. She stopped for a moment. Everything had moved so quickly since she arrived that she hadn't stopped to take it all in. It was no wonder Mr. Randolph had enjoyed his time in this place. She thought about him again. And then her thoughts turned to Arthur and Rowena Millstone. They had treated her terribly. Just as they treated everyone else, for that matter.

She looked beyond the porch as she walked to the gigantic sliding doors that led to the equally gigantic screened porch. From the porch, you stepped outside to a large wood deck that stepped down to several different levels. One was for grilling. One had a bar. Another was for lounging. From the lowest deck, a stone path wound its way to a long dock. At the end of the dock was another large deck area with Adirondack chairs. The late-summer sun was splashing pastel hues of lavender, pink, and orange. "It's quite wonderful here."

"It is. I can't get enough of it. Here. Sit." Clive handed her a beautiful stemmed glass of port and nodded to the teak sectional sofa with light gray cushions.

Colette smiled. "Again, my gratitude."

"Please. You drove all the way here to give me something from Randolph. It is I who owe you *my* gratitude."

Colette sipped on the port. "Max is quite taken with all of this. I was concerned he would be upset with everything being so frenzied and impulsive."

"He's a bright young fellow. He adapts easily," Clive noted.

Colette smiled. "I'm incredibly lucky. Most children would be a handful after a divorce, then moving without notice, then pulling him out of school to find you."

"Seems like he has an adventurous soul. Good-natured, too."

"Yes." Colette was thoughtful. "I hope I can give him some stability when we get back to Buffalo."

"Not to worry, dear." Clive gave her a warm smile. "Once

we get this notebook thing sorted out, and I can settle Randolph's estate, we'll discuss your future."

Colette looked surprised. "*My* future?"

"Yes. And Max's." Clive had some important information to share with Colette and was weighing when it would be appropriate to say something to her about it. It could wait. At least a few days.

"I don't understand." Colette looked worried.

"Don't be concerned. I'd like to know what your plans are. Your career ambitions. Your wish list for life."

"You have been truly kind to me."

"Randolph was very fond of you. He once told me that you were more respectful and caring than his son and that shrew, Rowena. Sorry. I shouldn't call people names."

Colette had a devilish look in her eye. "I can tell *you* something. The staff used to sing the song from *One Hundred and One Dalmatians*." Colette sang the first line. "Rowena-de-Vil, Rowena-de-Vil . . ."

Clive burst out laughing. "Now, that is funny. Wait until I tell Logan. Better yet, you can tell him."

"Where is he?"

"Trying to figure out how to get an Internet connection. He's a little less comfortable than I am without it. At least for a day or so. People need to unplug once in a while."

"Yes, I remember Mr. Randolph said before his heart condition got worse that he wouldn't allow any business to be conducted in the home. I don't know how he was able to build such an incredible business without working around the clock."

"Well, that's just it," Clive went on to explain. "When Randolph was younger, his father badgered him about taking over the family business. Which, by the way, was nowhere near as huge as it is today. Don't misunderstand. Millstone Enterprises was worth several million dollars when Randolph was in his early twenties, but he went on to prove himself to his father and expanded the company into what it is today."

"I still don't understand." Colette looked perplexed.

"The first forty years of his marriage he was a workaholic. Back then, there was no Internet. No digital communications. He had to spend most of his time at the office, traveling, or on the telephone. In 1969, when Arthur was twelve, his mother developed a serious drinking and drug issue, unbeknownst to most. The drinking was obvious, but her addiction to valium and amphetamines resulted in a horrendous death."

"Valium *and* amphetamines?" Colette looked shocked and surprised.

"Yes. Amphetamines to get her out of bed after a night of drinking and barbiturates. She was a disaster waiting to happen."

"Oh my goodness. I had no idea. No one ever spoke of it."

"Probably because everyone felt responsible. It wasn't a secret, but no one had the courage to speak up. People looked the other way, even when she would pass out in a chair during a dinner party. But it all came together in a horrendous climax when Gloria died of an overdose. It was a long time ago. As I said, Arthur was only twelve.

Colette was still in a state of disbelief.

"Everyone felt guilty. Except for Arthur. He was more peeved that his mother wasn't around to dote on him. I don't think he ever really mourned her, and he would have temper tantrums. People thought he was just 'acting out,' but he had always been a brat if you asked me. So, after Gloria died, Randolph decided that family was more important, and he would make it his mission to be home for dinner every night. No phone calls. No business. He wanted to focus on Arthur."

Colette murmured a hum.

"Yes. It boggles the mind. Randolph put the brakes on his business to concentrate on his son, who was always getting into one kind of trouble or another. Small things in his teens. He wrecked a few expensive sports cars and dropped out of college three years in a row. Randolph gave him a job at the company hoping he'd be able to teach Arthur something about responsibility. But then Arthur would go to Randolph and ask for an advance, a loan. Nothing major in their world of money. A few thousand here, a few thousand there. Randolph hoped against hope that Arthur would get his act together."

Clive paused, then gave a wry smile. "One evening after Randolph had bailed Arthur out of his gambling debt, he told me he thought maybe they had switched babies in the hospital, and he was given some hooligan's son instead of his own."

"Mr. Randolph must have been devastated." Colette shook her head in shock. "When did Arthur marry Sylvia?" Colette asked.

"Arthur met Sylvia when he was thirty. Nice woman. Randolph hoped that Arthur would settle down. Have a family. Be accountable. They tried to have children, but it wasn't in the cards, as they say. Things were relatively calm. Almost normal until a few years ago."

"Is that when he met Rowena?" Colette was putting the timeline together.

"Rowena and his gambling debt were like the perfect storm. They both hit Arthur within a year of each other. Arthur had joined a club the year before and got into serious debt. He had a penchant for poker. Unfortunately, he and the cards were not in a mutually admiring relationship. He was on a serious losing streak, to the tune of $100,000. Randolph had to bail him out for fear Arthur would end up in a wheelchair, or possibly a grave. The people to whom he owed the money do not mess around.

"It seemed that as soon as that crisis was averted, in blows the Rowena tornado. Randolph thought Arthur was going through a second midlife crisis. In retrospect, it's been a whole-life crisis with Arthur."

"So how did Rowena become a Millstone?" Colette was curious as to the means the obvious parasite had used to worm her way into the Millstone family.

Clive let out a guffaw. "Among other things, Arthur was a scoundrel when it came to women. He would go to his club, where a few of his buddies would meet up with"—he cleared his throat—"ladies of the evening."

"You mean prostitutes." Colette wasn't a prude, nor was she naïve.

Clive cleared his throat again. "Well, yes, I suppose."

"So was Rowena one of those 'ladies of the evening'?" Colette made air quotes.

"Not according to Arthur. She was a business colleague of one of his poker pals. Or so he said."

"But how did she get him to marry her?"

Clive smirked and tilted his head. "You mean aside from giving him genital herpes?" Clive couldn't resist punctuating Arthur's lack of decency with the incurable socially transmitted disease. Plus, Colette was a big girl.

Her eyes widened to the size of saucers. "What?" She was incredulous.

"Yes. It's true. When she told Arthur, he had to tell Sylvia, which is one of the reasons she divorced him."

"I see." Colette was zooming in on the picture Clive was painting for her. It wasn't pretty.

"Once the divorce was final, Arthur decided if he ever wanted to have sex again, he'd have to marry Rowena. That is, if he didn't want to be a total snake and not tell his sexual partners. Apparently, he hadn't been practicing safe sex. Why start?" he asked sarcastically.

"For the other person's safety?" Colette was both amused and horrified. "Wow. I often wondered why there was so much animosity between Rowena and Mr. Randolph."

"Randolph believed Rowena did it on purpose. She had a loaded pistol and waited for a good target. It was criminal if you ask me," Clive added.

"So Arthur went along with it because he felt he had no other choice." Colette made it a statement, not a question.

"Correct. Listen, I don't feel one iota of pity for him. He made that bed. No pun intended."

Colette chuckled. "This has been a highly informative conversation, sir. It explains a lot of things. There was always tension between Rowena and Arthur. A feeling of resentment. Often hostility. Now it all makes sense."

"I always felt that was the reason for Randolph's heart condition. It was one disappointment or bailout after another."

"That's terrible."

"Arthur never showed any remorse for being a bounder; nor did he show any appreciation of his father. He acted as if bailing him out of his messes was what Randolph was supposed to do. Save his arse. Each and every time.

"A sad, pathetic story. I always felt bad for Randolph. He lost his wife and blamed himself. He changed his life to focus on his family, which was the absolute right thing to do. But then he pampered Arthur to the point where Arthur acted like he was invincible. Spoiled rotten, if you ask me. Instead of being grateful and wanting to make his father proud, it was as if Arthur's mission was to take advantage of every situation."

"This is so much to absorb." Colette finished her port and proceeded to get up. "I don't know if I am going to be able to sleep tonight." She smirked.

Clive stood. "Colette, I cannot tell you how much your courage means to me. You were quite brave to come here."

"I had to do it for Mr. Randolph." Her eyes began to mist.

Logan came bounding into the room. "Got some Internet service back. I wouldn't push it, though."

"What do you mean?" Clive looked up.

"Don't download any movies, music, big files. It's like trying to thread a needle with a sausage."

Colette chortled. "That could be very messy."

Logan snorted. He thought she was charming, and there was a lot more to learn about this attractive, enigmatic woman who had appeared on their doorstep a few hours earlier. He had heard her name mentioned in passing but never had the opportunity to meet her. And she was far from ordinary-looking. Logan surmised she was also very bright. She had to be if she had been working for the Millstones. Either that or she was a total idiot and liked to be bossed around. He was certain it was the former.

Clive walked toward the kitchen. "I don't plan on downloading anything tonight, but I am going to take a look at that file Rowena sent. Probably should do it now. I downloaded it before the lines went down, but in case I need to do any quick lookups, it would be hugely helpful. Thanks, Logan." Clive patted his son on the shoulder.

"Sure thing, Pop."

"I shall say good night to you both. Sleep well." He turned to Colette and gave her a fatherly hug.

"Good night. Thank you again."

Logan looked at Colette. "Are you ready for some shuteye or can I talk you into a cup of tea?"

"Tea would be nice. After the story your father told me, I need something to soothe my mind."

"Coming right up. Take a seat." He pulled out one of the dining-table chairs.

Back in his den, Clive wiggled the mouse sitting next to the

keyboard of his computer. The Excel file came up. MILLSTONE
ESTATE SALE INVENTORY. At the bottom he saw the tab for SAL-
VAGE. One entry. George Nelson. He jotted down the phone
number. Now, if only the phone service was working, he
would leave a message for the man. He wondered if there
was a way for him to make a phone call from his computer.
Maybe Logan would know. He got up and went back to the
living-room area, where Logan and Colette were having a
cup of tea.

"Oh good. You're still up."

"Indeed I am. What's going on?" Logan asked.

"Do you know how to place a phone call from the Internet? Do we have WiFi?"

Logan laughed. "Sometimes. What are you trying to do?"

"I've got the phone number of the guy who bought the
contents of the garage."

"It's a little late to be calling people, no?" Logan asked.

"I want to leave a message. The sooner I can get in contact
with this guy, the better." There was a sense of urgency in
Clive's voice.

"Let's check it out. There might be a way to place a call
from the mobile phone through the Internet. Let me go get
it." Logan got up, went into the large side-entry area and
pulled his cell phone from a shelf, where they usually left
their cell phones next to a charging station. Since they didn't
work well in the house, this way they could grab them on the
way out.

"OK. Let's give it a try. As long as we still have an Internet
connection, it may be possible."

The three of them went into Clive's den. It also had a very
modern rustic look without being heavy. A small stone fireplace stood in the corner.

Logan went through a few settings on his phone. ENABLE
WIFI CALLING. Click YES. The little hourglass on his phone was

indicating there was something trying to connect. "What's the number?" Logan asked.

Clive called out the digits: 540-555-3491 as Logan pressed the buttons on the phone. Much to his surprise someone answered. "Yeah?"

"Uh, hello. Is this George Nelson?"

"You got 'im."

Logan gave the other two a strange look and shrugged. He handed the phone to his father.

"Mr. Nelson, my name is Clive Dunbar. I'm sorry to be calling so late."

"No problem. What can I do ya fer?" Clive wasn't sure if it was the connection or if Nelson had a wad of chewing tobacco in his mouth.

"I represent the Millstone estate. I was wondering if you still had the contents of the garage in your possession."

"That garage musta been somethin' special. Yer the second person to call about it tonight."

Clive was stunned for a moment. "Oh, I see." He was almost sure the other person was either Rowena or Arthur. Who else would be looking for something from the estate? "May I ask who the first call was from?"

"Jeez, don't know if she'd want me tellin' anybody."

She. Clive was sure that it had to be Rowena.

"I would make it worth your while, Mr. Nelson."

"Funny thing. She said the same thing. Like I says before. Musta been somethin' special in the garage."

"Let's just say there were some sentimental things that were discarded without notifying other members of the household."

"Well, I reckon if you want to make it worth my while . . ."

Clive veered from anything sounding incriminating. "What I mean is that I realize your time is valuable and I would want to compensate you for it. Whatever the woman gave you, I will double."

Nelson thought for a moment. Should he jack up the price? Nah. Somebody might find out. Shouldn't look a gift horse in the mouth. What he did know is that he was about to be $3,000 richer than he was when he woke up that morning. "She sent a grand through PayPal."

"And when was this?" Arthur asked casually.

"About an hour ago, I reckon."

"OK." Clive was well aware the connection for either the phone or Internet could go down any second. He had to get this negotiation over with as quickly as possible.

"Can you send me a payment request now, Mr. Nelson? Here is my e-mail address." Clive rattled it off to him.

"Sure can. Love this here kinda technology. Makes getting paid and payin' folks a lot easier."

Clive was thinking, *Enough of the chitter-chatter*, but he didn't want to push Mr. Nelson. He might sound like a bit of a hick, but he certainly wasn't clueless when it came to financial exchanges.

"If you could do that now, I would appreciate it. We're having a bit of wind where I am, and the power lines keep cutting in and out."

"You got it, captain. One sec." Nelson didn't want to lose out on his windfall.

In less than a minute, a ding on Clive's computer indicated an e-mail had been received. He clicked on it, then to PayPal. In a few seconds, the money had been transferred to George Nelson.

There was a long, empty silence, until Nelson declared, "OK, got the payment. Thank you. Here is the information. A guy named Cullen Bodman just outside of Asheville, North Carolina. He's in a place called the Stillwell Art Center." Clive was writing as fast as Nelson was talking.

"Thank you very much, Mr. Nelson. You've been extremely helpful." Clive rolled his eyes. Yeah, help to the tune of $2,000, plus the thousand Rowena had sent him. Mr. George Nelson had certainly hit the jackpot that evening.

Clive turned to Logan and Colette. "We have a name. Now we need to contact him." Just then, the small wheel in the search bar started to spin, and after a few seconds it spit out a notice:

NO INTERNET SERVICE. CHECK YOUR CONNECTION.

Clive let out a big huff. "If I know Rowena, she is on her way to Asheville by now."

"At this hour?" Logan seemed surprised.

"That woman will leave no stone unturned." Clive thought for a moment. "I'm going to have to get to a phone and call that Cullen fellow."

"Dad, it's past midnight. No one is open within thirty miles of here."

"Well, then, I'm just going to have to drive until I get cell service." Clive put the piece of paper in his pocket.

"Dad, are you sure this is a good idea? Can't it wait until morning?" Logan was almost pleading with his father.

"Son, you've met Rowena. She will stop at nothing. I need to warn those people." Clive started out of his den.

"You want me to go with you?" Logan was following him.

"No. You stay here with Colette and Max. I'll be fine. The wind's died down. The phone and Internet lines should be up and running soon, but I don't want to wait."

Colette was almost in tears. "Do you really have to do this now?"

"My dear young woman, someone went to a lot of trouble to find you. Where you worked and where you lived. And then he lied about who he was. Don't think for one minute that was the beginning or the end of this. The Millstones are desperate people. And if Arthur is in as much trouble as I suspect, they are beyond desperate, if there is such a thing."

Colette was shaking. Logan put his arm around her shoulders. "It's going to be OK. Dad can handle this." Logan looked at his father, hoping for a sign of encouragement. Clive gave a nod.

"None of us are in any danger here. It's the people in Asheville who need to be warned." Clive recalled the words of Winston Churchill when he was referring to Russia. "*It is a riddle wrapped in a mystery inside an enigma.*" But he was determined to sort it out, and as quickly as possible.

"Can't you call the police?" Colette asked innocently.

"Yes, but there isn't much I could tell them. 'I think a desperate woman is going to Asheville to harass some people'? I seriously doubt that would get their attention. No, warning these Bodman people is the best course of action right now. You sit tight. I should be back within the hour. I know I can get cell service once I get past the dead-zone hill."

"So what are you going to do? Call the Bodmans and tell them what?"

"I'm going to explain who I am and tell them to be on the lookout for Arthur or Rowena Millstone. I will advise him not to engage in any conversation or transactions until he and I have the opportunity for a person-to-person discussion."

"That sounds reasonable enough." Logan still had his arm around Colette's shoulder, and he had to admit that it felt good, even though he could feel her trembling. He walked her over to the sectional and wrapped a fleece throw around her. He looked over his shoulder. "Good luck, Pop."

As soon as Clive left, Colette began to sob. It had all been too much. She couldn't hold it together any longer. Logan poured her another port, grabbed a box of tissues, sat down, put his arm around her, and let her get it all out.

She started to hiccup. And then she started to laugh. "Oh my. This is so embarrassing." She blew her nose with gusto. "I am so sorry." Another snort and blow. She wiped her face with several tissues.

"No need to apologize. It's been a roller-coaster couple of months for you. Between losing Randolph, your job, having to move, and trying to find Dad, you've been on a rocky ride." He took another tissue and wiped her tears.

"You and your father have been so kind to us." She sniffled again.

Logan took the balled-up tissues from her hand and gave her a few fresh ones. The waterworks seemed to be subsiding. "I'll go check on Max. You relax." He took the glass of port that had been sitting on the coffee table and handed it to her.

Colette watched Logan leave the room and ascend the open staircase. Now *that* was the type of man she had been dreaming about. Kind, considerate, and competent. And good-looking, too.

Logan peeked in on Max, making sure he didn't wake the lad. He was sound asleep, clutching the stuffed bear that lived in the guest room. It had been Logan's as a child. Max must have spotted it and decided to make friends. Logan smiled. He remembered how much comfort he had gotten from that bear when he was Max's age. No matter how safe you feel, there's always that threat of the bogeyman. Logan knew it would be years before Max realized that the real bogeymen are grown-ups behaving badly. Not some spooky creature hiding under the bed.

He went back to where Colette was sitting, unsure how close he should get. He wanted to comfort her but wasn't sure how much comforting she required. He had to admit, it

felt warm and peaceful having his arm around her. Then Colette made it easy for him. "Please. Come sit next to me." She
was wrapped up in the blanket with only her hand poking
out, holding the port. Logan smiled. He tucked in the loose
parts of the blanket, making a cocoon for Colette.

"How's that?"

She sighed, tilted her head, and leaned back on the sofa.
"Wonderful."

Logan took the glass from her hand and sat next to her.
She moved her head from the back of the sectional and
placed it on his shoulder. She was asleep in a matter of minutes.

It was past midnight when Clive finally made it around the
big bend of the lake. His phone lit up with several bars indicating he was within reach of a cell tower. He pulled to the side
of the road and dialed Bodman-Antiques-Retro-Restoration
& Namaste Café. He checked the name quizzically. *Namaste
Café?* That was a new one on him. It rang three times and got
an outbound message. It was a man's voice. "You have
reached the BARRN-Bodman-Antiques-Retro-Restoration &
Namaste Café. Please leave us a message and someone will get
in touch with you as soon as possible." Then a woman's voice
finished with a lilting "Namaste."

Clive was brief. "This is Clive Dunbar, attorney for the
Millstone estate. Could you kindly return my call at your ear-
liest convenience? Thank you." He left both phone numbers,
his cell and landline. Just to be on the safe side, he forwarded
his cell phone to his landline. If Bodman tried the cell, he
might not get the call, but he wanted Bodman to have both
numbers regardless.

When Clive returned, he found Logan and Colette on the
sectional. Colette was propped up against Logan as he was
reading a book.

Clive whispered, "Everything OK?"

Logan gave him a thumbs-up.

"Max?"

Another thumbs-up. Clive retreated to his den to work on the Millstone estate. He knew there was a lot to be done, including deciphering the spiral-bound notebook, although he was relatively sure what the numbers represented. His task was to match it up with the other Millstone ledgers. That could take some serious forensic accounting.

Chapter Twenty-one

Boston, Massachusetts
Millstone Manor

Rowena returned to Arthur's den wrapped in a Neiman Marcus cashmere robe. Her hair was wrapped in a matching turban. She lit a cigarette and took a long drag. "Did he call back?"

"Yes, as soon as you went upstairs. Here's the information." Arthur slid the paper across the cocktail table. He still looked disheveled.

"I thought you were going to clean up." Rowena looked at the lump called Arthur Millstone.

"I didn't want to bring the phone into the shower, dear."

"Right." She looked at the address and phone number. "North Carolina?"

"That's what it says. I'm going upstairs." Arthur laboriously pushed himself up, using the arms of the chair. He looked like hell warmed over.

Rowena took to the computer and searched for Stillwell Art Center. Then she went to Google Maps. It was too far to drive. Then she checked the airlines. Only one flight per week from Boston. She would have to use the company jet. Randolph was against anyone's using it for personal transportation. It was a waste of jet fuel. But now he wasn't around to protest or deny her. Without waiting for Arthur to return from his shower, she phoned the hangar where they kept the Embraer Phenom 100. It could get her to Asheville on one tank and in less than two hours. She got the night dispatcher on the phone.

"Good evening. This is Rowena Millstone calling. I am going to need our jet for tomorrow morning."

"Hello, Mrs. Millstone. What time will you be departing?"

"Around nine."

"And what is your destination?"

"Asheville, North Carolina."

"One moment, please."

Rowena listened to the insipid music from being placed on hold. It felt like an eternity until the female voice returned.

"OK, Mrs. Millstone. We can get clearance for nine thirty. Your pilot will be Roger Murdock."

"That's fine."

"Please arrive here by nine."

"Yes. Thank you." Rowena clicked off the call.

Arthur came back, wearing a similar cashmere robe. His was navy blue. His hair was wet and uncombed. He was a cleaner version of his earlier hot mess.

"Who were you talking to?" He poured himself another scotch.

"The dispatcher at the airport."

"Why?"

"We're taking a little day trip to Asheville, North Carolina, tomorrow morning."

"On no, *we're* not. *You* are. I am exhausted. I'm sure you can handle the negotiation."

"We have to find it first, remember?"

"Right. So what's your brilliant plan?"

"I'm going to a place called Stillwell Art Center. A man by the name of Cullen Bodman bought the contents of the garage. He's in the restoration business. If we're lucky, he may not have started working on any of that junk yet."

"And if we're not lucky, he found the will, and he's going to make the connection if you tell him who you really are."

"Good point. I'll use some other name. I'll use Amber's. He's never met her, and I can use the same excuse we used on good old George Nelson, except Amber is working on behalf of the Millstones."

"But, as I said, he'll make the connection. Why don't you save yourself the trip and the jet fuel and just call the man?"

"What am I going to say to him? 'Gotta will I can burn?' No, this requires some serious investigating."

"Have it your way, Rowena. But I think you need to be anonymous at first and see if the junk is still there. Take a walk around. Feel it out."

"Since when are you the patient one?"

"Since we're close to recovering and destroying that will. I don't want anything to go wrong. Again."

"OK. OK. I'll be browsing, using an alias."

"Now you're using your head." Arthur gulped his scotch. "I'm done. Good luck tomorrow. Keep me posted." He turned and shuffled out the door. He felt the foreboding threat to his well-being hanging over him like a cloud. Not a heart attack. But a severe beating from the people to whom he owed money.

George Nelson could not believe his luck. Not only had he made a few grand selling the load of rubbish to that Bodman fella, he had just cleared another two grand from some guy, and a grand from some lady. Three grand in less than an hour. Heck, he was makin' doctor's wages. He wondered what was so special about that pile of junk. Maybe he should find out for himself. If he left immediately, he could be outside Asheville by sunup.

But what then? Try to buy the stuff back from Bodman? Then try to sell it to the highest bidder? He had to think on that. He racked his brain to remember what could be so valuable in a broken-down table, brass headboard, splintered dresser with missing drawers, and side table with a cracked leg. Was there something else he might have overlooked? As far as he could tell, there had been nothing worth anything in that garage. It would take a heck of a lot of days trying to reconstruct the rubble. He shrugged. Must be something important. He went back to the bar and asked his friend Leroy if he wanted to go for a joy ride. He even insinuated there could be some more money in it for both of them. Leroy bought a six-pack of beer from the bartender and jumped in the cab of George's pickup. They stopped at a drive-through burger joint. Leroy leaned over George and placed his order through the window. He stocked up on greasy, cheesy food, including several value meals, dessert, and milkshakes.

"What 'er you feedin' in there?" George spat at Leroy.

"We dunno how long were gonna be, so I's wants to be sure we have provisions."

George muttered something under his breath.

"'Sides, you got yerself some cash, what 'er you complainin' about?"

"Nothin'" George pulled two twenty-dollar bills from his wallet. He got a dollar back in change. "I swear that's the most money I ever spent here. You got 'nough to feed a small army."

"Quit gripin'." Leroy sat back in his seat. "Not sure what I should eat first. The fried chicken or the double cheeseburger."

"Eat the burger. Chicken ain't bad if it's room temp."
George pulled up to the window to retrieve their food order.

"Y'all have a nice night," said the woman with orange
hair and a gold front tooth who handed him the bag with
their food in it.

George grumbled, "It's gonna be a long one, that's fer
sure."

Chapter Twenty-two

Stillwell Art Center
Sunday

It was the crack of dawn when George and Leroy pulled into the parking lot of the Stillwell Art Center. It was also the same time Jimmy Can-Do brought his work into the shop. Jimmy had never seen anyone else in the area at that hour before and wondered what a beat-up pickup was doing at the far end of the parking lot. And he wasn't about to find out either. It was too far away to read the license plate, but if he ever had to give someone a description, it would be easy. *Old. Dark green. Wood railings on the flatbed. Duct tape on the front bumper.*

Boston, Massachusetts
Millstone Manor

Rowena was up earlier than usual. Her adrenaline was pumping. She had a good feeling about this trip. She'd take the company jet to Asheville and use a car service to take her to the Stillwell Art Center. Once she got there, she would browse, then casually pay Mr. Bodman a visit. Once she got the lay of the land, she would figure out her next move. Based on the condition of all the other items they had retrieved, she doubted that Bodman guy would have made any progress restoring all that junk. She also figured he hadn't found the will; otherwise, he would have brought it to someone's attention. No, she was fairly sure the document that threatened her lifestyle was still hidden somewhere. As soon as she could locate the salvaged pieces, the sooner she could plan her next move. She wasn't exactly sure what that would be, but she was too close to success to worry about it at the moment. She had to believe that once she found the document, she could destroy it and all the plans Randolph Millstone had made to terminate her cushy lifestyle.

For most of her life, she had gotten everything she wanted. Except herpes. Even now, she was not sure whether she had given it to Arthur or Arthur had given it to her. Either way, they were both contagious.

Rowena chose an elegant white pantsuit, a white Prada satchel, Loren sandals by Gina, and a white Hermès enamel bracelet. Her hair was slicked back. There had been no time to get a professional blow-out for her hair. Not that she couldn't do it herself. It was the principle of the thing as far as she was concerned. Her kind of principle. *Why do something yourself when you can pay someone else to do it?*

The town car came around to the front of Millstone Manor, and the driver rang the bell for Rowena. She pulled on a pair of Versace sunglasses. She looked expensive. Almost intimidating.

Nasty. Goes without saying.

They arrived at Boston Logan Airport in plenty of time. Rowena checked in at the small office that accommodated the private and charter jets. It was so easy. Walk in. Walk on. No regular people. No screaming kids. No security. Not that she was doing anything illegal. Not yet.

She boarded the jet with the company logo for Millstone Enterprises painted on the side. A huge M.E. She chuckled when she saw it. It hadn't occurred to her before. It spelled *ME*. Indeed it is. Just. For. Me. Ha.

She took a seat in the empty six-passenger plane. Even though it was a private jet, it did not come with all the amenities many others had. No big-screen television. No flight attendant. No champagne. Randolph had used it strictly for speedy transportation for business. If he had to go cross-country, he would take a commercial flight. It was cheaper and more comfortable. This aircraft was only for absolutely necessary short hops, not entertainment.

Within two hours, the plane touched down at the Asheville Regional Airport. Another town car was waiting to bring her to the Stillwell Art Center. She had hired it for the entire day. The minute she got in the car, the driver started babbling. "So, y'all going to that new art center?" He looked up into the rearview mirror.

"Yes." Nothing more. Rowena thought that if she kept her shades on, he would not engage any further. She was wrong. He kept prattling about all the excitement of the new place and how they had raffled off a Lincoln, and who won and on and on. It became white noise in the background until he pulled up to the main entrance, and shouted, "I asked if you wanted me to wait outside, come back in an hour? You tell me, miss."

"I'll call you. What's your number?" He rattled off the digits as she plugged them into her phone.

"Got any idea?"

"Not really." She sat there until he got out to open her door.

Rowena entered the Stillwell Art Center, turning heads from all parts of the courtyard. She almost looked like a movie star. Almost. Or one might guess a high-class hooker, which would not be all that far from the truth. In spite of the amount of money she was wearing on her body, there was something about her that said *fraud*. Her clothes were authentic couture, but there was something about the way she walked into Silver & Stone that immediately got under Chi-Chi's skin.

"Good afternoon. Thank you for visiting my shop. I hand-make all the items you see. All are authentic stones." Chi-Chi swept her hand across the room. "Please. Look."

"Uh. Thank you." Rowena couldn't help but notice the gorgeous jewelry, but she was on a mission. "Everything is beautiful." She pretended interest in a large amethyst piece. "That's awesome."

"My friend is very fond of it, too." Chi-Chi was getting a strange vibe from the woman. She retreated to the other side of the shop, trying to be inconspicuous.

The woman in white turned and said, "Thank you," and left the shop. Chi-Chi coolly watched the woman make her way over to Cullen's showroom. Chi-Chi knew that Cullen was on an errand, so the *femme en blanc* would have to speak to Luna. Chi-Chi snickered to herself. *If that woman is up to no good, Luna will suss it out.*

She saw the woman stop in front of the glass door of Cullen's showroom. Cullen's sign was hanging in the window, indicating that people should go next door to the Namaste Café for information. The woman went inside the café and looked around.

Luna walked up to the striking woman. "Hello. Can I help you?"

Rowena gave Luna the once-over. Big mistake. Luna caught every nuance and cocked her head, as if to say, *So?*

"Oh, hello. I'm browsing for restored furniture."

"Anything in particular?" Luna asked. *Most people were much more specific. I'm looking for a mid-century desk, or I'm looking for a sideboard.* Luna was immediately suspicious.

"Oh, you know how it goes. You look around until something grabs your eye?" Rowena hadn't rehearsed her spiel. She didn't think she was going to have to go through a watchdog first.

"My brother is running an errand. You are welcome to wait here. May I get you a cup of tea? Coffee?" Luna asked cordially.

"Thank you. I'll have a cappuccino, please." Of course, Rowena would request something that took a little extra time. Not much, but just enough. She didn't even like cappuccino. She just liked the idea that someone was doing something for her that took time and effort.

Luna offered the woman in white a chair. "Coming right up." As she turned, she caught Chi-Chi on the other side of the courtyard staring in her direction. Chi-Chi gave Luna an odd nod, but Luna got the message. Something about that woman. Luna had felt it the second Rowena had walked through the glass doors.

"Is this your first visit to Stillwell?" Luna asked loudly over the machine while she frothed the milk.

"Yes, it is." Rowena didn't want to offer too much information.

"Are you from around here?" Luna was pretending to make small talk.

Rowena wondered, *Which one is this hippie-looking chick supposed to be, Cagney or Lacey?* She almost laughed at her own joke.

Luna caught the snicker. "Sorry? Did you say something?"

"No. No. I thought I was going to cough." Quick save.

Luna brought the steamed coffee over to Rowena and set it down. "Can I get you anything else? Scone?"

"No, thank you." Now Rowena was thinking, *This one is more like Aurora Teagarden from the Hallmark Channel. Sweet, librarian-ish.* Rowena's polar opposite.

Luna decided to take the matter into her own hands and

stood on the opposite side of the table from where Rowena was sitting. "So, I'm an artist. I do sketches."

"Uh-huh." Rowena was trying to avoid Chatty Cathy by blowing across the foam on top of her coffee. *What's with people wanting to yack? Don't they have any friends?*

"I couldn't help but notice your profile." Luna was about to go into her supercharming mode. "You have a very regal look."

Rowena perked up at the compliment. No one had ever said that to her before. *Regal.* She liked it.

"Would you mind if I sketched you while you wait for Cullen?"

Rowena was flattered. No one had ever asked her that before either. "Really?" She was fascinated.

Luna knew that anyone who would dress the way Rowena was dressed had a high opinion of themselves. Not that wearing expensive clothing meant a big ego. It was the idea that everything Rowena was wearing had a logo on it. *Look how much money I spent!* was spelled all over her clothing, from Gina to Hermès to Prada. And it wasn't that the workmanship didn't deserve a high price tag, but Luna sensed that Rowena did it for the sake of bragging, not because she had any appreciation for the quality of the clothing. It was just a feeling she had about the woman, that's all.

"I don't know how long Cullen will be. Maybe another half hour. That will give me enough time to do a rough sketch. Come over to the easel." Luna nodded to the other corner of the café. "Make yourself comfortable." Luna turned the easel around so Rowena couldn't see what Luna was drawing. Luna realized she didn't know the woman's name. "By the way, I'm Luna. Luna Bodhi Bodman."

"I'm Ro . . . Roseanne." She caught herself just in time. The flattery of being called regal and having an artist want to draw her had caught Rowena off guard. She admonished herself. She had to pay better attention and not let this imp throw her off her game.

"Nice to meet you, Roseanne." Luna began to draw. They were heavy dark circles. Then the song "Cruella de Vil" from the Disney movie *One Hundred and One Dalmatians* started going through her mind. *How odd*, she thought. "Huh."

"What?" Roseanne/Rowena had to ask.

"Did a song ever pop into your head, and you don't know how it got there? I mean, you hear jingles or songs, and they stick with you. They call them earworms, brainworms, sticky music. But this song just popped into my head out of nowhere."

Rowena wasn't really interested. "Huh."

"Yeah. It's the craziest thing." Luna started humming the tune. *Cruella de Vil . . . Cruella de Vi . . .*

Rowena didn't know why, but she instantly became uneasy. Her skin was crawling, and her face was flushed. "Listen, I should probably go. I have a lot of things I want to see. Why don't I leave my phone number with you, then Cullen can call me. That's his name, correct?" Rowena knew darn well that Cullen was his name, but she was playing it for all it was worth.

Luna was relieved that the woman was ready to make an exit. She didn't know how she would explain the evil character on her sketch pad. Worst case, she would knock it over and spill coffee all over it. Thankfully, it hadn't come to that. "Do you have something I can write it down on?"

Luna handed the woman one of the café's business cards so she could write her number on the back. Luna looked down at the scribbled phone number and noticed the woman hadn't written down her name. She wondered why someone with her obvious social standing didn't have her own personal calling card. Another red flag. The woman's body language shouted "uncomfortable" and screamed "deceitful."

Rowena thanked her and turned her attention to the courtyard. She had to kill time until that Bodman guy returned. After browsing both levels, she checked her watch. It was after four and there was still no word from Cullen Bodman.

Rowena walked back over to the café. This time a dog greeted her at the door. Wiley had been in the dog park and was ready for a treat or a pat on the head. Rowena gave Wiley a snarly look, and he gave one right back at her.

Luna noticed her dog's body language, too. Wiley sensed something, and it wasn't that he was about to get a doggie treat. Luna was getting nervous. It wasn't so much that the *femme en blanc* was intimidating. No, it was more like bad juju emanating from her. Wiley got down on the floor and put his paws over his nose. He, too, wasn't feeling a love connection.

Rowena poked her head around the counter. "Hi again. Do you suppose I could browse around your brother's place? I know it's getting late, and I had hoped that he and I could chat. But meanwhile, could I maybe take a look?" Rowena was in a cordial mood.

"Of course. No problem. Follow me." Luna walked into her brother's showroom, feeling apprehensive. The woman wouldn't be able to steal anything by herself. But there was something suspicious about her. Luna would keep a close eye on Cullen's place without making it look like she was spying. Which, of course, was exactly what she was going to do.

Rowena meandered through the shop, pretending to admire several pieces. She casually worked her way toward the back, where Cullen had his workshop. She could always say she had gotten turned around if someone caught her. As she peered into the room, her heart skipped a beat. There it was. The table. The brass headboard. The old potting bench. Bingo! She had stopped in her tracks when a ding-dong sound indicated that someone else had entered the shop. She quickly moved back into the showroom area. It wasn't Cullen or Luna. Just two browsers. She smiled and nodded to the couple. They nodded back. After a few minutes, they left through the door that led to the café.

Rowena weighed her options. If the Bodman guy didn't return before they closed, she would have to come back the next day. She didn't want to risk time slipping through her hands. It would be risky, but she considered hiding in his showroom until after the art center closed. That would give her the entire night to go through the remains of the garage. There was a small lavatory in the back, so that solved one potential issue. Food? She decided she would go back into the courtyard and pick something up from the Blonde Shallot. Something she could fit into her purse. She stuck her head in the café. "Hi, again. I don't suppose you've heard from your brother?" Stupid question, but she had to ask.

"No, I haven't. It's not like him not to phone in." Luna dialed Cullen's cell phone number. She heard a distant ringing coming from his showroom. She followed the sound and found the phone on the desk in the back of the shop. She shook her head. Sometimes, he could be flakier than she. She walked back to where Rowena was standing and held up Cullen's phone. "He forgot it." Luna made a face.

"I see." Rowena tried not to act perturbed. "I'm going to grab something to eat. I'll be back in a bit."

"OK. We close at five," Luna reminded her.

Luna looked back at the phone and saw that he had messages. She didn't want him to lose a potential client, but she didn't have his password either. It would have to wait. She wondered where he was. He was supposed to be gone for about an hour. It had been closer to three. She didn't feel as if anything bad had happened to him, but she did have a feeling of something. She thought it might be that *mujer de blanco*.

But why? She watched the woman walk into the Blonde Shallot and noticed that Chi-Chi was also eyeing the questionable shopper. Chi-Chi nodded at Luna. Luna nodded back. They would discuss the situation after the center closed for the evening.

Luna noticed that the woman exited the sandwich shop empty-handed. She couldn't have wolfed down a panini in such a short amount of time. What was up with that? Perhaps she had changed her mind?

Rowena made her way back to the entrance to the café. "I'm going to take another peek if that's OK." Rowena went back into the showroom. She checked her watch again. She doubted the owner would be back in the next five minutes. She had to make it look like she had left the premises. She noticed an armoire with caned panels. She could easily fit in there and be comfortable for maybe a half hour. Enough time for the sister to close up shop. Rowena stuck her head back into the café one more time and faked an exit. "I'd better be going. Please ask your brother to give me a call. Have a good evening."

"Will do. Bye." Luna was clearing off the counter. As soon as Luna turned her back, Rowena dashed into the showroom, stepped into the cabinet, and closed the doors. She was glad it wasn't too tight. She could actually sit with her knees bent. *Clever move*, she thought.

George and Leroy had been staking out the rear entrance of the BARRN all day. The door was open, but no one had come in or out the entire time. Leroy was squirming. "Hey, boss, I ain't feelin' too good."

"What in blazes is botherin' you?"

Leroy let out a burp that practically fogged the window. George held his nose with one hand and tried to wave the odor away. "I think it was the fried chicken." Leroy burped again. George opened the door of the truck and stepped out. "For Pete's sake! Man, you stink like a garbage dump. You better keep all that food you ate to yerself. I don't want no puking or any other disgusting thing happenin' round here."

Leroy held his stomach. "Seriously, boss, I'm gonna be sick."

"For the love of all get-out, *get out* and go behind the pickup." George was getting frustrated, and he began to think that his good fortune was taking a turn for the worse. He had had no plan when they left the night before. The only thing George had on his mind was money. It had come so easily that evening, he figured he could get his hands on some more. He just hadn't figured out how, or even why that junk was in such demand. Even if he got it back, what would he do with it? Especially since he didn't know what all the fuss was about. Nope. The day had been long, and it was going to be nightfall soon enough. He had to figure out his next move. Driving with Leroy's gastrointestinal issues for hours was not appealing in the least. George kept staring at that back door. He peered to see if he could spot any security cameras. Nothing he couldn't get past.

George thought for a few minutes while Leroy regained some of his composure. He had a plan. He'd make Leroy wait in the pickup while he sneaked into the back of the workshop. He'd hide until the place closed, then he'd check everything out. Not having a clue about the layout, he knew he would be going in blind. He shrugged. He should have thought of that earlier. Check it out from the front? Too late now. If he got caught, he'd say he walked in the wrong way. No harm done. Now he had to plan his getaway. For sure, an alarm would go off when he came out of the building, so Leroy would have to be waiting for him. He told Leroy to rub dirt on the license plates so no one could read them. "Ain't that against the law?" Leroy asked, stupefied.

"No foolin', but we don't want anyone to ID my pickup either. We can clean the plates when we're far enough away. I'll ring your phone once. Do. Not. Answer. It. Got it?" George was questioning his own good sense and whether he had any left. George coolly walked toward the rear of the building, casually looking in both directions. Thankfully, he didn't look like a total mess. Just a worn-out handyman with a flannel shirt and a pair of jeans. Cowboy boots, scruffy beard. He surely didn't look like he was going to a black-tie event, but he didn't look like he had crawled out from under a railroad trestle either. He sniffed his armpits. *Ew.* He hoped he didn't run into anybody 'cause he was kinda stinky.

George finally reached the rear doorway and peeked in. Nothing too different from any other workshop. Tools, wood, table saw. Paint and brushes. Nothing different except the brass headboard that caught his eye. It looked familiar. He inched closer. And the side table. Yep. This was the stuff. But what of it? Nothing looked particularly special. If anything, it looked pretty much the same as when he had sold it. Faded, broken, and in a state of disrepair. So why would anyone want it? And more than one person at that. George was going to do his darnedest to figure out what was so valuable.

His first thought was that perhaps the brass headboard was really made of gold. Nah. Too much of a fairy tale. He heard footsteps outside. Someone bolted the door from the outside. It was a cylinder lock that required a key on either side of the door. If it was locked from the outside, you needed a key if you were inside in order to get out. Much to his dismay, the interior key was not in the lock on his side of the door. Unless he could bust the lock, he wasn't getting out that way. He thought they had done away with those types of locks. Fire hazard. He shrugged. Nothing he could do about it now. He'd call Leroy and tell him to meet him around front, but he remembered he had told Leroy not to answer the phone. He had to come up with a plan B or wait until morning. He knew Leroy wouldn't last that long. He'd be craving something deep-fried soon enough.

George decided to check out the front of the showroom. See if he could make his escape that way. He crawled along the floor of the showroom and looked out the big glass doors. He noticed some EXIT signs. He'd take the nearest one to the rear of the building. If he got caught, he'd tell them he had gotten locked in. Period. They couldn't prove anything different.

Chapter Twenty-three

Cranberry Lake—Cobblestone Hill

Clive had suggested that Logan take Colette and Max out for a boat ride while he waited for Cullen Bodman to call. He wanted the others to enjoy the day out on the lake. And he thought that Logan was showing some interest in Colette, which he wanted to encourage and facilitate. The Internet was back up, and so was the landline. He was certain he would hear something shortly. But the entire afternoon had gone by without a word. He couldn't understand why Cullen Bodman hadn't returned his call. Clive had said it was urgent.

It occurred to Clive that perhaps Cullen hadn't gotten the message yet. Strange thing in these techno-times. But then again, he lived in an area with sketchy cell service because of the mountains. Clive decided to phone him again. This time a woman answered. "Hello, the BARRN. This is Luna Bodman. How can I help you?"

"Yes. Hello. My name is Clive Dunbar. I represent the Millstone estate."

Luna started to shake. How could she be sure it was really him? "Oh?" She pretended ignorance.

"Yes. I understand Mr. Cullen Bodman purchased a container from the garage of the Millstone Manor."

Luna wasn't sure how to answer him. What if he was a phony? And where *was* her brother? "How can I help you?" she asked.

"I'm trying to locate the property. There was a mix-up during the sale." Clive wasn't sure how much information he should share. She hadn't acknowledged receipt of the goods.

"I believe you are going to have to speak to my brother about it, sir. Unfortunately, he isn't available at the moment. May I take a message?"

Clive felt a little more comfortable knowing it was Bodman's sister he was speaking to and not a clerk. He decided to share his concern about Rowena and Arthur Millstone. "Do you know if your brother received any calls from either Rowena or Arthur Millstone?"

"No. Not to my knowledge. May I ask why? Perhaps I can be of further assistance if I have more information."

Clive hesitated again. "It has to do with the late Randolph Millstone's estate. I'm not at liberty to discuss any details. However, should either of them get in touch with you, please do not discuss anything or have any transactions with them until you speak to me." Clive sounded as serious as a nuclear threat.

"Certainly, Mr. Dunbar." By that time, Luna was sure she was speaking to the attorney for Randolph Millstone, but she wasn't ready to turn over information or the goods. Not until she spoke with Gaines and Cullen. "I'll be happy to give him the message. I should be hearing from him shortly." She hoped.

"Thank you, Ms. Bodman." Clive hung up and continued pacing the floor.

It was just around five o'clock when Logan, Colette, and Max walked up the dock and climbed the decks to the main level. Clive was standing outside the porch. "Ahoy, mates!" He waved.

"Ahoy, Mr. Clive!" Max waved. Then Colette.

"Hey, Dad. What's the latest?" Logan set the cooler down on the deck.

"Not very much, I'm afraid." Clive heaved a big sigh. "I was able to reach the sister, but she wasn't very forthcoming with information. She said as soon as she heard from her brother, she'd let him know I called."

"Do you know if he got the first message?" Colette asked.

"I do not." Clive opened the wide screen door for everyone. "So how was your day?" He didn't want to put a damper on what he hoped had been a fine afternoon for them.

"Super!" Max cried out. "I caught a fish!" He was nodding like a bobblehead.

"And?" Colette urged him.

"And I threw him back." Max turned over his palms.

Clive chuckled. "What else did you do?"

"Logan took us to an island. We saw a bunch of lizards!" Max was ecstatic. "And we had a picnic."

"Yes, it was a lovely way to spend the day. Thank you, Logan." Colette smiled warmly. "I can't remember the last time I have enjoyed myself so much."

"It was my pleasure." Logan smiled in return. He was beginning to enjoy Colette's company more and more.

"Max, go upstairs and clean up. I'll see what I can whip up for dinner." Colette moved into the kitchen. She felt very much at home, enjoying the nurturing that was being shared. Food, company, fresh air.

"I took the liberty to thaw out some steaks. I thought we could talk Logan into firing up the grill."

"Sure thing!" Logan replied. "I'll go clean myself up, too. Be right back."

Colette investigated the pantry and found fingerling potatoes. She had a special recipe for them. Colette enjoyed cooking and took every opportunity when it was presented to her. Even if it was in a stranger's house. But they were no longer strangers. They had joined forces and were on a mission to see that Randolph Millstone's final wishes were carried out.

She went back into the kitchen and up the stairs to change her clothes, brush her hair, and check her makeup. She wanted to look her best for Logan. She was beginning to sense some interest on his part. And he really seemed to enjoy being with Max. *Could it get any better?*

Logan was the first to come down. "Any luck with the notebook?" he asked Clive.

"If the information I received from the accountant's office is correct, Mr. Arthur Millstone has been fiddling the family books. I found a number of transfers that coincide with entries in the binder."

"So you think it's a journal of payments to his loan sharks?"

"Possibly." Clive went into the kitchen and opened a bottle of wine. Tonight it would be a Séamus pinot noir. He took out a corkscrew and peeled the capsule from the top of the bottle. He removed the cork and poured the wine into a decanter. He turned to Logan. "And, I think he's been selling off some of the holdings."

"Doesn't he need the board's approval to do that?" Logan asked.

"Yes, he does. But maybe he was hoping he could buy them back at some point."

"Like a pawnshop?" Logan snickered.

"Indeed."

Stillwell Art Center

Luna was in deep thought as she tidied up the café. She was thinking about that strange phone call from the Dunbar man, or so he had called himself; that strange woman in white; and how strange it was that she hadn't heard from Cullen. She almost jumped out of her shoes when her cell phone rang. She looked at the caller ID. It was Marshal Gaines. She wondered if he would stop by. "Hey!" she answered lightly.

"Hey yourself," Gaines replied. "So, as I was heading over in your direction, I came upon a man who had a flat tire. To his dismay, he didn't have his cell phone with him. Apparently he had left it at his shop. I helped him unload the truck to get to the spare tire, which of course was flat as well."

Luna interrupted him. "Are you with Cullen?" The words rushed out.

"Well, I was about to say, the man was your brother. We've been sitting on the side of the road for the past two hours. You OK? You sound a little harried."

"Cullen got a phone call today. It was from a man named Clive Dunbar. He claimed to be the attorney for the Millstone estate."

"Isn't that who we were looking for? Millstone's attorney?"

"Yes, but he mentioned Arthur and Rowena Millstone and that we should not talk to them if they call." Luna was speaking a mile a minute. "And then there was a strange woman lurking about today. She said her name was Roseanne, but I think she was lying." Luna was running out of breath.

"OK. Take it easy. We should be there in about twenty minutes."

"OK. Hurry. I'm asking Chi-Chi to come over to the café."

"Good idea," Gaines said. "Here, tell your brother what you told me. I'm driving now."

Luna told Cullen about the woman who had stopped by looking for him. She described how the woman was dressed. Dripping of money. She seemed to be on a quest and was anxious to speak to Cullen.

"OK. Hold tight. We'll be there soon."

Luna clicked off the call and dialed Chi-Chi. She could see her across the courtyard pulling items off the counter and locking them up. "Hello, love," Chi-Chi answered.

"Chi-Chi, can you come by when you're done?" Luna was still out of breath.

"Of course, my love. You sound all wound up."

"Just a bit. I'll tell you all about it when you get here." They nodded to each other across the courtyard.

Luna finished putting everything away and poured herself a cup of tea. Chamomile. She sat at one of the tables, closed her eyes, and took several cleansing breaths. Such a wacky day.

Several minutes later, Chi-Chi tapped on the glass. "What is going on?" Her singsong voice was a balm to Luna's ears.

"You saw that woman who was creeping around today? The one all dressed in white?"

"Oh yes. Something about her did not feel right to me."

"Me neither. And she kept coming back, looking for Cullen, as if he might have been expecting her, although she didn't say so. And it he had been expecting someone, he would have told me before he went on his errand of no return."

"What do you mean, no return?" Chi-Chi became concerned.

"Well, he forgot his phone. He left it in the shop. On his way back, he got a flat tire. But, that's not all. Chris Gaines spotted him and was going to help him but they had to unload the truck, only to find the spare tire was flat, too." Luna slapped her forehead with the palm of her hand. "He's supposed to be the brainiac in the family. I'm supposed to be the ditz."

"Is everyone OK now? Are they on their way back?"

"Yes. They should be getting here any minute."

* * *

George made his way around the showroom, peeking into drawers, seeing what else was of interest. After his self-guided tour, he'd deal with the stuff in the workshop and figure out what to do next. Unless someone unlocked that back door, he was leaving empty-handed. He came upon a nicely finished armoire with cane-paneled doors.

Rowena heard his footsteps getting closer. She had nothing with which to defend herself. The footsteps stopped in front of the cabinet she was hiding in. The doors were pulled open, and both she and George started screaming!

It was hard to tell which one was more freaked-out. Rowena was beating George over the head, trying to push him away. He was covering his head, trying to shield himself from the large leather handbag being used to pummel his skull.

Hearing the shrieks coming from the showroom, Luna grabbed a fire extinguisher and marched in, holding the nozzle in one hand and the device in the other. "Call 911!" she shouted to Chi-Chi. Chi-Chi was already on it. Wiley was barking wildly, adding to the clamor.

"Stop! Both of you!" Luna yelled at the intruders. "Trust me. You don't want a CO_2 facial." She was directing her comment to Cruella de Vil. "And you," she said, looking at the pathetic man cowering on the floor, "don't you dare make a move or you will be picking sodium bicarbonate out of that beard while you sit in a jail cell."

Chi-Chi was on the phone with the police, describing the situation. "Yes, that is correct. We have two intruders and are holding them at bay with a fire extinguisher." Chi-Chi listened for a moment. "Yes, I did say a fire extinguisher."

Luna wanted to lunge at the wicked woman. The guy? A schlub. "What are the two of you doing here?" Luna demanded.

"I have no idea who this man is," Rowena said, her disgust that anyone would associate her with him evident.

"You sure do know who I am, lady," George piped in. "You sent me a thousand dollars last night to give you the name of the guy who bought the garage junk."

"How do you know it was me?" Rowena demanded.

"By your nasty tone, lady." George gave it right back to her.

Luna tapped the hose of the extinguisher against the armoire, then pointed it at Rowena. "Let's start with you, blondie. Answer my question. What are you doing here?"

"I, I, wanted to speak to your brother." Rowena was desperate to regain control of the situation.

"By hiding in an armoire." Luna was overstating the obvious. "Did you ever hear of making an appointment?" She was livid. She turned her glare to the dude. "What's your story?"

"Well, like I said, I was the one who sold the stuff to the guy who owns this place."

"So?" Luna was about to press the lever of the fire extinguisher just for the heck of it. Maybe make them dance around a bit. No. She had to invoke her inner spirit and remain calm. She spotted a roll of duct tape on one of the tables. "Chi-Chi. Wrap their hands behind their backs."

"My pleasure." Chi-Chi was as calm as a cucumber. Luna kept swinging the hose back and forth in case either of them tried to make a quick move. Chi-Chi grabbed Rowena's hands, pulled them behind her back, and began to wrap the tape. "Oh dear. This beautiful Hermès bracelet will be ruined."

Rowena started to protest. "You won't get away with this! My husband is an enormously powerful man!"

"Don't be absurd. How are you going to explain your presence in a showroom after hours? You had a blackout and don't know how you got here? You're going to have to come up with some kind of crazy excuse."

Luna turned to George. "So you sold the merchandise to my brother? What of it?"

"To tell you the truth . . ." he began.

"Yes, the truth. That would be a nice change." Luna looked over at Rowena. "Let me guess. Your name isn't Roseanne. It's Rowena Millstone."

Rowena stiffened but didn't answer.

"OK. Back to you, cowboy. What are you doing here?"

"I figured if two people was lookin' for the merchandise, it must be worth somethin'."

"You *sold* it to my brother," Luna said calmly, as she watched Chi-Chi wrap tape around the guy's wrists. "And you received payment for said merchandise. According to the laws of commerce, that means the merchandise belongs to my brother; he owns it, however valuable it might be. Other laws pertain to theft and larceny, which you could be charged with. For starters, you are trespassing."

George hung his head. He had no fight left in him. The woman who had come flying out of the cabinet had scared the bejesus out of him. And now this. Never in his life had he ever been bested by a woman. Maybe once when Shirley from the Road House beat him in arm wrestling, but he'd never been this close to being hog-tied before.

Luna turned her attention to Rowena again. "Let me guess. You are looking for something that was stashed away in one of the pieces?"

Rowena didn't answer her.

"Don't you worry your pretty little head. The document you were looking for is in a very safe place." Luna was relieved that she had listened to everyone about putting it in Chi-Chi's safe.

Rowena snapped to it. "What do you mean it's in a safe

place? You found it?" Rowena was slowly beginning to comprehend what was happening around her. What was she going to do? What *could* she do? She slowly looked at her surroundings. She was on the floor of a showroom with her hands tied together with tape, crumpled next to a repulsive, greedy scruff who smelled like Chick-fil-A.

"You seemed to have gone to a lot of trouble. What exactly were you looking for?" Luna wanted to hear it from the red-lipsticked harpy.

Chi-Chi spotted the security guard entering the courtyard with another equally disheveled man in handcuffs. "Oh dear. What do we have here?" She nodded in their direction.

On the other side of the courtyard, Cullen and Gaines rushed through the front entrance of the art center, Gaines with his hand on his weapon. They dashed to the showroom, then came to an abrupt halt.

Luna looked up at the two men. "Took you long enough." She waved the wand of the fire extinguisher at both of them.

"Seems like you have everything under control. I'll take that now." Gaines reached for the weapon Luna had been threatening her two intruders with.

Luna tipped her head toward Rowena. "Meet Rowena Millstone."

"Well, I'll be darned," Gaines said. "And who is this?" He turned to George.

"This is the man who sold the goods to Cullen."

"George Nelson?" Cullen looked flabbergasted.

"Yep." George was beyond humiliated.

"And who are you?" Gaines turned to Leroy.

"I'm with him." Leroy nodded at George.

"Where did he come from?" Gaines asked.

"We're from Reston, in Virginia," Leroy answered.

Gaines shook his head and rolled his eyes. Definitely not members of Mensa.

The security guard took the lead. "I got a call from someone saying there was a suspicious-looking truck behind the building. When I arrived, a man wearing a welder's mask was detaining Leroy with an acetylene torch."

"An acetylene torch?" Gaines looked stupefied. "I must say, you people are truly creative. Good thing we're at an art center." Gaines let out a guffaw. "Where is the masked man now?"

"He took off once I arrived and put this guy in cuffs," the security guard said.

Chi-Chi and Luna looked at each other at the same time, and exclaimed, "Jimmy Can-Do!"

"The baseball-bat guy?" Gaines was even more confused.

"That's the one," Cullen spoke up. "Odd. No one has ever seen him. He shows up before we open and comes back after we're gone."

"The honor-system dude." Gaines remembered leaving the note about the bat, getting a call a few days later, and giving the man his credit card number over the phone. At that moment, it occurred to Gaines that he, too, had had a leap of faith. It could have been a scammer. There was still hope for humanity.

Several police cars pulled into the parking lot, lights flashing, sirens blaring. Ellie's SUV was right behind.

The first one to get hoisted off the floor was Rowena. Luna nodded in her direction. "This is Rowena Millstone."

One of the police officers began to read her her Miranda rights. " 'You have the right to remain silent. Anything you say can and will be used against you in a court of law. You have the right to an attorney. If you cannot afford one, one will be provided for you.' "

"Next?" Gaines helped them pull George off the floor as the second officer read him his rights. Then on to Leroy, who was protesting, claiming he didn't do nothin'.

Ellie stood motionless and speechless. One thing was for sure, her security team had done its job splendidly. She surveyed the situation. "What on earth?"

"It's a very long story, Ellie. I apologize for all the trouble this may have caused." Cullen didn't know what else to say.

"Nonsense. As long as everyone is OK. I'm glad my guys were at the ready," Ellie replied.

"And you can thank Jimmy Can-Do as well," Chi-Chi added.

"What does he have to do with it?" Ellie was totally confused at that point.

"We have it on good authority he derailed part of the getaway plan," Gaines said.

"Getaway plan? Can someone please start at the beginning?"

As the police marched the three trespassers out to the squad car, Cullen explained the Millstone situation to Ellie, and how Luna had found a document that turned out to be the last will and testament of the fabulously wealthy Randolph Millstone, stuck in a table drawer, and the domino effect that discovery had had.

"And Luna saved the day with a fire extinguisher?" Ellie chortled.

"She did, indeed." Gaines looked at Luna. "Are you all right?"

"I'm just fine, thank you." Luna curtsied.

Cullen took the fire extinguisher from Gaines and placed it back on the wall.

"That was rather clever of you," Gaines said, admiring her quick-wittedness. Then he chuckled. "I can't wait to hear all the details as to how you got yourself into that situation."

"Well, if a certain person hadn't left his cell phone behind, we might have been able to avoid all of this."

In an effort to lighten the mood and change the subject, Cullen addressed the others. "Three Brothers?"

"Sounds good, but first you need to make a phone call," Luna said, pulling Cullen's cell from her pocket. "Mr. Clive Dunbar called twice. I didn't want to give him any information until I spoke with both of you."

"Yes, that's the lawyer for Millstone," Gaines confirmed. "And we found Colette Petrov and her son."

"But where? How?" Luna was astonished that Gaines had gathered so much information in such a short amount of time.

"I know people who know people." Gaines winked. "We followed the money. Clive Dunbar was the attorney of record for Millstone. One of the field offices got in touch with him at his cabin and told Dunbar they believed they had located a legal document signed by Randolph Millstone. They told him they did not have it in their possession but could make the document available. And Colette Petrov was with Mr. Dunbar."

Luna and Cullen gave the place the once-over and decided it was safe to leave the premises. They shut the lights, locked the doors, and the four of them exited the building. Ellie went back to her vehicle, where Ziggy and Marley were pacing in the back seat. She waved and called out to Luna, "I want more details in the morning!"

"For sure," Luna shouted back. "Scones and coffee."

When Rowena insisted on calling her lawyer, much to her dismay Clive Dunbar refused to speak to her, advising her to seek other counsel. Arthur met with a similar response. With the pending litigation, all the Millstone assets were frozen, forcing Rowena and Arthur to have a court-appointed attorney represent them. Bail would be out of the question unless Rowena hocked her jewelry. Such a dilemma. Arthur and

Rowena were sitting on their glorious butts with no lawyer in all of New England wishing to represent them. Too bad. So sad.

The reading of the will would move forward, as per Randolph's wishes, bequeathing his worldly holdings to several charities. Animal Care Sanctuary, St. Jude's Children's Research Hospital, the World Wildlife Fund, and several other foundations for the protection of animals or children.

As they left the Stillwell, Gaines continued to disclose the rest of Colette's involvement. "Turns out, Colette Petrov, who was Randolph Millstone's girl Friday, had stashed the letter in the table when her boss had his heart attack in the garage. She was also in possession of a spiral notebook that Randolph had given her. When someone impersonating a lawyer from Dunbar's firm came looking for her in Buffalo, she got spooked, so she took her son out of school and went in search of the Dunbar cabin."

"Wow. That is quite a story. That was very brave of her, going in search of Mr. Dunbar."

"Hmmm," Gaines mused. "Seems like good things come from search parties."

Luna blushed and looped her arm through Gaines's as they walked toward his Jeep. Chi-Chi did the same with Cullen. It seemed like the natural thing to do. And it felt that way to all of them. Natural.

The four piled into the Jeep and headed to their favorite pizza restaurant. When they finally settled in at their table, Luna noticed a man sitting at the bar. He was looking in their direction. He smiled and lifted his glass. Luna raised her glass in return and smiled. She was willing to bet that he was the enigmatic Jimmy Can-Do.

Gaines looked over in the man's direction. "Recognize someone?"

Luna twisted her mouth. "Not exactly." She motioned for the waitress. "Could you please buy that gentleman a drink on us?"

"Of course," the waitress responded.

"I thought you said you didn't *exactly* recognize that guy."

Gaines wasn't jealous, but curious. It had been an enormously curious day.

"Let's just say I think I know who he is." Her eyes went around the table. Chi-Chi was the first one to pick up on it. Then Cullen.

"What?" Gaines looked left out. "What am I missing?"

Luna leaned in toward the middle of the table, trying not to be too conspicuous. "I think that's Jimmy Can-Do. Don't look!"

"How do you know?" Gaines asked. She gave him a sideways glance.

"OK. OK. Your woo-woo, voodoo." He leaned back and pulled the menu up to his face.

"Such a baby." Luna tapped his foot.

"Oh, and you're Annie Oakley with your rootin'-tootin' fire extinguisher," Gaines teased.

"Well, you were nowhere to be found. You, too, mister." She focused her gaze on her brother.

Chi-Chi finally chimed in. "I think your sister was very brave. She had no idea what was going on in the showroom, yet she ignored all of her own fear and marched ahead with what was at her disposal. I think we should toast her."

Gaines and Cullen looked just a tad embarrassed. They weren't sure if Chi-Chi was totally serious or if she was admonishing them for not moving fast enough. It didn't matter. Everyone was caught up in the joy of the moment. Mr. Millstone would get his final wish. Rowena and Arthur were certainly going to jail.

When Gaines asked for the check, the waitress told them it

had been taken care of. Evidently, the man who had been sitting at the bar earlier had picked up the tab.

Gaines helped Luna out of her chair. "Well, missy. It seems as if every time I'm around you, there is a whirling dervish about to hit."

"You should be so lucky." She squeezed his arm.

The four of them got into Gaines's Jeep, and he proceeded to drop each of them off. Luna was the last one. When he pulled into her driveway, he turned off the ignition. Luna unbuckled her seat belt, waiting for him to come around and open the door. Instead, he unbuckled his seat belt, turned her head toward him, brushed the hair from her face, and landed a kiss on her lips. He didn't miss the mark this time. That would have easily scored a 10.0 in the Olympics.

Epilogue

Ellie was excited about two new tenants coming into the art center. One built birdhouses, another made wind chimes. The holidays were around the corner, and the center was bustling with shoppers, all in anticipation of the tree-lighting celebration. Cullen was busy trying to get things done for impatient customers. Luna was her usual ball of fire, lending advice for holiday decorating and creating a little holiday magic for her special clientele. The big holiday festival was on the horizon, and it included a date with Marshal Christopher Gaines.

Colette and Max spent a few more days at Cobblestone Hill, planning their next adventure. Clive offered Colette a job at his law firm. She would have to move back to Boston, but the opportunity to move back home made her very happy. Her parents were still there, and Max had friends. Her relationship with Logan was blossoming. He helped her find a nice, comfortable, ranch-style house in a good neighborhood with an excellent school. Once Randolph's will was read, Clive gave her an envelope with a check for $100,000. "This is from Randolph. It was not a bequest, since he could not have you mentioned in the will and also witness his signature. That would be a conflict of interest. So he instructed me to transfer this money to you after his will was read. And, in addition, he set up a college fund for Max with a deposit of $50,000." Colette was over the moon. She knew for certain that Randolph had been truly watching over her and her son.

Rowena and Arthur remained in jail as the charges of fraud, tax evasion, and embezzlement were stacked against them.

And Rowena verified what she had always thought was true—orange was not a good color for her.